LADY VIOLET INVESTIGATES

THE LADY VIOLET MYSTERIES—BOOK ONE

GRACE BURROWES

GRACE BURROWES PUBLISHING

DEDICATION

This series is dedicated to my nephew, Jackson, and to all those who have the courage to speak the truth—and to those who don't have the courage but speak up anyway

CHAPTER ONE

Two mortal afflictions befell me the night of the Robertsons' ball. The first arrived as a pounding agony spreading from the nape of my neck around to the left side of my skull. The megrim would be gone in a day or two—sooner if the fates were kind.

The second undeserved penance stood before me in the person of Sebastian MacHeath, his arctic-blue eyes full of disdain I'd done nothing to earn.

"Sir." I offered him a curtsey.

"Lady Violet." His bow mocked even as it sketched exquisite grace on a grand scale. "What the hell are you doing here?"

He still had the burr, the one that had been nearly unintelligible when he'd first been sent down from Scotland at the age of ten. His accent was a soft growl now, but to my ear, discernible. The better to vex him, I took him by the arm.

"I'm socializing," I said, "a quaint custom among the higher primates. What has induced you to inflict your person upon polite society?"

"I'd heard you were in mourning." No emotion colored that

observation, not gloating and certainly not concern. Once upon a youthful time, Sebastian had been kind and generous. That endearing fellow had apparently died a figurative death at some point during Wellington's Peninsular campaign.

For me to regret the passing of that younger version of Sebastian was folly, though I did. The taciturn officer he'd become was sadly in want of charm.

"I put off second mourning months ago," I said. "Shall we discuss the weather, or glare daggers at one another to liven up this otherwise genteel event? Lady Robertson would doubtless prefer the latter."

We were making a circuit of the ballroom, a tedious exercise intended to show off a lady's finery and her partner. My escort could not help but turn heads. Sebastian met every criterion for a young maid's most fanciful dreams—tall, sable-haired, possessed of an aquiline nose that stopped just short of hooked. Heavy brows, an angular jaw, and an incongruous dimple on the left cheek. Broad shoulders narrowed to a trim waist and lean flanks. The term broodingly attractive came grudgingly to mind.

If he ever smiled, which evidence of humanity I had not seen for years, he'd be gorgeous. In his present perpetual glower, he would frighten every unmarried woman in the room straight back to her chaperone's side.

"How did Belmaine die?" Sebastian asked.

"I did not poison my husband." In my worst, most wounded moments, I'd wanted to, but those moments had passed as the marriage had become a functional alliance. My late spouse had been the apple of my eye when we'd plighted our troth, but then, a seventeen-year-old's eyes are easily deceived. After a year of marriage, I'd realized that Frederick Belmaine's real fondness had been for my settlements and for the fact that I was the first female born to the Earls of Derwent for nearly eighty years.

"Belmaine was too young to die of an apoplexy," Sebastian said, "and too healthy to succumb to a heart seizure."

"Also too unlucky to avoid bad fish." That Sebastian was ignorant of the details told me he'd only recently returned to London, which raised the question: Why was he here?

Not that I cared. Curiosity, however, had ever been my besetting sin.

"I heard he died in a questionable location."

A brothel, but let it be noted Frederick had expired at an *exclusive* brothel in *exclusive*—expensive—company. I had paid Madam's bills myself after the funeral and taken care of other pressing obligations resulting from Frederick's demise as well.

"Why does it not surprise me," I said, "that you'd bring up such a sordid detail in the very middle of a Mayfair ballroom?"

"You do not deny the rumor."

Nor could I deny that some stupid, callow part of me wished that Sebastian had never gone to war, wished that the tolerant young man with the winsome burr had married some sweet young lady and was now the father of more winsome young fellows, one of whom I might call my godson.

"Why would I bother confirming or denying such twaddle?" I replied. "How is your sister?"

Sebastian ignored that question, steering me deftly into an alcove lit by a single sconce. As a widow, I had earned the freedom of alcoves and closed carriages, provided I was discreet.

"Clementine is up to four weans, all of them loud, opinionated, and impertinent, much like their mother."

He fell silent, his gaze not searching so much as accusing, though I knew not of what. To his family's horror, Sebastian had stormed off to buy a military commission when all loyal subjects of the crown with the blunt to do so had been similarly engaged. More than once, I'd wondered why.

If men had simply *stayed home* when the call to arms had sounded, half of Europe would not be in ruins and half the lower orders not reeling from wounds and widowhood. Of course, my strategy required that the Frenchmen stay home as well, and in that regard, the Corsican had failed to oblige me.

"Are you well, Violet?" Sebastian snapped off the question like a salute before battle.

"I am quite well." Though what battle were we about to join? "And you?"

"Thriving."

"On a diet of anger and vexation, apparently." War could do that to a man. I respected Sebastian enough not to deliver more than a glancing poke to the hornet's nest of his temper.

One dark brow swooped aloft. "You believe I'm angry?"

"Vexed about something. You were never very good at hiding your emotions." I'd treasured that about him. Sebastian had been an honest, openhearted fellow. English public schools had muted his inherent good cheer to philosophical humor, but even Headmaster's fondness for the birch rod did not explain the ill-tempered warrior pacing the alcove like a caged tiger.

He came to a halt before a floor-to-ceiling window that looked out on the torchlit terrace. In the shadows of the single sconce, Sebastian might have been a demon liberated from the pit for some nefarious purpose.

"I am attending the house party at Bathvale." He said this quietly, more of an admission than an announcement. "Uncle passed away last year. I am to take my place in Society, or Clemmie and the aunties will do me a grievous injury."

He'd inherited a marquessate, then. The Scottish peerage was of lesser precedence than the English peerage, but still, I had not heard of this development. The obscurity of widowhood suited me, though lately, I'd also suffered a curious restlessness even amid the endless glories of my conservatory and greenhouse.

"Sebastian, I am sorry for your loss." He'd hated his uncle, whose lofty station and lack of sons had dictated Sebastian's remove to England as a boy.

"Not half as sorry as I am." A hint of Scottish self-mockery laced his words, a ghost of the old Sebastian.

"A quarter of polite society will attend the Bathvale gathering." Myself included. Widows were ever so handy when a chaperone needed a little privacy for her own diversions, or a hostess wanted extra eyes and ears among the mamas.

"I did not want to ambush you," Sebastian said.

He faced the garden, suggesting that perhaps—possibly?—he had not wanted to *be* ambushed by a reunion with me amid the gossips assembled at the typical house party.

The shock of seeing him had been considerable. I ignored the pounding at my temples and searched his words for any meaning beyond the superficial. We were not enemies that I knew of, to waylay each other or spread tattle. Once upon a time, we'd been friends.

Good friends, with the heedless, trusting intimacy of the young.

Then his earlier admission swam past the unanswered questions that thoughts of Sebastian always provoked: *I am to take my place in Society.*

"You will begin your search for a marchioness." That hurt, not because this was Sebastian, confidant of my girlhood, splendid soldier, and wealthy aristocrat, but because courting rituals would always have the power to wound me, even if I were indifferent to the parties involved.

Which I was in this case, or nearly so.

He glanced at me over one muscular shoulder. "One marries when afflicted with a marquessate."

For another man, that word choice—*afflicted*—would have been ridiculous, but for Sebastian, who'd loved nothing better than roaming the fields, reading poetry in a treehouse, or sinking a line in the brook only to throw back everything he caught, the title was a dreaded sentence come to pass.

"I will wish you the joy of your campaign," I said, trying to mean it. "I expect you will achieve your objective long before the house party's closing festivities." Perhaps the right wife could banish the shadow that had fallen over Sebastian's soul in adulthood.

I was neither equal to nor interested in that task.

Sebastian studied me, which required that I meet his gaze without flinching. I'd always loved his eyes, so blue, so bold. Windows not only to his soul, but to his heritage as a Highland laird taking his place in a long and courageous succession.

"You have a headache," he said. "What the hell are you doing at this farce when a megrim is upon you? You'll only make it worse, and then you'll be laid low for three days. Violet, *you know better.*"

Of all people, Sebastian alone had the power to discern, simply by looking at me, when my head pained me. He'd always had this ability, claiming my eyes gave away my suffering. My eyes had never given away my suffering to my husband, my parents, or my dear brothers.

Only to Sebastian.

"The headaches pass," I said.

He stepped closer. "And then they return. You are an idiot to bring needless suffering upon yourself for the sake of a few waltzes."

"I am." But how could I convey to him, a familiar who'd become a stranger, the subtle threat that another quiet evening among my orchids presented? The yawning abyss of ennui that the retiring widow was supposed to fashion into something pleasant and meaningful?

I had no wish to remarry—none—but lately, even my conservatory was losing its charms.

"So go home," he said, his hand settling on my nape. His grip was warm—he'd always had warm hands—and firm. He squeezed with an exquisitely calibrated pressure that brought blessed relief of my pain. I'd tried fashioning a clamp to emulate the sensation of Sebastian's grip on my neck, to no avail.

His touch was a forgotten balm, a small miracle that reminded me of life beyond the seemingly endless purgatory of a nascent megrim. My thinking mind knew the pain would pass, but my body believed fervently in the suffering.

"I'll send for your coach," Sebastian said, gently circling a thumb at the join of my neck and shoulder. "Whatever possessed you to attempt this gathering when you know the pain will only worsen is beyond mortal comprehension. Do you want to end up in Bedlam?"

I stepped away. "Your solicitude is appreciated, but I have promised the supper waltz to Dr. St. Sevier." We'd spend the set talking about botany, as agreeable a use for a waltz as any.

"Who is this St. Sevier? The name is familiar."

None of your business. I might have flung that inelegant retort at Sebastian's scowling face, except that a scream—high-pitched, prolonged, terrified—rang out across the ballroom. The violins straggled to a halt as the screaming went on, and the murmur of a hundred conversations fell silent.

"That's coming from the gallery," I said, trying to push around Sebastian, who'd planted himself in the alcove's archway like an inconveniently positioned sculpture.

The screaming ceased, leaving a shocked stillness in its place.

"Stay here," he muttered. "Better still, have your coach brought around and get the hell home."

He strode off, every inch the officer wading into battle, and I, no longer one to heed any man's orders, followed immediately in his wake.

～

A tearful maid amid a sea of shattered glass gibbered into her apron, while a scruffy man stood barefoot three yards from her. The fellow was, in fact, entirely without clothing, his earthly temple as free of habiliment as the day he'd taken his first breath.

Lady Robertson's guests were crowding up the steps, the gentlemen trying to shoo the ladies off and having little success.

"You two," I said to a pair of gaping footmen, "give him that table-cloth. Now."

Lace-trimmed damask was the best I could come up with. Sebastian stepped across the shattered glass and stood immediately before the man, shielding him from some of the onlookers. The intruder was wretchedly skinny, none too clean, and gazing about as if he'd no idea how he'd arrived in the gallery.

"Damned riffraff," Lord Godbey groused to my right. "A body isn't safe in his own home."

"That man is no threat to anybody," I countered, which earned me a look widows knew well. Displeased, slightly contemptuous, but not offended enough to take such an ill-bred creature as I in hand. I was an earl's daughter and a comfortably well-off widow. Even a viscount took me in hand at his peril.

"He's an offense against decency," Mr. Ketchum sniffed. "I vow he should be tossed from the window. Not a fit sight for a lady, I should think."

The footman passed Sebastian the tablecloth, which he wrapped around the naked fellow's shoulders.

"He's bleeding," I said, for a trickle of blood tracked through the grime on the man's gaunt face. "He's doubtless a victim of the very lawlessness you deplore, gentlemen." And as for a man's unclothed form being an unfit sight...

I had been raised with four brothers who had perhaps a teaspoon of modesty between them, and that teaspoon only rarely in evidence. My late husband, Frederick, had considered himself quite the Corinthian, though his charms had paled in light of how selfishly he'd wielded them.

Lady Robertson arrived at the top of the steps, her expression a blend of consternation—naked men generally did not frequent ball-rooms—and poorly masked glee. Her otherwise staid gathering would be the talk of London for a week at least.

Sebastian tucked an arm around the man's waist and half lifted him over the broken glass.

"Ruffians," he said, setting the fellow down near a harpsichord. "Ruffians who not only steal a man's clothes, but beat him nigh senseless. Lady Robertson, I suggest you close the curtains about the ballroom, and the gawkers and thieves will likely disperse."

She didn't want to, clearly, for spectators were an important aspect of any glittering affair's cachet, but she gestured to the footman who sidled off toward the servants' stairs.

"Shall we send for a doctor?" I asked. "A blow to the head should never go untended." And what was wrong with these people that all they did was idle about and ogle another's ill fortune?

The victim remained next to Sebastian, and—was I the only person who noticed this?—Sebastian remained next to him.

"I'm sure the guests would rather be about their entertainments," Sebastian said, "and Mr....?"

"Upjohn, sir. R-Rhys Upjohn."

"Mr. Upjohn would rather confer with a physician after the demands of modesty have been more thoroughly tended to."

That scold had some of the guests wafting down the steps, for gossiping about a man wearing a tablecloth was more important than gawking at him, now that he was decently covered.

"My coach is available for transport to a surgery," I said when nobody else seemed inclined to make that offer. "Lady Robertson, if you'd have my carriage brought around?"

"Thank you, Lady Violet," Sebastian said. "Please have the coachman pull up in the mews."

Lady Robertson went swanning down the staircase, all but a few guests hurrying after her.

I approached Mr. Upjohn, my handkerchief in hand. "Have we brandy? Spirits of any kind? That wound should be cleaned."

Mr. Upjohn shrank closer to Sebastian, as if I intended to resume the beating he'd apparently just suffered.

"Please, ma'am," he said. "I'll manage."

"One doesn't manage an infection," I retorted. "One suffers and dies from it. Ask his lordship here. He was a soldier, and he's seen infection do more harm than pitched battle."

If Sebastian was discommoded to have a disheveled, bleeding, half-naked stranger pressed to his immaculate evening attire, he gave no sign of it.

"A blow to the head can leave a man disoriented," he said. "Mr. Upjohn's wounds will be tended to, but *not here.*"

Upjohn was shaking minutely, though the gallery itself was warm.

"Might I be of service?" Hugh St. Sevier sauntered across the gallery, looking as genial and relaxed as he did among his lilies and potions. He was slightly more than six feet of chestnut-haired, dark-eyed elegance, an exquisite exponent of the deposed French aristocracy. In the present political climate, that status wasn't always an asset.

"Lord Dunkeld," I said, addressing Sebastian by his late uncle's title, "may I make known to you Monsieur Hugh St. Sevier. Monsieur, I give you Sebastian, Marquess of Dunkeld. Mr. Upjohn has apparently been set upon by ruffians who stole his clothing and delivered more than a few blows to his person. I would be indebted if we could call upon your medical training."

"You're a doctor?" Sebastian asked. "I believe you served under Wellington on the Peninsula."

St. Sevier's geniality became somehow more formidable. "I had that honor," he replied. "And this fellow needs ice or cold beefsteak for that eye, which any fool could tell him." He held up his hand. "Follow the movement of my fingers."

Upjohn complied. What choice did he have?

"Might we continue this elsewhere?" Sebastian asked, unknotting the linen tied just so at his throat.

"My coach should be in the mews any moment," I said. "I'll just get my cloak."

"You will do no such thing," came from Sebastian at the same time St. Sevier murmured, "Perhaps we can send the coach back for you, my lady?"

The two gentlemen had just been introduced, Upjohn's head wound had left him dazed and bruised, and yet, all three fellows were apparently united in their determination to render me useless.

"You have a headache," Sebastian added, stripping off his cravat and handing it to St. Sevier, who soaked the cloth with the contents of a silver flask.

"Headaches benefit from rest," St. Sevier so helpfully added. "We'll send the coach back for you as soon as we've seen to Mr. Upjohn. I'd offer you my vehicle, but I chose to walk tonight."

"As did I," Sebastian added as the apples-and-vanilla scent of brandy filled the air.

I was being dismissed, which provoked me to an inordinate rage, and that reminded me of my headache, which was, predictably, growing worse.

"I'll have a footman deliver your cloaks and hats to the mews," I said. "The servants' stair is just there beside that portrait, and..." *I want a full report in the morning.*

I had no authority to make that demand. I was being humored, three times over, and Mr. Upjohn needed medical attention—also, clothing.

"You are the soul of generosity," St. Sevier said, "to lend your conveyance to our unfortunate friend. *Au revoir*, my lady. We'll have the coach back to you in no time." He held open the door to the servants' stair, and Upjohn, clutching his tablecloth with pathetic dignity, shuffled through the doorway, St. Sevier following after.

Sebastian tarried at the door. "He'll be fed, clothed, tended to, and given a safe place to sleep. He has the look of a veteran about him, and head wounds, as you say, take time to manifest their full misery. Trust me to do at least this much right."

I trusted Sebastian. I no longer knew him and didn't much care for the person he'd become, but I trusted him.

"St. Sevier was trained in Edinburgh," I said. "He's seen battle and is quite competent, for all his manners."

"Imagine that, a waltzing physician. I'll bid you farewell."

"Good night, but not farewell. We'll doubtless see each other at the Bathvale house party." An eventuality that seemed to please neither of us.

Sebastian withdrew to the lower reaches of the house, and now I was stuck at this infernal ball for the next half hour at least and I wasn't even to have St. Sevier's fine dancing to help me pass the time.

"For God's sake," I said to the single hovering footman, "please clean up the broken glass."

CHAPTER TWO

Bathvale Abbey was a Byzantine pile at the edge of the South Downs. I had learned in the course of my marriage to view such edifices not as charming monuments to tradition, but as expensive vanities. The central structure had been a monastery once upon a time, the property awarded to some Bathvale knight or baron upon the Dissolution for rehabilitation into a stately home.

The project had yet to conclude. At various times, wings, gargoyles, an occasional flying buttress, and even some Egyptian friezes had been added, giving the whole façade the air of a building in a bad mood and unable to decide what to wear.

The weather on the day of my arrival put me in a similarly unpleasant humor. Relentless rain turned the roads into instruments of torture for human and equine alike, and an unseasonable chill added to my misery.

Belinda, Lady Bathvale, nonetheless greeted me with the same sunny demeanor that had characterized her throughout our years at finishing school.

"Violet, my dear." She took both my hands the moment I gained entry to her soaring foyer. "Why is it I catch not a glimpse of you for years, but when I do see you, you look as fetching as you did at Miss Harmon's Academy?"

We brushed cheeks, as women do, and I caught a faint whiff of citrus. "I never looked fetching at school, my lady. I looked bored, as did we all."

The countess slipped her arm through mine and steered me toward a grand curving staircase. "And then we got married and found the true meaning of the word. Were it not for the little ones, I'd have to take up cutwork. You truly do look wonderful."

Her ladyship had endured several years of childlessness before the hand of providence had seen fit to bless her with two children in rapid succession.

"The baby has a birthday coming up, doesn't she?" I asked. "It has been nearly a year since you were last brought to childbed."

We mounted the steps, which offered an ideal view of the cavernous entrance hall. Life-size full-length gilt-framed portraits covered the walls with renderings of various progenitors of the present earl. White marble adorned the floors, and pink marble half columns graced the corners of the octagonal space. The newel posts were more carved marble—birds of prey—and the bannisters were oak fashioned into profusions of leaves and flowers.

More carving decorated lintels and door panels, and no less than four liveried footmen stood at attention near the front door.

Miss Belinda Putnam had done quite well for herself when she'd accepted Lord Bathvale's suit, but then, Belinda's papa was in the lucrative business of supplying arms to the Crown. Male guests, upon entering Bathvale and admiring its appointments, doubtless concluded that Lord Bathvale had done quite well for himself to marry one of the Putnam heiresses.

"How is Clara?" I asked, referring to her ladyship's twin sister.

"Looking forward to seeing you, though even Bathvale will be crowded by her standards when all of my guests arrive. My sister has grown more shy with time, not less."

Clara Putnam had missed a significant part of each school year due to illness, though I was never exactly sure what ailments befell her. She and Belinda were identical twins, both having blond hair, blue eyes, and the same approximate height. Nonetheless, most of the girls at school had had no difficulty telling them apart.

"Is Clara well?"

"As well as ever," Belinda said, taking the left-hand corridor when we reached the first floor. "I am very fortunate to have her company when his lordship is kept so busy, but Clara seldom leaves the estate unless she's traveling with us. Tell me of London, and if you have a moment before supper, perhaps you'd give the sleeping arrangements a glance. Several of the bachelors don't arrive until tomorrow, and I'm never certain who should be placed conveniently close to whom, if you take my meaning."

Lord Bathvale had doubtless benefitted materially from the Putnam marriage settlements, but he'd also taken a bride who had the knack of genuine warmth despite holding a high station. Belinda enjoyed the sort of good humor that never insulted others, even as she poked general fun at the human condition.

I liked Belinda, and I'd forgotten how much. "As long as you don't put me too close to the Marquess of Dunkeld, Bathvale Abbey should remain standing."

"You and the marquess were once great friends, Violet. Has he offended you?" She stopped before a door carved to show a pair of lambs curled up amid foliage and trees.

"War changes some men," I said. Sebastian puzzled me more than he offended me. "Whatever friendship we had has faded past recognition, though I wish him the best in his search for a marchioness. Who else have you invited from among the bachelors?"

"I'm told you are acquainted with Dr. St. Sevier, though apparently not many people here know him well." She led me into a sitting room that epitomized the word *charming*. The sofa and reading chair matched, both sturdy, with tufted blue cushions and a profusion of embroidered pillows. An afghan or shawl lay folded over the back of each, again matching, but this time in cream wool.

The carpet was a darker blue edged with pink flowers, but more than the room's comfy appointments, its modest size rendered it cozy. This parlor would be easy to keep warm, and—when the usual house party intrigues tried my patience—hard to resist.

"This is a corner of heaven," I said, pushing open the drapes. A pair of French doors led out to a balcony that overlooked the rolling green countryside beyond the back gardens. On sunny days, the view would be restful, and on rainy days, the room would still have more light than most.

"This is one of the smaller guest rooms, to be honest," Belinda said. "I thought you'd like it. The rooms nearest you house others whom I judged to be of a quiet demeanor, but I'm afraid I did put Lord Dunkeld two doors down across the corridor."

Meaning, I might glimpse some enterprising widow joining Sebastian late at night, or catch him returning to his room at dawn from a similar venture. I had no cause to judge him for such behavior —I might well be indulging similar impulses—but the idea was still... odd.

Disquieting. "As best I understand etiquette at house parties," I said, "discretion is mandatory for the sake of all concerned, and Lord Dunkeld's discretion remains—I am confident—utterly trustworthy."

Belinda rearranged the pillows on the couch so two sat against each armrest, and the fifth occupied the center.

"Lord Bathvale won't allow this gathering to degenerate into a bacchanal. My husband is not without warmth—he dotes on the children—but he holds propriety dear. Then too, some of his parliamentary cronies are attending, and they will doubtless hide away with him in the estate office, smoking vile cigars and drafting bills to regulate shoeblack manufactories."

A soft tap on the door heralded a pair of porters with my largest trunk.

I motioned them into the bedroom, and two footmen trooped in behind them, each man carrying a smaller trunk. The four of them bowed smartly and marched off, their day promising to be long and exhausting.

"You have uncommonly handsome footmen, my lady." The leader of the procession had been of above-average height, his features very pleasing, his hair a dark auburn. Trifling with the help was bad form, though I did not doubt that fellow received more than his share of offers.

"Footmen should all be blond and blue-eyed, I know," her lady-ship said, "but Samuel's people have been at Bathvale for ages, and he's a hard worker. Samuel is our first footman. If you need anything, and you can't find me or the butler, Samuel will oblige."

I had unpacking to oversee, provided my maid hadn't gone missing in the bowels of the house. "We will manage splendidly, I'm sure. What time is dinner?"

"The buffet will open at eight of the clock." Lady Bathvale surveyed the room, which wanted only a cat to make it domestic perfection. "The tea tray should be here any minute. I'll leave you for now. Doubtless, more guests have arrived."

She hugged me again, a fleeting, fierce, orange-blossom-scented embrace that took me by surprise. Not until my maid, Miss Lucy Hewitt, had arrived and the smaller trunks had been unpacked did I realize what about Belinda's welcome hadn't felt right.

We'd discussed her sister, Clara, of the quiet disposition and uncertain health.

We'd discussed Bathvale, his standards of morality and his parliamentary bent.

We'd even discussed Sebastian and a passing footman, but Belinda had shown no interest in me personally, nor had she shared anything regarding her own recent doings or even about her children.

One of whom was soon to celebrate her milestone first birthday.

~

Lucy Hewitt's past was a mystery to me, but she could bring order to chaos more effectively than any authority since all of creation had been fashioned in six short days. She flung open my trunks, arranged dresses about on the furniture, and ordered me from the room.

"You want to finish off that tea tray," I said, "and you aren't about to ask my permission to do so."

Lucy came up from rummaging in the largest trunk, a peacock paisley shawl in her hands. "I *want* to do as I've been told and sort out your wardrobe, my lady."

"You want to find some obliging young footman to interrogate in the kitchen." Lucy was younger than I—so many women were—and pretty in a blond, sturdy way. Men liked her, and more to the point, I liked her.

"And if providence is kind," she said, folding the shawl over her arm, "we won't take a fancy to the same footman."

"Trifling with the servants is the best way I know to start talk. I wish you the joy of new acquaintances." I took the shawl from her and wrapped it over my shoulders, the silk a pleasure against my bare arms. The shawl was an old favorite, one I'd been given at the time I first put up my hair.

"The first footman's name is Samuel," I said, "and he's quite attractive. I don't know if Samuel is a given name or a family name, but Lady Bathvale specifically commended him to me. I'm off on an exploration."

Lucy dove back into the trunk. "Looking for stray French doctors, my lady?"

"I'm not sure St. Sevier is the straying kind, but he's good company. If I remain here, you will never have a chance to enjoy your tea and croissants."

Lucy straightened, a lacy blue dressing gown in her hands. "Be careful, my lady."

Lucy was nothing if not practical. "Is the Abbey haunted?"

She folded the dressing gown and laid it on the bed. That Lucy would choose her words when we were private meant she'd likely heard something belowstairs, something unfit for a lady's ears.

"The house is haunted with gossips," she said, "or it soon will be. With jealous mamas, feuding chaperones, and gentlemen who aren't worth the name. This is your first house party as a widow, and some of those gentlemen may get above themselves. Have a care, my lady, for I don't look forward to ending up in Newgate, but needs must when gentlemen forget their manners."

She smoothed a nonexistent wrinkle from the bedspread, the gesture conveying an odd, wistful quality.

"Nobody need go to jail on my account," I said, heading for the door. "I'm merely orienting myself before I must change for the evening. In a house of this size, I like to know where I am and how to get from one place to another."

By the end of two weeks, I'd likely know my way around the Abbey better than Lady Bathvale herself did. This was a peculiarity of mine, that orientation to my surroundings was both necessary and easy for me. I tended not to get lost whether on foot or at the reins, and mazes usually presented little challenge.

The building's footprint resembled the traditional Elizabethan *E*, with the central wing shorter than the top and bottom wings. The ballroom, half sunken beneath ground level, occupied the central wing. Tall windows meant that guests could peer into the ballroom from many vantage points on the upper floors. A conservatory projected from the central wing, coming level with the ends of the top and bottom wings. Two open courtyards lay between the arms of the *E*, one formal, one informal, and both opened onto a long back terrace that ran the length of the building and turned the *E* into a squared-off *B*.

For the servants, tunnels and cellars likely connected the three wings, else traveling from one to the other would be prohibitively time-consuming.

I patrolled my own floor first, exploring doors obscured by clever paneling, examining the view from various windows. When I was confident that I grasped the layout of my immediate surrounds, I descended one floor, where I expected to find some of the public rooms. The corridors were devoid of other guests at this hour, which suited my purposes exactly.

I rounded a corner that should have taken me toward the middle of the house and came upon an open pair of imposing white doors. Shelves and shelves of books were visible through the doorway, and my heart gave a happy sigh. Bathvale Abbey had a large, well-stocked library situated close to my quarters.

Give me good books, and I can endure even the most tedious gathering.

The library was occupied. A man and a woman stood at the far end of the room, silhouetted against floor-to-ceiling windows. The lady was remonstrating with the man, based on her tone. I could not hear her words, but because I had come upon my hostess apparently scolding a footman, I attempted to retrace my steps.

I was denied a discreet retreat, for the lady gestured to the door and looked up, catching me three steps shy of my objective.

"Lady Violet?" she called. "Lady Violet, is that you?"

I advanced into the room. "You have found me out, my lady. I was rambling about the Abbey, enjoying a chance to move after spending all day—*Clara?*"

Lady Bathvale's younger sister approached me, her arms outstretched. "Oh, Violet, Violet, how good to see you. It has been an age and a half, and of all the guests Bathvale has summoned for this occasion, you are the one I've most looked forward to seeing."

She hugged me, which familiarity I endured while Samuel, the first footman, pretended to arrange the fronds of a large potted fern sitting in the window.

"You look to be thriving, Clara," I said when I could extricate myself from her embrace. She had put on weight since school, not a lot, enough to round out her curves and create a silhouette that more nearly resembled her sister's.

"I am in great good health, thank you. Samuel, we will continue our discussion later."

The footman bowed and withdrew, though something in his

regard for Clara struck me as *off*. Not disrespectful, but certainly unservile. But then, he was a senior retainer of long standing and might enjoy a more familiar relationship with the family than did others in their employ.

"When did you arrive?" Clara asked, twining her arm through mine and drawing me along the rows of shelves. "We could not have arranged for worse traveling weather, could we? And nobody would think to disappoint the Earl of Bathvale by arriving a day or two late, despite the state of the roads. His lordship sets great store by the civilities."

She said this as if it were a confidence.

"I have not yet met his lordship," I replied. "If his house is any indication, he will be conscientious, dignified, and well turned out."

Clara patted my arm. "You always were perceptive. You describe my brother-in-law to the life. I never thought Belinda would end up with such a proper fellow, but he is easy on the eyes. Speaking of handsome men, when is Lord Dunkeld to join the gathering?"

Clara might be living the quiet life of a rural spinster attached to her sister's household, but she clearly kept up with the London gossip.

"I am not privy to the marquess's movements," I said as we left the library. "He and I have seen little of one another in recent years."

"Now that is a shame," Clara said. "He's another fellow who's easy on the eyes, isn't he?"

I had noticed with other friends from school that we tended to revert to our girlhood selves when we first reestablished a connection. The young lady who'd been fluent in French had to offer greetings in that language. The one who'd been mad for bonnets opened the conversation with a reminiscence about some special hat.

Clara was in the mood to notice the handsome men at the gathering, as the younger unmarried women would, but then, why shouldn't she? Clara was still a Putnam heiress and of marriageable age, for all that she chose to dwell as her sister's companion.

"Some people might enjoy an eternally stern countenance on a man," I said, "but regarding Lord Dunkeld, I miss the smiling young fellow I knew years ago. The present incarnation of the marquess is too forbidding and serious for my tastes."

Clara and I were progressing down a corridor in the direction of what I assumed was the center of the house. The grand foyer likely lay ahead, along with the entrance to the ballroom.

"But surely you admit that Lord Dunkeld is a fine specimen of a man?" Clara said as we neared an intersection of two hallways. "He's titled, wealthy, in good health, a war hero, and well educated. What else could he have to recommend himself to a lady, except good teeth and fine manners, which as I recall, he also possesses?"

We came to a halt, and I cast around for a means of changing the subject. "Lord Dunkeld's sense of humor was a casualty of the Corsican's guns. As far as I can tell, the marquess has become arrogant, sour-natured, much taken with himself, and prone to handing out scolds. What matters a man's appearance when the rest of him is so disagreeable?"

Clara cleared her throat, she looked past my shoulder, she stared at her slippers.

A prickling up my nape suggested the Abbey was indeed haunted by ghosts, but no such luck. I turned to find Sebastian lounging against a sideboard, arms crossed over his impressive chest.

He made us an elegant bow. "Lady Violet, Miss Putnam."

My mortification was without limit, for though I could not like the man Sebastian had become, neither did I wish him any awkwardness.

I curtseyed, despite the blush flaming over my features. "My lord. Forgive my unguarded tongue."

Clara watched us as if a glove might be slapped against a cheek in the next moment.

Sebastian swept me with a magnificent glower, but I held my peace. I'd spoken honestly, if unwisely. The youth who'd charmed me all those years ago had never come home from the war, and I could do nothing but regret that.

"Perhaps your ladyship would agree to join me at dinner," he said, "that I might humbly endeavor to improve your opinion of me."

If I refused the wretched man I'd reveal myself to be the more sour-natured and arrogant of the two of us. "Thank you, my lord. I would be honored to share supper with you."

He nodded—regally—then turned on his heel and disappeared down the corridor.

"Oh dear," Clara said softly. "I do hope you haven't made an enemy of an old friend, Violet. His lordship has so very much to recommend him."

I took her arm and resumed our progress. "Perhaps the right wife can sweeten his disposition. I have it on the very best authority that he's considering taking a marchioness."

And may God have mercy upon her soul, whoever she might be.

CHAPTER THREE

I did not recognize the man before me in large measure because he was fully clothed. The only time I'd seen him previously, he'd been wearing nothing but lacerations and bruises, which he'd then covered with a tablecloth.

"Mr. Upjohn," I said. "That is Lord Dunkeld's livery you're wearing, isn't it?"

He tugged his forelock, bowed, blushed, and then found it necessary to stare at his shoe buckles. "Ma'am. Milady, rather. I am wearing Lord Dunkeld's livery. You are correct."

I'd seen Upjohn naked, bleeding, disoriented, and injured, and none of that was his fault. "You look to have recovered from your ordeal." In fact, he had a fading bruise above his right eye, though his blond hair obscured most of the discoloration.

"I am on the mend, my lady. Thank you."

Mr. Upjohn did not make a very convincing footman. His hair was still in need of a trim, his features were more homely than handsome, and he stood well under the requisite six feet required of the ideal male house servant.

"Would you happen to know if his lordship has gone down to

dinner yet?" I was making my way to the gallery, where the evening's buffet would be laid out.

"He has already gone down, ma'am. Shall I escort you below?" A proper footman would not have asked. He would have waited for direction from me, or excused himself with an offer to find an escort for me.

"I can find my own way, though I must say, that livery becomes you."

He darted a glance at me, likely to see if I was making a jest of him, which I had not intended to do.

"Never worn livery before, ma'am. Between you and me."

"The secret to success as a footman is to see all and say nothing. Be friendly with the other servants but not flirtatious, and don't take yourself too seriously."

"Sounds like being a good publican to me. Serve the ale with a smile, offending none and collecting payment from all."

A *publican?* "As good a comparison as any. You will find my maid, Miss Lucy Hewitt, ready to provide answers or assistance should you need either. If you will excuse me?"

One did not ask a servant to excuse one, but Upjohn was so clearly new to his station that I deemed a passing courtesy permissible.

"Thank you, ma'am," he said, bowing again. "And thank you for the tablecloth."

"I don't recall any tablecloth, sir, this being the first time you and I have met."

His smile was lopsided but charming, perhaps the smile of a publican or a publican's son. "My mistake."

I hurried on my way, the final dinner gong having sounded before I'd left my room. Lucy had been muttering about a musty smell in the wardrobe, though with all the recent rain, the entire south of England had a musty smell. My evening attire, by contrast, bore the scents of cedar and lavender and sported nary a wrinkle.

Sebastian's person bore the fragrances of sandalwood and cedar.

He'd always been fastidious as a boy, and army life must have been a trial in that regard. I found him lurking near a portrait of the Dowager Countess of Bathvale, though his height alone made him conspicuous.

"She looks sad to me," I said, considering the painting. "What sort of countess sits for a portrait with her lapdog? Why not with her offspring, or at least with their likenesses smiling from the walls of her private parlor?"

Sebastian offered his arm. "She had only the one son, in addition to a daughter who died in infancy. Our host was the last of his line until a very few years ago."

As Sebastian was the last of his line—or was he? "Can your title be preserved through the female heirs?" This was more often the case with Scottish titles than English or Irish titles.

"Preserved, yes, but that would mean trustees appointed to oversee the properties and estates. I wouldn't like to see that happen. Are you hungry?"

"Peckish. I ran into your Mr. Upjohn." I kept my voice down as we sauntered along the row of portraits. Talk of Upjohn's ordeal had made the rounds in London, but I saw no need to bring gossip down on the man here.

"He needed employment."

"He needed a decent set of clothes, and you put him in livery. Was that wise, Sebastian?"

"No."

I nodded to Lady Everett and her daughter, the fair Lady Priscilla. They smiled at me, and had I given the least indication, they would have approached me for an introduction to Sebastian.

"Don't," he murmured while appearing fascinated by a painting of the first Viscount Bathvale.

"She is said to be well dowered, and I can attest to her agreeable nature." Though, in truth, Lady Priscilla had a bland nature, which was to be expected when Lady Everett was her mama.

"According to an impeccable authority, "Sebastian countered. "I do not have an agreeable nature. She would bore me silly in a week. Upjohn has no recollection of the incident that resulted in his unusual circumstances when last you met him."

The first viscount cut quite a dash in his ruff and hose, though he looked far too serious for my tastes.

"Upjohn suffered a blow to the head. What did St. Sevier say about the memory loss?"

"That it's not unusual to have no recollection of such a trauma, though Upjohn might eventually recall what happened. I've known soldiers to come off their horses and also have no memory of the fall. Upjohn says he's from Nottingham, but doesn't know why he was in London other than to look for employment."

"Give it time. St. Sevier is here somewhere if you'd like to consult with him again. What did your valet say when you presented him with a new footman?"

"I took Upjohn into service in part because I haven't a valet at present."

We moved on to the next portrait, a young woman in panniers and powder, though she at least looked to have a spark of humor about her.

"Did you gobble your valet up with a sauce of virgin's tears?" I asked. "Have him fed to the monster at the bottom of your loch?"

"He refused to leave Scotland. I inherited Uncle's retainers, and they are gradually finding ways to pension themselves. I know how to dress without assistance. If Upjohn can manage an iron or wield a needle, he'll be adequate."

"Said the man who has a disagreeable nature. You hired a valet with no references and likely no experience, who can't even tell you how he came to be in London. Upjohn also let you come down to dinner without a pin to secure your cravat." Though other than that oversight, Sebastian looked very well turned out indeed.

His evening attire was the requisite black with white linen, and the fit was exquisite. He wore a waistcoat of burgundy silk with black embroidery, and his sleeve buttons sported small, bright rubies cut in the elongated oval of the French marquise style.

"I had a cravat pin made to go with this ensemble," he said, ignoring a smiling blonde hovering near the punchbowls. "I must have left it in Town."

"You packed your own trunks?"

"I packed my own jewelry," he said. "Don't you dare ask me to fetch you a glass of punch."

"Mrs. Albright likes Scotsmen, I'm told."

"Served in a sauce of bachelor's tears, no doubt, with a side of dower properties and a liberal garnish of pin money. Do you suppose Upjohn stole my cravat pin?"

Our progress took us to a painting of a pair of small children, possibly the current earl and his now-deceased sister. "Why would you think that?"

"I know I packed that pin. I haven't many rubies, and this is my favorite formal waistcoat. I can wear plain gold with it, but the rubies are more impressive."

If Sebastian were any more impressive, Lady Priscilla would have swooned at the sight of him.

"Have you become vain, my lord?" He'd been a handsome boy, but the years had filled him out and given him gravitas. If he ever smiled... I might regret that we were no longer friends.

"As a Scottish peer without a wife, I am judged for my appearance, just as I am judged for my accent, for my antecedents, for my dancing, and for the company I keep. Whoever painted this didn't like children."

"Does anybody like children?" St. Sevier had taken the place at Mrs. Albright's side, and he cut a fine figure in his formal attire.

"You did, once upon a time. Your Frenchman is either brave or foolhardy."

"He's not my Frenchman, Dunkeld, and hunger must be making you more irritable than usual. Let's fill our plates, and I will regale you with what little I know about the unmarried young ladies among the guests." That had to be why Sebastian had sought my company for dinner. Whatever else might have gone amiss between us, he still trusted me to be truthful regarding polite society's eligible young women.

"Wait until after we've eaten to offer that discourse, please," he said. "Spending all day in a coach has put my digestion off enough as it is."

"And then you saddled yourself with me for a dinner companion. Really, Sebastian, what were you thinking?"

I expected a rejoinder—sarcastic, ironic, or simply grouchy—but Sebastian merely led me to the buffet table, passed me a plate, and began heaping food upon it. The evening promised to be long, the house party interminable, and yet, I had at least set foot beyond my own property and found company other than my cats and my orchids.

Progress, however modest, was cause for rejoicing.

～

By the time I finished my meal more than an hour later, I'd puzzled out in greater detail why Sebastian had chosen me for his dinner companion.

"If you'd wanted a bodyguard," I said, "you might simply have asked me. I'm happy to keep the matchmakers in their places."

The mamas and chaperones had circled us as relentlessly as starlings flitting around a tea tray left unguarded on a garden terrace. The ladies would swish past us, glance over their fans, pause to smooth their skirts or take a sip of their punch, and all the while Sebastian focused determinedly on his meal.

Clara had not initially been among them, but even she had eventually made a circuit, pausing to adjust the drape of a bright orange shawl that did not particularly flatter her coloring.

As the parade continued, I'd told Sebastian what I knew about the half-dozen unmarried young women among the guests. I was no longer Frederick Belmaine's hostess, and thus my store of intelligence was not as deep or current as it would have been otherwise.

"And what of Mrs. Albright?" Sebastian asked as we set our empty plates aside and rose from the bench we'd occupied. "Did the late Mr. Albright leave her pockets to let?"

"The late Mr. Albright was a gun dealer who had the foresight to die before hostilities on the Continent concluded. A nephew inherited the business, while the widow is rumored to be quite well fixed."

Helene Albright was also astute, pretty, and practical. She would not trouble Sebastian with needless domestic drama, and she'd be faithful at least until the requisite heir and spare arrived.

"You do not like her," Sebastian said, placing my hand on his arm.

"I like her quite well, but I do not like your mercenary approach to matrimony. At least pretend to look for some compatibility with your prospective marchioness."

He led me from the music room, where we'd taken our meal, and I kept him moving toward the grand staircase.

"My title and wealth will be compatibility enough," Sebastian said. "I don't recall you being much concerned about compatibility when you leaped upon Freddy Belmaine's offer of marriage."

Sebastian's tone was sardonic, though he slanted a glance at me that suggested his observation was more than casual.

"I was seventeen at the time of my engagement, and the offer was made to my father, who had coveted the Belmaine water meadow since his youth. You can afford to choose carefully, and I hope you do."

The first footman, Samuel, hurried by in conversation with Marple, the Bathvale butler.

"He reminds me of somebody," Sebastian said as we reached the bottom of the staircase.

"The butler?" Butlers tended to be butlerish, in my experience. The good ones, whether young, old, short, or tall, had a certain consequence to their bearing that combined dignity with an air of cheerful discretion.

"That footman, Samuel. He's a good-looking devil, but not in the way footmen usually are."

Meaning Samuel wasn't a tall blond whose first obligation was to fill out his livery with muscles.

"Befriend Samuel," I said, "within the limits of your station, and he'll keep an eye out for Upjohn. That one strikes me as much in need of guidance." Particularly if he was already pinching his employer's jewelry.

"You are going up to bed?" Sebastian asked, scowling down at me.

"I am nearly asleep on my feet, meaning no reflection on present company. If I don't rest tonight, I will spend a sennight yawning my way from one entertainment to the next. Tomorrow morning, we start the day with a walk in the deer park, followed by a picnic lunch. The afternoon is nominally free, but if Lady Bathvale has any odd jobs to tend to, I will be expected to assist her with them."

His scowl became a glower. "Why?"

"Because that's what widows do at these house parties." I twitched my shawl higher on my shoulders—white silk for evening—because the staircase had a draft. "Good night, my lord."

"Shall I see you up to your room?"

"No need for that. Why don't you crook your little finger at Mrs. Albright? I'm sure she's willing to admire the stars with you, *or something.*"

I left him at the bottom of the steps, and when I took the turn on the landing, Sebastian was still monitoring my progress. What did I care if he was comparing my retreating figure to its girlish counterpart? I'd borne no extant children, I was still quite active. I doubted my figure had changed much. Nonetheless, I would never again be the happy, outgoing young woman who'd spoken her vows with Frederick Belmaine.

I found my room on the first try—part of the reason I'd bothered with reconnaissance earlier in the day—and let myself in. Lucy had doubtless finished unpacking and was well on her way to learning the names of the horde of servants thronging the house's lower reaches. She had a good memory for details, which had been invaluable to me in the early days of my widowhood.

Grief and shock had fogged my mind, or perhaps relief and guilt had.

I sat on the sofa to remove my slippers when a noise from the bedroom caught my ear. "Lucy?" A door banged shut as I crossed the room. "Lucy? Are you still—? Who are you?"

A plump young woman in a maid's mobcap and full-length apron stood before my wardrobe. "Just tidying up, ma'am." She shoved at her cap, tucking a dark curl out of view.

"I am *Lady* Violet, and as you can see, the room is already quite in order. Who are you?"

More to the point, *what* was she? A maid indulging her curiosity? A thief? A thief's eyes and ears? A spy for some ambitious gossipmonger?

"I'm Haines, your ladyship." She bobbed a curtsey. "I'm assigned to the guest rooms on this side of the corridor. I was making sure you don't need anything."

"If I need something, I'll have my maid ask the housekeeper, butler, or first footman for it. You are excused, and while I understand that you might find it necessary to sweep the hearth or retrieve a tea service, there is no need for you to set foot in my bedroom in the future."

Another curtsey, along with a mutinous gleam in her eyes. "Of course, your ladyship. As you please."

She flounced out of the bedroom and kept going, closing the parlor door behind her. I opened the wardrobe, though Lucy would have to tell me if anything had been disturbed. My collection of jewels looked to be complete, but then, I seldom wore fancy adornment and never brought expensive pieces with me when I traveled.

I had changed into my nightgown and robe and taken the braid down from atop my head when a soft tap on the door interrupted my fuming. Very likely, Lucy had returned to see me to bed and to share whatever news she'd picked up belowstairs.

I opened the door to find Hugh St. Sevier looking splendid in his evening attire. He held a bottle in one hand and two crystal glasses in the other.

"A nightcap," he said, holding up the bottle. "Doctor's orders."

"I'm not in need of a nightcap."

"I most certainly am."

I stepped back, took the bottle from him, and allowed him into my sitting room.

~

Hugh had brought Armagnac, which would have been my choice. Like most proper young ladies, I'd been brought up without gaining a close acquaintance with strong spirits. My brothers had occasionally entertained themselves by allowing me a tot of this or a sip of that, and I'd carried the requisite flask into the hunt field, but I'd developed a taste for spirits only since becoming a widow.

"I did not see you at dinner," I said, taking a seat on the sofa.

Hugh came down beside me and poured us each a serving. He passed me one and held out his glass to me. "To your health and my continued bachelorhood."

"To the health of bachelors everywhere." I touched my glass to his. "Was dinner awful?"

"I am not a coward, my lady. I sallied forth at the appointed hour and had barely made it to the bottom of the steps when I was accosted. The woman claimed we had been introduced, but I have an excellent memory, and I can assure you the honor of her acquaintance had not yet been mine."

Hugh's English was impeccable, but subtly accented. He was of émigré stock and had come to England in childhood. His intonation was French, his sense of style was French, his air of amused tolerance for all he surveyed struck me as French as well.

Also… attractive, particularly when he wore evening attire. His boutonniere was a white rose wrapped together with a few violets, and his gold and amber stickpin complemented his brown eyes.

"Did this lady who accosted you become your dinner companion?" The Armagnac was well aged with traces of chocolate and cinnamon on the tongue. Hugh had likely brought it with him, for I doubted even Lord Bathvale would have had access to such an exquisite brandy.

"I fear this woman has become my wife," Hugh said, studying his glass. "Perhaps I have forgotten the wedding ceremony. Age and abject terror take a toll on a man's recollection."

He had the ascetic features I associated with a native Gaul, as well as thick chestnut hair and brows with a slightly imperious arch. I'd seen him at the theater once or twice with a woman I assumed was his mistress, for he had not introduced us.

"While you might forget an introduction and even a wedding ceremony, I doubt you'd forget the wedding night. What was her name?"

"Mrs. Bonaventure, though I was to call her Pamela. She has been bereaved these five years and adjusted to her loss like—what is the saying?—a duck to a pond?"

"A duck to water. Some women do." I was not one of them.

He studied me over the rim of his glass. "How are you, my lady?"

"Is that a medical inquiry?"

"The question is friendly, Violet."

And *that* was a gentle scold. "I'm here. I very nearly sent my regrets."

His regard was patient and kind—also unnerving. Hugh would know if I lied, even if I were convincingly engaged in self-deception.

"As I chose which items to bring with me," I said, "as I made arrangements to be away from home for two weeks, my sense of unease grew greater and greater. As if I were leaving on some dangerous mission, rather than preparing to while away a fortnight in the country."

He sat beside me, and though his closeness was a presumption, his very presence—substantial, masculine, acquainted with some of my foibles—was also soothing. He wore a gardenia or honeysuckle scent that would have been too much on most men, but on him the fragrance was subtle and pleasing.

"Packing upset you?"

"I don't physically pack my trunks, St. Sevier. I tell Lucy what to bring, and she decides which outfits go in which trunks."

"When was the last time you were away from home for two weeks?"

Visiting the Belmaine family seat didn't count, nor did occasional forays to call on my brothers in Town. "You mean travel to someplace where I was unfamiliar with the other guests? Unfamiliar with the surrounds?"

"Someplace new and different, where you were unsure of your allies."

Odd word choice. "My wedding journey."

He squeezed my hand. "Did you resort to the poppy to get you here?"

Had there been any doubt, that question confirmed that his concern was medical. "I wanted to." Merciful days, had I wanted to. The sweet oblivion afforded by a bit of laudanum had seen me through the early days of my widowhood. Natural caution and Lucy's vigilance had prevented temporary aid from becoming a permanent problem.

"Did you partake prior to your departure?"

My glass had become empty. I set it on the low table, knowing Hugh would not offer me another serving.

"I did not. I instead did as you prescribed. I went for walks in the park. I read in the garden. Once, I took my mare out for a hack. I caught up on correspondence, and I distracted myself from the upcoming journey."

"There, you see?" he said, patting my back. "Your courage was sufficient to the challenge. I am proud of you."

I longed to slap the smile from his handsome face. I did not want his approval. I did not want to *be here*. I most assuredly did not want an interrogation from him every time I traveled.

"The ordeal becomes no easier," I said instead. "The whole way here, I was nearly sick with unease. I want right this minute to call for my carriage and return home. I want to be gone from this place and away from these people." Even as I spoke, I knew that such cowardice was not *me*.

"And away from me most of all," he said, saluting with his drink. "But you are here, and it will get easier. Six months ago, you could not have done this."

"But a year before that, I did not have these problems."

This prodigious capacity for worry had come over me slowly, gaining ground like a malodorous fog creeping off the Thames. The suspicion that I was in difficulties dawned on me when all four of my brothers called upon me in the same fortnight. They had rarely called upon me prior to Frederick's death and only occasionally thereafter.

I had become a recluse and not even noticed, much less cared.

"A year from now, you might again go about as freely as you once did," Hugh said. "Courage is like a muscle. The more you use it, the stronger it becomes, but there is strength for swimming, strength for rowing, strength for galloping on horseback. All exertion is beneficial, but specific challenges require specific training."

He was quoting somebody, probably a medieval hermit or an ancient Greek philosopher.

"There is also strength for throwing presuming men out of my boudoir," I said, rising. "You are a dear to pay this call, but it wasn't necessary." I gathered up the glasses and the bottle, lest the nosy maid find them in my quarters.

"To me, a little visit was necessary," Hugh said, getting to his feet. "I goaded you into accepting this invitation because I knew I would be here too. If the excursion had overtaxed you, I'd be to blame."

I did not correct him. "The excursion is just beginning, sir."

"And at any time, you can summon your carriage and leave—if

you must. I am five rooms down on this same side of the corridor. My door has a griffin couchant carved on the door."

Griffin couchant. I would remember that, for it suited him. I passed him the bottle of Armagnac and the two empty glasses. "Give my regards to Mrs. St. Sevier."

"Such a wit, you are. Good night, my lady." He brushed a kiss to my cheek and sauntered toward the door. He halted halfway across the room when a soft knock came from the other side.

"Open the damned door, Violet," growled a soft burr. "I cannot be seen lurking out here, for God's sake."

Hugh set the bottle and glasses on the table by the door and darted to the left, where the door itself would shield his presence.

I opened the door a few inches. "Sebastian?"

"This is yours." He held up my peacock silk shawl. "I found it in the library."

I could not take the shawl from him without opening the door wider. I unfurled the fabric enough to confirm that the garment was mine.

"I did not leave this in the library, Sebastian. I was wearing it when I returned to my room, because the corridor was and is chilly." I had also worn the shawl because I liked the feel of the silk on my bare arms, not in a sensuous way, but in the manner of a child taking comfort from a favorite blanket.

"It's yours, then?"

"Most assuredly. My thanks for returning it to me." That snooping maid—what had her name been?—was due for a severe dressing down.

Sebastian's gaze fell on the opened bottle and the two glasses. He swept me with a visual perusal, reminding me that my hair was in a single braid, and I was attired in a dressing gown. I was decently covered, of course, but very much in dishabille.

He bowed slightly and marched away.

I considered calling after him. *It's not what you think...* But Sebastian had spent supper interrogating me about the eligible young ladies at the gathering, while using my company to deflect their mamas and chaperones.

How could his opinion of my social habits possibly matter? He was hunting a bride, while all I sought was a pleasant two weeks in the country. I wrapped the shawl about me, endured another kiss to my cheek from St. Sevier, then sent him on his way with his dratted truth potion.

CHAPTER FOUR

"She said her name was Haines. I'm not sure I believe her." I offered that observation as Lucy made an inventory of the contents of my wardrobe. Outside my bedroom window, demented tree pipits and other avian saboteurs prevented sane people from sleeping until a decent hour of the morning. I occupied a small table positioned near the window, the tea tray before me, but I was far from awake.

"Everything looks to be here," Lucy said. "I can ask belowstairs about a maid named Haines, but these house parties..." She refolded my paisley shawl, the silk shimmering in the early morning sunlight. "Everybody but the goose girl is recruited for inside work, and the house staff can't be expected to know all of the guests' servants."

"Ask Samuel," I said, taking a sip of tea that was suspiciously weak. "He seems like an intelligent fellow. Did we bring any China black?"

"Of course."

"I do believe the Bathvale stores should be supplemented from our own. This tea wouldn't keep a preacher's sweetheart awake through his Easter sermon. What is the news from the servants' hall?"

Lucy laid out a walking dress of blue muslin sprigged with lavender violets and dashes of greenery. "Where shall I start?"

"Must I truly trudge about the park half the morning pretending fresh air and chattering company agree with me?"

Lucy unearthed my traveling tea service, the pot being half size and made of silver rather than porcelain. "Somebody's company was agreeing with you last evening."

Talk, already. Of course. "Lord Dunkeld was an agreeable dinner companion."

"Not him." She swung a kettle over the coals on the hearth. "I came up here to turn down your bed and heard voices, one of them male."

"Hugh St. Sevier stopped by to make sure I was still speaking to him. He dared me to attend this house party, and here I am." On a pretty spring morning, I could be a little proud of myself for that, though I was still unhappy with St. Sevier.

Taking my hand, patting my back. I liked his affectionate nature, maybe a little too well.

"The Bathvale staff isn't very chatty," Lucy said, settling onto the raised hearth, which a properly respectful domestic would never have presumed to do. "Much is going unsaid, and that's unusual. A crowd like this usually means everybody is run off their feet, tempers flare, and decorum—if any there is—wears thin. This lot at Bathvale... They aren't happy, and they aren't exactly loyal. I'm not sure what's afoot here."

"Could money be a problem?" Tea was dear. Good tea, anyway. In my travels about the house, I hadn't noticed any shabby corners, but then, I hadn't half begun to explore the place.

"With the Quality, money can always be a problem." Lucy rose and added silk stockings, garters, and a knitted shawl of lavender merino wool to the outfit on the bed.

"I'll wear a straw hat rather than a bonnet," I said. "I wish I'd brought a lock for the wardrobe."

Lucy busied herself filling the teapot. "Somebody nicks your shawl and then leaves it in the library. That's odd, that is."

"Haines probably had it secreted under her apron before I came upon her. When I surprised her, she knew I could identify her as the thief. She had no choice but to surrender the contraband in a manner that wouldn't incriminate her."

"Makes sense."

"But why take my shawl when she could have taken jewels?" The shawl was valuable enough that its theft alone constituted a felony, but the jewels were easier to sell and of greater worth.

"Maybe you interrupted her scheme."

I rose and shed my dressing gown, hanging it on a hook on the bedpost. "Or maybe, like a smart thief, she was merely perusing what was on offer. She'll purloin the truly valuable items the night before we depart, when everything is packed for travel. We won't discover anything missing until we're back in London. Then we'll believe we've simply left a few items behind, polite notes will be exchanged, and nobody will be accused of anything."

I traded my nightgown for a chemise and began the process of dressing for the day. I was not as particular about my clothing as some women, but I did like to look presentable. Then too, Society judged a lady for her appearance, and I had no wish to be labeled a widow who'd allowed herself to go to pot.

Lucy brushed out my hair, did it up in a single braid, and secured it in a bun at my nape.

"I refuse to wear a snood," I said when she would have affixed a crocheted contraption around my chignon. "I am too young for snoods, and they never behave as they ought. Even the word 'snood' sounds old and prim."

Lucy passed me my half boots. "Monsieur St. Sevier isn't old and prim."

"He's a friend." Also my physician, albeit informally. More or less.

"He's a handsome friend."

"I am not in search of a dalliance, Lucille." Though was I to spend the rest of my life without intimate companionship? I had no wish to remarry, on that I was quite clear. Still, the prospect of decades of widowhood filled me with as much unease as the prospect of another spouse did.

"The best dalliances aren't the result of searching," Lucy said. "They spring up unbidden, like volunteer daisies. You will please *wear* your hat today, my lady. Don't simply carry it, or you'll get freckles."

"Freckles—horrors! And at my age. Don't let the tea go to waste." Lucy did set great store by a fresh, hot cup of tea.

I slipped on my boots and left her debating what I should wear for dinner that night. Breakfast awaited, and I did not intend to miss it. I made my way down the main stairs, visions of warm toast slathered with butter and jam filling my head. I might fortify myself with a pot of chocolate in anticipation of the morning's exertions and help myself to a cinnamon roll for later in the day.

I was still several yards down the corridor from the breakfast parlor when the buzz of multiple conversations confirmed that the house party was off to a chatty start. Miss Clara Putnam intercepted me outside the door and took me by the arm.

"Sit with me, please, Lady Violet. I am simply not up to small talk with forty people."

"As lively as the gathering is, I doubt we'll have to make conversation. We can nod and smile and stir our tea without having to say a word."

The closer we came to the breakfast parlor, the louder the din grew.

"What can they all be going on about?" Clara asked.

"Heaven knows." But whatever was afoot, this was not the cheerful banter of a house party off to a merry start.

~

Clara had offered to be my walking partner, which suited me quite well. I'd seen Sebastian halfway down the breakfast table, in earnest conversation with a blond woman of mature years—meaning a trifle older than my own five-and-twenty years—and ample endowments. Mrs. Pamela Bonaventure had appeared to be enjoying the marquess's company. St. Sevier was nowhere in evidence, but then, the French breakfasted differently from the English.

I slipped out through the doors of the music room and made my way across the gardens. I wanted to see my windows from outside the house, another quirk of my nature. I liked being able to see out across the park. I did not like thinking some fellow with a spyglass could lurk in a tree and see in.

The nearest such vantage point was a hedgerow of oaks that separated the park beyond the garden from a shallow stream. The oaks were centuries old, and climbing into their boughs would have required a rope or a ladder.

The walking path that ran between the oaks and the banks of the stream was probably as old as the trees, and quite peaceful, though I was not to enjoy it in solitude.

"Good morning, my lady."

The head footman, Samuel, held the hand of a sturdy little lad who'd clearly been wading in the shallows.

"Good morning, Samuel. Won't you introduce me to your companion?"

"Master Owen, make your bow."

The child flopped over from the waist, wheat-blond curls bouncing. "Owen Braithwaite, at your service." He came up grinning, clearly not a fellow afflicted with shyness.

"Braithwaite is the Bathvale family name," I said. "Do I have the pleasure of addressing the heir?"

Samuel's smile was rife with genuine affection. "The heir, and the despair of his nanny. Master Owen is blessed with high spirits, and with the house all at sixes and sevens, the nursery routine has been tossed to the wind."

"Children thrive on routine," Owen said, swinging Samuel's hand. "Papa says that all the time."

What would Bathvale think of this early morning departure from decorum? I heartily approved, being of the opinion that children needed fresh air more than scholar ever needed Latin verbs, but then, I had no children of my own.

"You are very fortunate, Master Owen, that Samuel can spare the time to take the air with you. The houseguests will soon be thronging the park and then picnicking beneath the trees."

"May we picnic?" Owen asked, turning a pleading gaze on Samuel.

"Perhaps in the garden, though that's up to Miss Chandler. Her ladyship will keep this little excursion to herself, I'm sure, but only best behavior will win you a picnic, my boy."

Owen's little shoulders slumped. "Best behavior is hard. Will Sissy come on the picnic?"

"No more talk of picnics," Samuel said, hoisting the boy onto his back. "First, we must get you back to the nursery, then you must comport yourself like a perfect gentleman until noon."

"Shoes would help," I said, scooping up a pair of tiny boots into which wool stockings had been stuffed. "Most gentlemen prefer to go about shod when in company."

"Thank you, my lady."

"Before you go, Samuel, can you tell me if Bathvale Abbey employs a chambermaid named Haines?"

"We do. If she's overstepped, my lady, please say so."

"She's apparently assigned to the rooms on my side of the corridor, but I've instructed her not to venture into my bedroom. My own maid is territorial and will see to me well enough without assistance."

"What little consequence we in service have, we guard jealously. I'll have a word with Haines. She's not one to get above her place, usually."

Master Owen yawned and settled his cheek against Samuel's

broad shoulder. They made a sweet picture, though I would not have bet on an entire morning's best behavior from the cherub dozing on Samuel's back.

Samuel offered me an awkward bow. I curtseyed to the heir—Master Owen was probably a courtesy viscount—and debated tarrying on nearby stone bench.

"One last question," I called to Samuel's retreating back. "What color is Haines's hair?"

He smiled, looking as mischievous as his young charge. "As red as the coals of Old Scratch's forge, according to our housekeeper, but Haines is even-tempered for all that. Enjoy the outing in the park, my lady."

I took the bench and let the burbling stream soothe me, though Samuel's disclosure was unsettling. Given the whispers I'd overheard at breakfast, the house party was apparently hosting at least one very bold thief.

And her name was not Haines.

~

"House parties are such a lot of foolishness," Clara said. "Entertaining oneself is challenge enough, but to entertain several dozen people, many of whom have never met before, is asking for a disaster."

We strolled along a path that bordered the edge of the park. Most of the party was ahead of us, though a few of the dowagers and chaperones were straggling, likely intentionally, the better to give the young people a chance to flirt. St. Sevier was escorting two young ladies, one on each arm, while Mrs. Bonaventure had taken Sebastian captive. Lord Bathvale escorted Mrs. Albright, while Lady Bathvale was in the company of an earl's bachelor heir.

"I'd hardly call a missing pair of earbobs a disaster," I said. "Miss Waltham either misplaced her earbobs or forgot to pack them." Another theory presented itself: Miss Waltham claimed to have been robbed so that she might garner the concern of other guests—this was a house party, after all.

But the simplest theory, the only theory for which I had any supporting evidence, was that a thief was at large. I did not dare confide my experience with the snooping maid to Clara, who appeared all too ready to add to any drama.

She leaned nearer. "Lord Hempley said he couldn't find his lucky cravat pin either."

"Lord Hempley's valet probably forgot to pack it. Why steal an amber pin when more valuable items were likely stored in the same jewelry box?"

"Because," Clara said, "an item of smaller value is less likely to result in a thorough search or a hue and cry. Lose a penny, you shrug and go about your day. Lose a sovereign, and you turn the house upside down."

Her reasoning was sound and explained why my shawl had gone missing rather than my jewelry, though the shawl had sentimental value far in excess of that possessed by any trinket.

"Let us turn our imaginations to happier matters," I said. "Will there be any matches made at this house party?" Every hostess liked to claim that she had brought together the halves of a perfect couple, and the Bathvale gathering was abundantly blessed with unmarried guests.

"What matters a match to a widow?" Clara asked. "You can disport as you please, and nobody judges you for it."

A familiar resentment bloomed, and I saw no reason to keep my feelings to myself. "Do you know how irksome it is for half of Society to accuse you of panting after every man you see, while the other half assumes you will be perpetually bound by grief to the husband who's gone forever?"

I'd kept my voice down, but this was another reason why I hadn't looked forward to this gathering. The status of widow had consolations, but they were consolations for a very great loss even beyond the actual spousal bereavement.

A woman lost wealth, status, security, often her home, much of her dignity, and the right to parent her own children when a husband died, and the law—in the hands of men who suffered none of those burdens—was happy to consign her to such suffering when she was also dealing with grief.

Frederick, for all his faults, had been enlightened on the matter of my fate in the event of his death, but too many widows were not as well situated as I was.

"I am sorry," Clara said. "I did not mean to speak intemperately. Perhaps being a widow is somewhat like being a spinster. I'm neither dead nor elderly, and yet, certain people treat me as if I ought to be one or the other. Instead, I make the best of my lot, avoid the company of matchmakers, and affect good cheer that's seldom genuine."

How hard did a spinster sister find watching Lord and Lady Bathvale move in Society as a wealthy, titled couple, their heir thriving in the nursery with a little sister besides?

"Do you get along with Bathvale?" I asked. He'd disengaged himself from Mrs. Albright, or rather, she'd taken Sebastian's free arm, leaving Bathvale at large. He was a good-looking man, with thick auburn hair, and slightly above-average height. He would age well, but I had yet to see him smile.

Clara walked along in silence until we came to a stile. She popped up the steps and over the fence and waited while I followed. We crossed into another grassy meadow, where honeysuckle was making a good effort to obscure the bordering stone walls. Clara led me to a bench in the sun, and I was reminded of Lucy's warning regarding freckles.

"Bathvale is a gentleman." Clara sank onto the bench, and I joined her. The wood was sun-warmed and smooth, and the location begged for a lady to get out her favorite novel or book or verse.

"Do you damn Bathvale with faint praise?" I asked.

"I neither condemn nor praise. He's old-fashioned."

The sound of the guests' chatter faded as the cavalcade meandered toward its destination. In the secluded meadow, all was peace and quiet, but for the drone of honeybees going about their rounds in the hedges.

"Your description—old-fashioned—could mean your brother-in-law is a courtly swain, or that he believes in burning witches."

Clara twirled her parasol, a frilly, girlish affectation that probably did little to shield her complexion from the sun.

"He's a little of both. He and Belinda were not a love match, but he's not the love-match sort. Women are ornaments to him, expensive, valuable ornaments. We're to bear children out of the sight and hearing of men so as not to disturb the important business of running the realm, or the equally important illusion that the ceaseless toil of our fathers and husbands results in lives of unfettered ease for us."

A younger Clara Putnam would never have formed, much less voiced, that sentiment.

"Frederick was of a similar persuasion, but he did know how to laugh at himself." The day was so lovely, the meadow so splendid, that to discuss the great disappointment that marriage could become felt blasphemous. "Does Bathvale at least treasure his children?"

I had not reconciled myself to my childless state. The one great accomplishment expected of a wealthy man's wife was that she'd produce healthy sons. Had my husband lived, I might have fulfilled that duty—our marriage had been moving toward cordiality, despite his peccadilloes—but fate had decreed otherwise.

"Bathvale was enormously relieved when Owen arrived. We all were. The staff dotes on that child, but he's only one small boy."

Not much to stand between a vast estate and a family's ruin. "More children might come along. Have any of the bachelor guests caught your fancy?"

Clara laughed, though her mirth sounded sad to me. "I'm not that sort of spinster, Lady Violet. Shame on you. Perhaps you can be a bad influence on me. Shall we join the others? All the best picnic spots will be taken, and we'll be forced to share a blanket with those chatty Baxter boys."

The Baxter boys—who were well past university—were a pair of lively rascals. Hostesses adored them because they were excellent dancers, witty dinner companions, and wealthy enough not to be fortune-hunting.

Clara and I returned to the path in the park. When we arrived at the edge of the lake, we found blankets laid out under pavilions in the shade of stately oaks and maples. Footmen were setting up a buffet under a long white awning, and Lady Bathvale was conferring with Samuel.

"I met Master Owen," I said, "earlier today."

"Stumbled into the nursery by accident?" Clara asked.

"No, I came upon the boy with Samuel by the stream at the foot of the back gardens. They had gone wading, apparently."

"*Samuel* was with the boy?"

Oh dear. "Owen was pleased with the outing and entirely charming."

Clara was clearly no longer listening. She was glowering at Samuel, who was in conversation with Lady Bathvale. "We've had problems with Samuel before. He knows better."

The last thing I wanted was to get an innocent man in trouble. "I can't see that any harm was done, Clara. I'm sorry I mentioned it. Samuel said the house party had disrupted the nursery routine, and he'd merely taken Owen out for a breath of fresh air."

"Since when do footmen cart children about?"

What on earth had vexed her? "Since always? My brothers were often attended by footmen when their tutors, nannies, governesses, and governors needed a respite. I beg you not to make too much of this."

Lord Bathvale joined the conversation with Lady Bathvale and Samuel. Both men listened to her ladyship and wore identically attentive expressions.

"You are right, I suppose," Clara said. "But with a possible thief on the loose, any servant behaving oddly bothers me. It appears the dowagers and chaperones have all paired off. I suppose I must sit with the Baxters after all. Perhaps you should join us?"

Lady Bathvale discreetly beckoned to me.

"Thank you for the invitation, Clara, but it appears I'm needed. I'll see you at supper."

Lady Bathvale asked me to sit with Lady Fulton and her son. Lady Fulton had just put off mourning, and her son was at the age when assuming the role of head of the family was a painful fiction.

I settled in for an hour of asking the young man about his studies, his political opinions, and his favorite sports—thank you, odious brothers—but I was perplexed by something Clara had said. If a servant put on airs above his station or failed to take direction well, then in no large English household I knew of would that servant achieve the status of first footman, much less while still a young man.

～

"If I'd known that a bee sting was all that was needed to free us from crawling ants, tittering schoolgirls, and Baxter's bad puns," Sebastian muttered, "I would have volunteered myself for the ordeal two hours ago." He stalked along at my side, casting the occasional glance over his shoulder.

"For a man intent on finding a bride, you seem determined to be disagreeable."

"I'm honest," he said, "in present company."

"Was that a compliment, my lord?"

"A confession, perhaps. Whoever decided to spread picnic blankets beneath oak trees was not thinking clearly."

"Has our gracious king decreed that a marquess is forbidden to get up, move his blanket, and settle somewhere acorns would not trouble his lordly backside?"

That question kept Sebastian quiet for perhaps a half-dozen steps. "What do you make of the missing items?" he asked.

We'd come to the stile that led to the peaceful meadow. The

rest of the party was spread out, some guests lingering by the lake, some wandering in the direction of the house. We were free until dinner, the first formal meal of the gathering, and many hours away.

"We don't know for a certainty that they are missing. Neither the cravat pin nor the earbobs are particularly valuable, and they might both turn up packed in the wrong trunk three days hence."

Rather than use the steps, Sebastian vaulted the stile one-handed. This display of casual athleticism impressed me for its grace and power, despite my current disaffection with my escort.

"Hempley claimed he packs his own traveling jewelry box," Sebastian said, "and he recalls including the amber pin in the baubles chosen for this trip."

"Hempley also claims that Wellington turned to him for advice before half the major battles on the Peninsula."

Sebastian resumed pacing at my side as we wandered in the direction of the old bench. "I long to correct that falsehood. Old Hookey had no time for Hempley. The staff referred to him as Hem-and-Haw, and the men had worse names for him than that."

This was the first mention Sebastian had made of his military service. "What did your men call you?"

When we sat, he ranged an arm along the back of the bench and crossed his ankles. "I was plain MacHeath when in uniform. The title had yet to be secured around my ankle. The men called me sir or, eventually, colonel."

"I thought every officer was christened with a nom de guerre or two." Sebastian had been mentioned in the dispatches, a signal honor for a plain mister, but then, Wellington had known exactly who was in line for a title and who was not.

"Is St. Sevier an intimate friend, Violet?"

What a shame the day was too pretty for my first foray into homicide. "That's twice you've attempted a clumsy change of subject in five minutes, my lord. Are you perhaps realizing that taking a bride means acquiring a living, breathing female for a wife? Seeing her across the breakfast table most days, worrying for her when she's in childbed?"

Sebastian would worry. Despite Clara's contention otherwise, good men did worry over a woman's travail. When Sebastian's sister Clementine had first got with child, I'd thought he'd call his brother-in-law out for putting the lady at risk of harm.

"If a woman cannot abide a few acorns under her picnic blanket," Sebastian said, "if she goes into strong hysterics over a bee sting, how can she contemplate motherhood with any seriousness?"

Miss Waltham of the missing earbobs had had the misfortune to be stung by a bee, or so she claimed.

"You were considering Miss Waltham for your marchioness?"

"No." He uncrossed his ankles, then crossed his arms. "Yes. I must consider them all. They are certainly considering me, but then I think, *She's silly.* I would make her miserable with my focus on the ledgers, correspondence, and tenants. Then *I* will be miserable because a sulking wife is not to be endured. Another young lady strikes me as sufficiently dignified, but she's overly religious. I cannot abide excessive displays of judgmental piety, and I do occasionally swear."

"Quite colorfully."

"Another young lady has a grating laugh, yet another cannot seem to raise her voice above a whisper. They are lovely young women, I'm no great prize, and yet…"

To hear the marquess express anything less than confidence in his objective was surprising. As a boy, Sebastian had been rashly convinced of every goal he set—until he failed or succeeded spectacularly—a characteristic my mother had attributed to Scottish stubbornness.

"Dunkeld, get hold of yourself. Frederick and I did not suit in every particular, but we were learning to muddle along in a somewhat friendly fashion. I was not called upon to adore him, only to perform loyally in public, a courtesy he reciprocated. We contrived, my lord. You will find somebody you can rub along with as well, though attempting to accomplish that task by sundown might be overly ambitious."

"I thought you were quite fond of Belmaine."

Most people had liked Frederick. "I enjoyed his company well enough for the purposes of a cordial marriage." Most of the time, eventually. I hoped.

Sebastian rose, towering over me. "Shall you tarry here, or allow me to escort you back to the house?"

Three changes of subject. Truly, I beheld a marquess rattled by silliness and acorns. "I'll return to the house with you. I'd like to put a few questions to Samuel."

Sebastian apparently still knew better than to offer me assistance to get to my feet. "Why pester the head footman now, when he's likely needed in four places at once?"

"Because I did not leave my shawl in the library, my lord. I wore it there, true, but I returned to my room wearing it."

Sebastian again hoisted himself over the stile in a single lithe bound. "You're certain?"

I stood higher than he by virtue of the steps that led over the fence. "Do you have on a coat right now, my lord? Are you certain?" I finished my descent. "Perhaps you should solicit the opinion of a knowledgeable adult female to confirm your own sense of the matter. Coats can be deceptive. On one minute, slipping off the next..."

"Violet, I didn't mean—"

I started walking up the path. "And the fact that the corridors here are as cold as an icehouse, and a lady risks a lung fever going abroad without a shawl, is of course irrelevant when considering if I know whether I'm dressed or not."

"That's not what I meant."

"You meant that I'm an imbecile, incapable of recalling even the clothes on my person the same day I've worn them. If you did not mean to imply as much, then you offer a lady an apology rather than a scold, Dunkeld."

"I am sorry, but I am also concerned."

"I am concerned as well if that's your version of an apology, sir. Any apology followed by a 'but' is seldom the genuine article."

We rounded a corner of the park, and Bathvale Abbey in all its sprawling glory came into view. I counted windows, found my rooms, and let go of an anxiety I hadn't admitted.

"I am sorry," Sebastian said. "I should never have implied that you could mistake your own wardrobe."

"The sullen tone rather diminishes the gallant effect. Why are you worried?"

"I did not find your shawl in the library."

I slowed my pace, which had been rather headlong. "I beg your pardon?"

"I found your shawl in my bedroom."

Sebastian was many things, most of them annoying, but he was honest. "Then somebody is attempting to throw this house party into chaos."

"You haven't been in my bedroom? Didn't open the wrong door by mistake?"

I stared at my half boots and counted to ten in both French and Latin. "You concede that I know what clothes I'm wearing, but not what rooms I've occupied?"

Sebastian stared past my shoulder, easy to do when he was nearly a foot taller than me.

When he did gaze down at me, his expression was puzzled. "When did you grow so prickly, Violet? I'm trying to make sure of my facts before I accuse anybody of anything. The items that have been misplaced—or stolen, or simply moved about for the sake of inciting chaos as you put it—are of sufficient value to land the perpetrator in very great trouble."

True enough. Theft could result in hanging. Transportation was also a possibility, and surviving the journey, much less the term of penal servitude, was far from assured.

"We cannot be seen to argue," I said, linking my arm through Sebastian's and steering him in the direction of the back gardens. "I did not leave my shawl in your bedroom. To place it there would be the work of a moment for whoever sought to cause this uproar."

"Whoever moved the shawl could not know that, of all the guests, I alone would be able to recognize that garment as yours. I'd think instead that some woman had been pawing through my effects, and when I produced the shawl, the finger would have been pointed at you."

"I expect Lord Hempley's cravat pin will turn up where it ought not be," I said, "and possibly Miss Waltham's earbobs as well, but why?" I explained to Sebastian about finding the strange maid in my bedroom. "She had dark hair, Sebastian, but the actual maid named Haines has flaming red hair. Samuel confirmed that much."

"Is that why you're seeking him out now?" Sebastian asked. "To interrogate him about dark-haired chambermaids lurking precisely where chambermaids are likely to be?"

"The chambermaid doubtless doesn't realize that I glimpsed her hair and can catch her out in a lie. I feel I ought to say something to Lady Bathvale." Exactly what to say, I did not know.

"I feel you ought to keep your door locked at all times. Somebody has already attempted to embroil you in unsavory talk."

Another possibility made more sense. "Or attempted to imply that you and I are having a liaison."

Sebastian wrinkled his lordly beak. "It's a house party. We're of age and unattached. Who would look askance, even if that outlandish fantasy were true?"

We were alone in the garden, but in full view of the manor and park. A raging set-down for the marquess, followed by a grand exit on my part, would not do.

"In your opinion, I don't merit a man's intimate appreciation, my lord?"

He led me up the steps into the first of the tiered parterres. "There is a curious creature in the northern woods of the New World. It looks like a larger version of a hedgehog, but can do significant damage by embedding barbed quills in the flesh of any who approach it."

"First you ask impertinent questions, then you bungle an apology. Now you call me a porcupine. I fear for the Dunkeld succession."

"In the name of all that's plaid, Violet Belmaine, I state the obvious. You'd no sooner dally with me than you'd sing an aria in public."

I not only *could not* sing in public, I *would not* sing in public. Sebastian had learned that from one of my traitor brothers when I'd been fifteen. I'd had the usual lessons in voice, and my natural talent was above reproach—until I had an audience. The results then were the stuff of my nightmares and probably the nightmares of all who'd heard me.

"I will talk to Lucy about making sure my effects cannot be plundered," I said. "Will you mention the situation to Lord Bathvale?"

"I will, assuming I can find a moment alone with him. Men have been hung or flogged to death on the strength of accusations that at the time made perfect sense, but were later found to be misguided."

He was doubtless referring to some tragedy from his military career. "This is not the army, my lord. For whom do you fear?"

The garden was of the older, formal style, all low hedges and statuary, with only an occasional urn of heartsease to give it color. Clara's comments about Lord Bathvale came to mind. The garden was geometric, tidy, and utterly boring, but doubtless met his lordship's standard for what the garden of a grand estate should be.

And somebody was trying to bring scandal to this stately, sunny corner of the Downs, but why?

"Fear is too strong a word," Sebastian replied. "I do have a valet in my employ about whom I know little, one who has no friends among the staff. Upjohn strikes me as the honest sort, and he took the king's shilling for six years. He'd make an easy target, with nobody to vouch for him and a memory that's less than sound."

Oh dear. As snobbish as the aristocracy was, domestics could be snobbier. "I will ask Lucy to befriend him, to the extent a maid and a valet can be friends." I would ask Samuel for the same consideration, assuming I could find the head footman and have a private word with him.

Sebastian offered me a parting bow on the back terrace. "You never did explain your relationship with St. Sevier."

I patted the marquess's chest. "And I'm not about to now. Until dinner, my lord." I curtseyed and took my leave of him.

CHAPTER FIVE

At a formal dinner, strict propriety dictated that I converse with only the companions seated immediately to my right and to my left. Over the course of a long meal, sheer boredom and successive glasses of wine usually resulted in that rule being honored in the breach.

The widow of a mere mister apparently did not rank among the earls and heirs, even if her papa had been titled. I thus ended up seated between St. Sevier and Lord Hempley at dinner, a juxtaposition of the charming and the insufferable.

Hempley smelled strongly of cigars with an undernote of brandy. His hand found its way to my arm nearly every time he turned to speak to me, which was constantly. His beefy thigh occasionally brushed against my leg, until I contemplated spilling my wine on myself to cut short my tribulation. I liked the dress Lucy had chosen for me, though, a pale blue velvet that did nice things for my eyes. A wine stain would ruin the frock, and any moment, I expected Lady Bathvale to liberate the female guests from the dining room.

"Ruddy damned shame," Hempley said, for perhaps the third time. "We're not even safe under our own roofs anymore." He took a gulp of his wine. "Pardon my language, your ladyship, but the rabble have got above themselves ever since the Corsican was packed off to that island."

Hempley was what most would have called a fine figure of a man, meaning he had a prosperous belly, an extra chin, and a nose that would grow more veined and bulbous by the year if he didn't moderate his drinking. He brushed thick white hair straight back from his brow and likely prided himself on his aim with a fowling piece.

"Please enlighten me," I said. "How does Napoleon's defeat result in more domestic crime, my lord?"

"The riffraff," he replied, lowering his voice and breathing foul fumes on me. "We rounded 'em up and paid 'em to march. Now they're back, calling themselves the saviors of the realm, but once a scoundrel, always a scoundrel, I always say. Today, it's a pair of earbobs. Tomorrow, a lady's person will be plundered."

He'd spoken loudly enough that Lord and Lady Bathvale exchanged a look down the length of the table. On my right, I could feel the quality of St. Sevier's silence shift from patiently amused to something quieter and less gracious.

Several of the diners were still eating, which meant the ladies could not leave yet. I cast around for a change of topic, but Mr. Thaddeus Baxter, who sat across from Hempley, spoke up first.

"Being a bit premature, aren't you, Hempley? A few missing baubles hardly means brigands are roaming the corridors. No need to alarm the ladies, is there?"

Hempley gestured with his wineglass, which had the unfortunate result of sloshing a few drops of claret on my hand.

"Better to be alert to the thieves and scalawags among us now," Hempley said, "than to wait for them to steal us blind in our sleep."

The sheer rudeness of that remark toward our host and hostess had everybody studying their plates, the candles, or the fresco on the ceiling.

"Do you," St. Sevier said softly, "happen to know who the thieves and scalawags might be, my lord? I am under the impression that until a culprit has been identified—if indeed there is a culprit—that wild accusations will only serve to inflame tempers and insult the innocent."

Too late, I recalled that Hugh St. Sevier was French, and Hempley had lost a son on the Peninsula.

"I have no wish to hear accusations," I said. "Not over a pair of earbobs that will likely turn out to have been misplaced rather than stolen."

"My cravat pin was *stolen*," Hempley said in the too-loud tones of the semi-inebriated. "Anybody who says otherwise is calling me a liar, madam."

"But let us ask ourselves," St. Sevier said in cool tones, "who had the most ready access to your personal effects, my lord? You and your manservant, or some unnamed thief risking his life in a house crowded to the rafters with guests and servants? And why steal such a commonplace item when every guest room offered more valuable jewels?"

Other conversations died. The clatter of cutlery on china fell silent, and across the table, Sebastian's gaze had become watchful. Beside him, Clara Putnam's expression was a cross between horrified and rapt.

How many people here knew that Sebastian's valet had served on the Peninsula, among the *riffraff who'd been paid to march?*

Hempley set down his wineglass. "You damned Frenchie. You *damned*, upstart Frenchie. Are you accusing me of fabricating a tale from whole cloth? You, whose self-crowned emperor tried to steal all of Europe for his own? Sneak thieves, the lot of you. I can assure you—"

I stood before any challenges were issued. "I can assure the entire assembly that I am more than ready for a hot cup of tea among the ladies in the parlor." Because I'd sat between Hempley and St. Sevier, I became a physical barrier between them when I stood. I chose that ploy rather than the less obtrusive coughing fit. The last thing I wanted was to give Hempley an opportunity to solicitously put his hands anywhere on my person.

"Quite so," Lady Bathvale said, getting to her feet. "Lady Violet has anticipated my own suggestion. Ladies, shall we leave the gentlemen to their port?"

The men rose en masse, Lord Bathvale and the Baxters escorted the women to the parlor, and I said a small prayer that Lord Bathvale would intervene between two guests who'd nearly come to blows.

"Why on earth would St. Sevier antagonize a man so clearly not worth the bother?" Clara murmured as we filed into the parlor. Folding doors had been opened, so the music room next door and the guest parlor flowed together, creating a space sufficient to accommodate more than a dozen women.

"Why remain silent when Hempley was being an ass?" I countered. "First he accuses our gallant infantrymen of turning up criminal, then he turns suspicion on St. Sevier merely because his parents were French. Such behavior is inexcusable, particularly when St. Sevier also served under Wellington on the Peninsula." And yet, only Baxter had spoken up to intercede.

"Bad form, I do agree," Clara said, joining me on a love seat in a corner. "But Hempley's an old blowhard, and nobody takes his maunderings seriously. Is Dunkeld truly, truly looking for a wife?"

"Apparently so."

Clara and Sebastian might well be a good match. She was unencumbered by romantic notions, he was... Sebastian had called himself no great prize, and that comment bothered me. He was grouchy, arrogant, moody, and difficult, but he would die to protect those he loved, and his integrity was unassailable. He was a prize, if an imperfect prize.

"I do believe the question of his lordship's bride-hunting will be moot before I find a moment alone with the marquess," Clara said. "Which of the Baxter boys do you think will fall into Miss Waltham's arms?"

Across the room, Lady Bathvale presided over an elegant service of Sèvres porcelain. Ornate cups and saucers, gilded plates full of cakes, and pretty embroidered table napkins were passed out as guests organized themselves into small groups. The tension in the dining room had been put aside, but only for the juicier game of matchmaking.

"Why not set your cap for one of the Baxters?" I asked. "They are charming, the family is much respected, and you would have your own household."

For that matter, why didn't *I* consider marrying one of them? But I knew the answer. I'd already had one charming husband, and while Frederick and I had made a go of our marriage, more or less, the experience had cost me the last of my romantic inclinations.

"I could not leave Bathvale," Clara said. "This is my home now, and my sister needs me."

She spoke with simple conviction, though I doubted her conclusion. Lady Bathvale seemed supremely comfortable in her role as a titled man's hostess, and an army of servants, as well as Lord Bathvale, were on hand to see to her needs.

Clara drifted away, and when I looked around for her a few minutes later, she'd apparently left the room. I was about to do likewise when Lady Bathvale took the place beside me on the love seat.

"Thank you," she said. "I was waiting for Mrs. Bonaventure to finish eating, lest I appear rude, but those men..."

"St. Sevier was publicly maligned, and Hempley had been far too liberal with the wine."

"Which is why St. Sevier should not have taken offense. But he did."

An accusation, or at least a suspicion, lay in her ladyship's words. "You think St. Sevier protests too much?" The notion was outlandish.

"No, but I do wish he hadn't antagonized Hempley."

"Hempley antagonized *him*, my lady." Should I explain that for the two previous hours, Hempley had been blustering and cursing, when he hadn't been making free with my person? The man was a disgrace, even if he had lost a son on the battlefield.

"Well, Hempley wasn't wrong," Lady Bathvale said quietly. "Somebody among my guests has taken to thieving. I've a notion to call for the magistrate, but Bathvale won't hear of it."

Good for him. "I meant to tell you that I came across a maid in my bedroom, one who identified herself as Haines."

"Haines?"

With dozens of inside maids, I could not expect her ladyship to know each one by name. "A young woman with dark hair. Samuel told me that Haines has bright red hair."

"When did you have occasion to discuss this with him?"

That was the wrong question for my hostess to ask. Instead of focusing on a lying maid who could well be our thief, Lady Bathvale had seized on my conversation with Samuel.

"Earlier today," I said. "Samuel is quite busy, but I caught him between duties for a moment."

Lady Bathvale glanced around at her other guests, who were chatting in small groups and looking entirely harmless.

"In future, you may bring such inquiries to me. There's more afoot here than I can comfortably disclose."

And that was also odd, given that she'd specifically recommended Samuel to me as a source of ad hoc assistance.

"There's something else you should know, my lady." I explained about my shawl magically secreting itself in the quarters of a bachelor marquess. "And I hope my recitation absolves Monsieur St. Sevier of any suspicion in your eyes."

The gentlemen had begun to arrive, suggesting the session over port and cigars had been extremely brief.

"I'm not sure I follow your logic, Lady Violet. How does this situation with your shawl absolve anyone of anything?"

"The only guest at this entire gathering who would know I own that shawl is Lord Dunkeld—I've owned it that long, and it's a distinctive item. I've worn it once so far outside my rooms, when no other guest was wandering the corridors. The only person at this entire gathering who knows how well Dunkeld and I were

acquainted in our youth is St. Sevier. If St. Sevier were attempting to
embroil me in gossip, why would he put my shawl in the rooms of the
only man with whom that plan was doomed to fail?"

She studied me for a long moment, and I could not divine her
thoughts. Did she *want* to make a scapegoat of St. Sevier?

"I tell you this in strictest confidence, my lady," she said,
keeping her voice very low. "Mrs. Albright's mourning locket has
gone missing. Her quarters were searched from sheets to shoes, to
no avail. I don't particularly care what happens to a cheap cravat
pin or pair of earbobs, but a widow's mourning locket is an item of
great sentimental value. We either find that locket in the next day
or two, or I summon the magistrate, and Bathvale will not gainsay
me."

~

I excused myself from the gathering when Mr. Bertram Baxter came
up with the brilliant suggestion to finish off the evening with "a few
hands of cards." I had never been fond of cards or of the drama that
could accompany deep play.

I bade the company good night and made for the door at what I
hoped was a ladylike pace.

"I will escort you to your room," St. Sevier said, taking a carrying
candle from among a dozen sitting on the sideboard. He lit the candle
from a sconce in the drafty corridor and offered his arm.

"You were naughty," I said, wrapping my hand in the crook of his
elbow. "Hempley wasn't worth the bother and should have been left
to drink himself under the table."

"I would not trust that slobbering hound under any table where
ladies were taking their meal."

The note of genuine anger in St. Sevier's voice surprised me. He
was usually so urbane and self-possessed.

"Hempley insulted Wellington's infantry before he got around to
insulting you," I pointed out. "The 'riffraff' who died in droves to

keep us safe. Somebody should have planted him a facer for that comment alone."

We mounted the stairs, the temperature dropping as we reached the higher floor. Bathvale Abbey really was a mausoleum of a building. I could only imagine what Yuletide guests endured if the corridors were chilly even in high summer.

"Before Hempley insulted anybody else," St. Sevier said, pausing at the top of the steps, "he insulted you."

"He was friendly."

"He was a pig."

Well, yes. "I've been fending off pigs since I left the schoolroom, monsieur. If I took exception to every man who allowed his leg to bump mine, or put his hand on my arm without invitation, I would soon be invited nowhere."

"I do not understand Englishwomen," St. Sevier said, leading me down the corridor toward my room. "You would benefit exceedingly from losing your tempers from time to time, but no. Instead, you smile, nod, pass the teapot, and make me want to vomit. Hempley had no business touching you."

"None at all, but what does it profit me to call attention to his behavior when I know Lady Bathvale seated me beside him precisely because I can manage his pathetic overtures without losing my composure? Wait a moment, would you?"

Something had wedged itself into my slipper, and I'd ignored the irritation long enough. I took a chair in an unlit alcove and untied the ribbon holding the shoe on my foot.

"That her ladyship expected you to fend off the old rhinoceros makes it all the worse."

I shook out my slipper and put it back on. "He lost a son in Spain, St. Sevier."

"I lost three brothers to the Corsican's madness, one of them in the infirmary of a British camp. I saw good men of many nationalities die by the thousands. Does that give me the right to comport myself like a troglodyte?"

Three brothers? "I am so sorry for your loss, and I do take your point. Hempley behaved disgracefully. If he doesn't learn some manners, I will reprimand him privately."

St. Sevier's smile was crooked and, by the dim light of the single candle, wan. "That is the very point, though. You should not have to *be* private with a man who cannot observe proper decorum even in public, should you?"

"Is that why you argued with him? To stop him from groping my leg?"

"He groped your—*mon Dieu*, I do not understand Englishmen either. How can Lord Bathvale allow such a cretin among his guests? I will sit next to Hempley in your stead in the future, are we agreed?"

"We are not. Everybody would remark the disruption to the seating order, and you would call further attention to yourself." The alcove was chilly, and I had not worn a shawl to a formal dinner. I rose, looking forward to the sanctuary of my room.

"He would have seized on Upjohn," St. Sevier said. "That unfortunate is a destitute veteran, raised above his station only recently and only by the largesse of Lord Dunkeld. Because Upjohn suffered severe blows to the head, his ability to recount his recent activities could be faulty. Hempley would bluster that into an inference of guilt, and I simply cannot abide a bully."

St. Sevier spoke softly, but both his voice and his gaze held a flat, soulless quality that added to the corridor's chill.

"I had hoped Upjohn might have been spared Hempley's aspersions," I said, though both Sebastian and St. Sevier had seen the possibility. "Have a word with Dunkeld, and he'll make sure Upjohn stays out of sight. My thanks for your escort."

"My pleasure." St. Sevier bowed, the light bobbing with him and casting odd shadows. "I would tell you to be careful, but I have concluded that lecturing you is pointless. Would you be very upset if I departed from this gathering?"

Well, yes, I would. "You can't leave now. Mrs. Albright's

mourning locket has gone missing. If you return to London, you will look as guilty as Hempley would like you to be."

St. Sevier cupped my jaw with his free hand. His touch was warm and, in some way, an antidote to Hempley's drunken pawing. "You do not need me."

Whatever did that mean? "I would not be at the house party without your encouragement," I said. "I do need my friends, Hugh."

"On that tactful note, I will take my leave of you, my lady." He kissed my forehead, a gentle brush of his lips that soothed even as the spicy scent of his shaving soap reminded me that he was a gentleman of means *and experience. "Bonsoir, Violette."*

"Good night."

He sauntered on his way, leaving me in the gloomy little alcove a few doors and one turning away from my bedroom. An odd, unwelcome thought joined me: Would a man who'd lost three brothers to war with Britain take satisfaction from relieving English aristocrats of their gems and baubles? I did not think so—St. Sevier had taken the British side, in at least a medical capacity—but revenge played a role in many a foolhardy undertaking.

Somebody was creating havoc at this house party, and they were doing so with increasingly valuable personal items—a shawl, a cravat pin, pearl earbobs, and now a mourning locket. I wandered up the corridor to my room, pondering if that list of items revealed any significant connections. The missing effects were all personal, meaning one of a kind and easily identified.

The thief was being either stupid or purposely provocative.

I arrived at my room only to find Lord Hempley had propped himself against the wall opposite my door, his arms crossed. At the sight of me, he pushed away from the wall and approached.

"If it isn't Lady Violet. Did you tarry on the landing with your pet Frenchie?"

Lord save me from aging sots. "I'll bid you good night, sir." I stayed out of pawing range, because however much Hempley had overimbibed, he'd also waited for me outside my room, and he'd seen me leave the guest parlor with St. Sevier. He wasn't falling-down drunk, he was recklessly drunk.

"If you fancy a tumble, you needn't soil yourself rolling in the mud with the likes of him," Hempley said, stepping closer on a blast of foul breath. "You're a widow. You have needs."

"I *need* a good night's sleep." I *wanted* a bullwhip. "Let me pass."

He smiled, a ghastly, wet-lipped horror of a grin. "Playing coy, are you? You're all cool and proper at the dinner table, but I know your kind. You're a hot little piece of fluff beneath the sheets, and I know exactly how to give you what you want."

He watched me with the fixed, predatory gaze of the stray dog who'd decided to make an unsuspecting rabbit his next meal.

But I was not a rabbit. When Hempley lunged at me, I was ready for him. He was surprisingly fast, and he had the good fortune—or the guile—to tromp on my hem. Using my knee to destroy his rutting inclinations was thus difficult, and as I struggled, my annoyance flared into the beginning of fear.

"Hold still," he snarled, yanking on my arms. "You can flirt with that frog by the hour, but you begrudge a peer of the realm so much as a little—"

Lord Hempley flew across the corridor like so much dirty linen tossed down a laundry chute. He hit the opposite wall with a dull thud and slumped there, glaring at me as Sebastian came up on my right side.

"Bid the lady good night." His burr had thickened to the consistency of a lethal threat.

"Dunkeld." Hempley pushed himself upright and jerked down his waistcoat. "You misconstrue what was merely—"

"Bid the lady good night, or name your seconds."

I ought to have been appalled by that reckless talk. I'd been accosted in dim corridors before, and I really should have known better than to part from my escort even a few yards shy of my door. Even so, Hempley had disrespected me, as St. Sevier had said, and then he'd sought to do me bodily harm.

I glowered at Hempley when what I wanted to do most in the whole world was slink off to my room and indulge in a fit of the weeps.

"Beg pardon," Hempley said. "Meant nothing by it."

Sebastian jabbed a finger in the direction of the staircase. "Go, and do not presume to address her ladyship again in this lifetime. If I find you've forgotten that warning, when I'm done with you, all four of her brothers will take a turn, and they won't leave enough of you to poison a lapdog."

Hempley strutted off, and abruptly, my knees threatened to fail me.

"Come along," Sebastian said, wrapping an arm around my waist. "You might well be coherent enough to scold me for my presumption, highhandedness, and interfering male behavior, but I, for one, need a drink."

"A drink right about now sounds lovely," I said, but then, Sebastian's arm around my waist, supporting me and anchoring me to his side, felt blessedly lovely as well.

~

I slept surprisingly well, considering that Lord Hempley had made such a pest of himself. When Sebastian had returned me to my room, he'd lingered long enough to make me finish a serving of Madeira and explained to Lucy exactly what had transpired. I had sipped my nightcap and let Sebastian lecture me about drunken fools, presuming toads, and heaven knew what else.

I was sufficiently rattled that his *interfering male behavior* endeared him to me, though that aberration was doubtless temporary. And yet, when I ventured from my room the next morning, Sebastian was loitering outside my door, and I was glad to see him.

"I was just on my way to breakfast," he said. "We can go down together."

"No, we cannot. Not unless you *ask* me to join you."

He tugged at his cravat, which was off-center, then heaved a long-suffering sigh. "Violet, dearest companion of my halcyon youth, would you be so good as to endure my company on the hike down to the breakfast parlor?"

"Hold still." I batted his hands aside and untied his cravat. "Upjohn's work leaves something to be desired. What knot do you prefer?"

"A simple mathematical, please. I tied this myself. Upjohn has apparently become lost in the catacombs that pass for servants' quarters in this place."

I drew the ends of his cravat even, then positioned them for a knot that would be symmetrical once completed.

"Do you truly want a mathematical, or is that the only knot you know?"

Sebastian lifted his chin, allowing me to deal with his linen. His docility was either a random miracle or a measure of his vanity. "I like the plainer styles, and if I did ask you to tie something fancy, then Upjohn would try to replicate it on his own, and the result would render me fodder for the Baxters' attempts at humor."

"Better," I said, fluffing the lacy ends of his neckcloth once I'd tied the knot. "You don't think Upjohn has scarpered, do you?"

We struck off in the direction of the breakfast parlor, though I was certain that the servants' stairs would have seen us there sooner.

"Why would Upjohn leave the first stable employment he's had in months?" Sebastian asked. "He's miles from London, has yet to receive any wages, and has only my livery to wear."

"You hired him without a character, Dunkeld. You must admit that finding a man naked in a Mayfair ballroom is not a sound recommendation of his talent for domestic service."

"He's trying to do his best, and that's all I ask of any man."

"You heard Hempley referring to the enlisted men as riffraff?" I asked.

Sebastian stopped to admire his reflection in a pier glass.

"Upjohn is not a thief, Violet. I know him to be possessed of at least common sense."

"Thieves are likely sensible, even cautious, people. Don't ruin my handiwork, Dunkeld."

He gave the cravat a tug without pulling it askew. "If Upjohn is a thief, then he's chosen the worst possible place to embark on his life of crime. Better to steal a winter coat from my town house. It won't be missed for months, getting it to a fence or a pawnshop is the work of a quarter hour, and nobody would connect him joining the household now with the coat disappearing when the theft is discovered this winter."

I resumed our progress toward good food and hot tea. "You have a point, my lord."

"I liked it better when you called me Sebastian."

So had I. "I must thank you for intervening last night with Hempley. He's faster than he looks."

Sebastian paused at the head of the stairs. "I saw his lordship leave the parlor after you and St. Sevier had bid everybody good night. I did not care for the way Hempley looked at you."

I was torn between gratitude for Sebastian's vigilance and frustration with a code of gentlemanly conduct that meant Hempley could grope a woman and leer at her in public, and the response of his peers would be simply to keep an eye on him. At the next house party, Hempley would accost some other widow—or worse, a spinster or companion who lacked the connections I could claim.

"Thank you," I said again. "I will talk with Lady Bathvale regarding Hempley's conduct. He will not be invited back, I'm sure." I stopped on the landing, which had a large arched window that overlooked the back garden. "Somebody has escaped the nursery again."

Samuel and the Bathvale heir were once more at liberty, the boy skipping along and tugging on Samuel's hand.

"I've often thought that children should be given an hour of fresh air to tear about and yell and get dirty first thing in the day," Sebastian said. "Then they could settle to their book learning, instead of pining away all day in the schoolroom and hoping for good weather when they eventually earn their parole."

He was pragmatic. I'd always liked that about him.

While we watched, Samuel swung the boy up onto his back, which struck me as unfootmanlike behavior when in full view of the house.

"They appear to be great friends," I said. "I suppose it speaks well of Lord Bathvale that his staff is so fond of the heir."

Lord Bathvale himself was coming up the walkway from the stables. He was in riding attire, suggesting he'd begun his day with a morning hack. An argument ensued, with Bathvale gesturing toward the house and Samuel making an equally emphatic gesture in the direction of the stream.

"Do your footmen remonstrate with you like that?" I asked quietly. And what sort of doting papa failed to even acknowledge his only son upon first seeing him in the morning?

"Not if those footmen want to keep their jobs," Sebastian replied. "They might suggest, point out, or discreetly raise a question, but they wouldn't challenge my authority in front of my own child, much less before a house full of guests."

The disagreement continued for another few moments, the two men curiously unlike earl and footman. They were of an age, approximately the same height, and of much the same physique. Attire alone distinguished them.

The boy buried his nose against Samuel's neck, and the discussion ended with Bathvale making a dismissive gesture, then stalking off toward the house.

"The boy gets his outing," Sebastian said as Samuel set the child on his feet and continued with him into the garden. "I do admire nursery staff who will take up for their charges."

"Samuel is not nursery staff," I said, starting down the stairs. "He is the first footman, but if we are to believe the evidence of our eyes, he also has sufficient standing to countermand the wishes of the head of the household." At least when it came to Bathvale's son, about whom no one, not even the boy's mother, should have had more authority than Lord Bathvale.

"I can hear you thinking," Sebastian said as we reached the ground floor. "Does a footman with the audacity to defy his employer have enough boldness to steal from the employer's guests? Have you been reading too many Gothic novels, Violet?"

"I've decided to write one," I retorted, "about an irascible Scottish marquess whose eccentricities include hiring a naked valet and rescuing intrepid damsels from the clutches of sniveling Englishmen."

Sebastian laughed, a hearty, merry sound that stirred many a happy memory. "I like the sniveling-Englishmen part, but I'm not irascible. I'm simply confident of my conclusions, as a Scotsman among Englishmen must be if he hopes to survive the ordeal of inferior company."

We approached the breakfast parlor, and the scent of fresh toast and bacon assailed me. I realized that I was hungry, famished, in fact. I had not eaten much of the evening meal. I also realized that Sebastian had done me a significant kindness by entering the breakfast parlor at my side. If Hempley had been spreading slander in my direction, the morning meal would become a gauntlet of whispers, nods, and sly smiles.

As it happened, Lord Hempley wasn't even present among the guests enjoying their first meal of the day.

I took my seat, accepted a cup of tea from Mrs. Albright, and added a third realization to my list: I had missed Sebastian's laughter. Had missed it terribly and was delighted to have provoked him to mirth.

CHAPTER SIX

Breakfast posed a conundrum.

Sebastian had seated himself closer to the head of the table and next to Miss Fredericka Peasedale. Fredericka's younger sister had stolen a march on her and married a viscount's spare last Season. Fredericka was thus understandably flirting nineteen to the dozen with Sebastian, while her mother cooed and smiled at the would-be couple from across the table.

I buttered my toast and pondered whether I ought to intervene, and if so, how? Sebastian had chosen to sit next to Miss Peasedale, but did that mean he'd chosen to have her breast mashed against his arm in public? Chosen to have her all but whispering in his ear before the entire company? Was her thigh pressed against his under the table, or was her hand even now *accidentally* wandering north of his knee?

Not that any of that was my business.

Thaddeus Baxter, on Miss Peasedale's other side, was attempting to offer the lady a distraction, but Sebastian was a marquess, a war hero, wealthy, and not bad looking—in a dark, irascible sort of way.

Mr. Baxter's charm and ten thousand pounds a year could not compete with Sebastian's greater standing.

"May I join you?" Hugh St. Sevier stood to my right, a full plate in his hand.

"Your bacon might suffer for proximity to my appetite," I said, "but I would appreciate the company. How did you sleep?"

He slid into the empty seat and held up his plate for me to take a snitch of bacon. The gesture would be remarked, while Miss Peasedale's assault on Sebastian's person would likely merit nary a raised eyebrow. Unmarried women attended house parties to attach the interests of unmarried men and conversely.

"I slept well, my lady. And you?"

"I am not an early riser, but needs must when a pot of chocolate beckons. If you'd walk with me to the library after we break our fast, I'd appreciate it." I wanted him to hear of Hempley's bad behavior from me. Sebastian would keep his mouth shut, of course, but Hempley's discretion wasn't to be trusted. He'd been the worse for drink, and who knew what imagined slights he'd concocted when swilling away the dregs of the evening?

"I will happily escort you anywhere you please to go."

St. Sevier's comment landed in the middle of one of those pauses that occur when members of a group chatted among themselves. Miss Peasedale scowled at her cinnamon bun, for St. Sevier's offer had apparently caught Sebastian's attention.

St. Sevier's good looks held up to morning light, which could not be said for every gentleman present. He was no boy, but his habits were moderate, and perhaps as a result of his medical training, he believed in fresh air and regular exercise too. Hugh was charming, reputed to be wealthy, but also something of a mystery to polite society.

And to me. Did I want my name linked to his at a gathering like this?

"My lady, the butter, if you please," Sebastian said, "and I do believe we're almost out of toast at this end of the table."

A footman scurried from the sideboard, a rack of golden toast in his hand. The conversation resumed, and St. Sevier tucked into his meal as if nothing untoward had occurred.

"Are you never afflicted by anxieties or worries yourself?" I asked, keeping my voice down. "Does nothing ruffle your calm?"

He held up his plate again, offering me more bacon. "You ask that after last night?"

We were not about to plow that ground again, not in a full breakfast parlor. "No more for me, thank you. If you could pass the raspberry jam?"

Lord Bathvale joined the gathering, bending to kiss Lady Bathvale's cheek before taking his seat. The gesture struck me as perfunctory. Not the morning greeting of a couple with two small children in the nursery. Perhaps his lordship was vexed with Samuel, perhaps he was vexed to cut his morning horseback ride short.

"Today's diversion will be an archery tournament," St. Sevier said. "Do you wield the bow and arrow, my lady?"

"I have four brothers. What do you think?" Too late, I recalled him telling me that he'd lost three brothers and regretted my comment.

"I think I will try to be assigned to whatever team you are on and thus improve my chances of victory. I understand the Baxters are effective marksmen too."

Thaddeus Baxter confirmed the rumor and tried to draw Clara Putnam into the conversation. She claimed to eschew all activities involving weapons, which prompted an inane discussion of whether good looks were a weapon or a curse or both.

I took another strip of bacon, lest my mouth get me into trouble so early in the day.

"Excuse me, all," Lord Bathvale said, raising his voice slightly. The table grew quiet, for Bathvale's tone was far from jovial. "Some of you are aware that a few items of sentimental value have gone missing since we began our gathering two days ago. As your host, I'm asking you each to keep a sharp eye out for a pair of pearl earbobs, an amber cravat pin, and—I regret to add—Mrs. Albright's mourning locket, which shaped like a golden heart. If the missing objects are not found by suppertime tomorrow, I will have no choice but to turn the matter over to the local magistrate."

A quiet shock traveled up and down the table. Beside me, St. Sevier said nothing, but he and Sebastian exchanged a fleeting glance.

"I am certain," Lord Bathvale went on, "that the issue is one of misplaced property rather than anything nefarious, but Sir Randall Hatcher, as the king's man in these surrounds, has been helpful in recovering lost property before. We consider him a friend and neighbor and will seek his advice if necessary."

Lady Bathvale asked for the teapot and the cream pitcher. St. Sevier went back to eating his omelet. Across the table, Sebastian looked positively thunderous. He rose abruptly, bowing to Miss Peasedale though she was in midsentence.

"What has the resident Highlander in a temper?" St. Sevier asked quietly. "And where do you suppose Hempley is? He struck me as a man who took regular sustenance as a religious obligation."

"Hempley is doubtless nursing a very sore head," I said. "As for Dunkeld, he and Sir Randall have a prior acquaintance. They do not care for each other."

The two men nearly hated one another and had since adolescence. Something to do with schoolyard politics, as best I recalled.

"And what of you?" St. Sevier asked. "Do you have an opinion regarding Sir Randall?"

"He's charming, shrewd, and well-favored. He enjoys a good opinion of himself." *Don't turn your back on him.*

"Splendid," St. Sevier muttered. "Another Englishman prone to tantrums and sulks. Exactly what the situation does not call for."

~

A man's library revealed a lot about him. Was his collection organized? Was the room itself clean? Were the chairs comfortable? Or did musty books line the shelves mostly for show, a testament to wealth and arrogance rather than to learning?

Lord Bathvale's library was a sizable room, situated, as most libraries were, to take advantage of natural light. The windows overlooked the back garden, and three fireplaces ensured the space would be reasonably warm, at least in certain areas. The faint smell of coal smoke suggested the fires were frequently lit, and in addition to that scent, I detected the worn-leather fragrance of old books.

If the collection had been acquired for show, it had not been acquired recently, though the globe, massive desk, and busts of former kings suggested no one had exercised any imagination in this room for at least the last century either.

"What do you seek here among the learned tomes?" St. Sevier asked.

"Privacy," I replied, traveling a good distance from the door to ensure no guest would overhear our discussion. "Samuel, good morning."

The head footman, who an hour earlier had been arguing with the master of the household, now stood with his nose in a book between two rows of shelves.

"My lady, monsieur. Good morning." His bow was worthy of a ducal heir. "May I help you find a particular title?"

Had Samuel been waiting for another guest? Perhaps a female guest?

"I fancy a good Gothic novel," St. Sevier said. "A terrifying adventure distracts the mind from bunions, wrinkled linen, and other burdens, do you not agree?"

"I favor travelogues myself," Samuel said, "but if it's novels you prefer, we are well supplied."

St. Sevier dutifully followed Samuel to a set of shelves closer to the far end of the room, while I took up the book Samuel had been reading. A travelogue, true enough, recounting the great capitals of the Continent from the perspective of their architectural, artistic, and ancient glories.

"Do you have a moment?" I asked Samuel as St. Sevier took to perusing the novels.

"Of course, my lady. How may I be of service?"

"Lord Dunkeld has brought a manservant by the name of Upjohn with him to this house party."

Samuel grimaced. "Very trim fellow, new to his livery. New to service, I fear."

"Why do you say that?" Upjohn bore little resemblance to the unkempt unfortunate I'd met in the Robertsons' ballroom. He was clean now. His cheeks were clean-shaven, and—lest I overlook the obvious—he was clothed in more than a tablecloth.

"His livery is new, ma'am, for one thing, but more to the point, he's not sure how to go on."

"How to go on? In what sense?"

Samuel looked as if he wasn't sure how much to tell me. "The organizing principle of life belowstairs is that we take our consequence from those we serve. Your lady's maid is given considerable deference, for example, because you are an earl's daughter. Only Lady Bathvale's abigail outranks Miss Hewitt among the junior female domestics. The governess, housekeeper, and cook rank above Miss Hewitt, but will treat her most cordially nonetheless."

I'd been aware of this reality, but hadn't considered the ramifications at a large gathering.

"You are saying Upjohn has considerable consequence belowstairs because he's attached to the highest-ranking gentleman guest."

"Precisely, my lady. Upjohn should sit at the butler's right hand at the second table. He should be first in line at the breakfast buffet in the servants' hall. He should leave his boots and shoes out for the boot-boy, not sit up with the boot-boy as they both work at the same labors."

The other servants, clearly, had remarked Upjohn's eccentricity.

"Upjohn is former military," I said. "He takes the care of his kit seriously. He is new to service, but Lord Dunkeld hired him personally. If you'd take a friendly interest in him, I'd appreciate it."

Samuel's gaze fell on the travelogue in my hand. "I'll do what I can, but a valet who needs help with his own neckcloth will be considered an odd duck."

"Lord Dunkeld is not without his eccentricities and doesn't care for fancy linen."

Samuel leaned nearer. "I came upon Mr. Upjohn in the stables last night, ma'am. I was... I thought he'd been drinking, but detected no evidence of overindulgence about his person. He was simply disoriented. I suspected hashish, but again, I caught no hint of the scent about his person, and one doesn't go to the stables to smoke."

Hashish? *Gracious ministers of the Almighty.* "I assure you, Samuel, that Upjohn is as upstanding as you or I, but he recently suffered an injury to the head, and it apparently still troubles him. Your efforts to smooth his way will be appreciated, and I will let Lord Dunkeld know we've had this chat." Samuel was a canny fellow. He'd grasp that Lord Dunkeld's appreciation would take the form of a generous vail at the conclusion of the gathering.

"I'm happy to help, my lady. May I reshelve that book for you?"

"Please," I said, passing over the tome in question. "I'll join Dr. St. Sevier among the Gothic novels and perhaps borrow one for myself."

"I'm sure Lord Bathvale would want you to enjoy his collection. Lady Bathvale is an avid reader, as is Miss Putnam." He bowed and withdrew, taking the travelogue with him as he left the room.

"Have you found a riveting tale to distract you from your bunions?" I asked St. Sevier.

St. Sevier left off pretending to search for a book. "Thanks to an exorbitantly well-compensated cobbler, I do not yet suffer bunions. You had the right of it, you know."

"I was correct about something? Where is a royal herald when one has news? What was I right about?"

St. Sevier tapped his temple with a finger. "A head injury can result in lingering disorientation. Also in dizziness or lack of control over the limbs that might at a glance resemble inebriation. There's another explanation as well."

"You will ensure Lord Dunkeld knows of these symptoms?"

The collection of Gothic novels was indeed extensive. Either Lady Bathvale or Clara was adding regularly to the titles on the shelves. I chose one at random, lest anybody conclude I'd come to the library merely to spend time privately with St. Sevier.

"I already told the marquess what to expect from Upjohn's recent injury," he said, "but it had not occurred to me that wartime service might have added to the man's troubles."

Sebastian had offered Upjohn employment when he'd known Upjohn was in less than reliable health. Sometimes, recalling that the marquess and I were no longer friends really was an effort.

"How does wartime service add to Upjohn's current troubles?"

St. Sevier took me by the hand—presuming of him—and led me from among the bookshelves. "Shall we sit?"

I would have preferred a brisk walk along the stream or in the deer park, but a stroll with St. Sevier in addition to accepting his escort the previous night would have been remarked. I took one of two reading chairs flanking a spotless hearth.

St. Sevier took the other. "Have you ever come upon a moment when you thought your late spouse was still alive? Then you stop, reconsider, and remind yourself that he's passed on. You aren't sure, though, so you look in the Bible on your bedside and see the date of his death noted."

I knew from the bleakness in St. Sevier's eyes that he had first-hand experience with the sequence he'd recited.

"I understand the reference." I'd never had to go so far as consulting a Bible, but I had momentarily forgotten that my husband had died. "I've also been known to forget what day of the week it is, or where exactly I am expected when I march out of my house, certain that I have to be some specific place at a specific time."

"Just so," St. Sevier said, crossing his legs at the knee. An Englishman would rarely have adopted such a posture in the presence of a lady, but on him, the look was casually elegant. "We operate on a continuum, sometimes quite aware of the specific moment we inhabit, sometimes wandering far afield from it. In my experience, those who have gone soldiering are more likely to dwell on the wandering end of the spectrum. They can think themselves back on the battlefield, or at least back in the army."

"Like being drunk on bad memories."

I'd known one such occasion about a month after Frederick's death. I'd awoken deep in the night, convinced that I was waiting for Frederick to come home. I had awoken in that state many times previously when Frederick had been out enjoying his usual diversions. For an agonizing eternity, I hadn't known which reality was the true one —that of the confused widow, or that of the anxious wife who'd so frequently feared her husband had come to harm.

"A soldier who took the king's shilling for six years would have many bad memories," St. Sevier said. "Who knows what a blow to the head does to those memories, particularly when followed by a change in circumstances that unmoors that former soldier from all that's familiar to him?"

Again, I had the sense that St. Sevier was speaking from experience.

"Upjohn was a very poor choice for a marquess's valet, wasn't he?"

"Disastrous, one might say, and now items of value are going missing. I was relieved not to have to deal with Lord Hempley's bile at breakfast, but I do not look forward to my next encounter with him."

I explained to St. Sevier what had transpired the previous night.

By the time I finished my recitation—a sanitized version—he was muttering in French and pacing before the hearth.

"The hypocrisy is stunning," he said, rounding a bust of German George. "Hempley behaves like the lowest knave, accosting you in a deserted corridor when the rest of the guests are entertained elsewhere, and yet, he accuses me, by virtue of my French heritage, of being intent on crime. I might have to shoot him, my lady. I truly might."

What an endearing sense of honor St. Sevier had. "No, you truly might not. You would bring scandal down on all concerned, and I do not comport myself as the pattern card of feminine dignity so you can indulge in histrionics for the sake of misguided chivalry." Besides, Sebastian would want first crack at Hempley, followed by my brothers—and by me.

"If Hempley disrespects you further in any way," St. Sevier said, "I will not answer for the consequences."

"Duly noted. I'm off to consult with Lucy regarding my wardrobe for the rest of the day. I'll see you at the archery tournament."

St. Sevier smiled, the mantle of the witty raconteur settling upon him like a signature scent. "Let us hope Cupid makes an appearance as well. I do believe Miss Peasedale fancies herself as Dunkeld's marchioness."

"I wish her the joy of that pursuit," I said, leaving the staid, formal library for the chilly gloom of the corridors. St. Sevier parted from me at the stairs, though his room was on the same floor as my own. Perhaps he was off to have a word with Sebastian.

I wanted a moment with Sebastian myself, for my discussion with Samuel had raised a few questions that a marquess, who employed many footmen, might be able to address. I'd read the inscription in the travelogue that Samuel had taken with him from the library rather than reshelve: *To my dear Samuel, best of luck as you embark on your adventure at public school. Love, Papa.*

What manner of footman attended public school, and what manner of footman's father had the blunt to send him there?

~

"He's gone," Clara Putnam said, testing the tension on a bow at least six inches too long for her with a grip sized for a larger hand. "Hempley, that is. He departed before breakfast, muttering about brigands and thieves. My lady's maid had it from the underbutler, who saw him off. Will you participate in the tournament?"

Handling a weapon in my present frame of mind would not be prudent. "I'm woefully out of practice. I'll cheer on the rival teams. Try this one." I passed her a bow more suited to her stature.

"I like it," she said, flexing the string. "Not too tight, not too light. Did Hempley make a pest of himself to you?"

Other guests milled about on the back terrace, some near the punchbowl, others lounging on the benches and balustrades. Miss Peasedale occupied a seat immediately to the right of the main doors, her mother at her side. Mrs. Albright sat fanning herself on the bench to the left of the doors, Mrs. Bonaventure beside her.

"Why would you inquire about Hempley?" I asked, collecting a quiver of arrows from a footman passing them out.

"Because as I went for my constitutional before breakfast, I overheard a certain Scottish marquess delivering Hempley such a rebuke as would singe your ears, Lady Violet. Dunkeld makes quite an impression when he's in a passion."

"Hempley was not entirely sober last evening. He forgot himself, and the marquess's intervention was timely and much appreciated."

Practice butts had been set up at the foot of the garden. I preferred to have this discussion where we were less likely to be overheard, and thus I steered Clara down the steps.

"Why is it," she said, "that the randy old goats make advances we wish they wouldn't, but the handsome young fellows are all on their best behavior when we wish they'd stray a little—or more than a little?"

That was such an unspinsterish thing to say that I took it as a joke. "And very likely, over their port, the men wonder why the managing widows make uninvited advances, while the delicate flowers never so much as put a slipper wrong. Tell me about Sir Randall Hatcher." I knew him by reputation and a few passing social occasions, but my path and his hadn't crossed for years.

We approached the practice butts, having the range to ourselves. The firing lanes were marked off with yellow cord, as was a safety zone to either side. The worst fate a stray arrow could suffer was to end up in the stream some distance past the targets.

"Bathvale and Belinda are having a row," Clara said. "Their disagreements are always civilized, but I've learned to spot the signs. He goes for a gallop by himself, won't take even a groom. She dresses with particular care and flirts with other men. They never raise their voices, but this business of a thief among the guests has caused discord."

I passed her an arrow. "We're sure it's a thief? Perhaps Lord Hempley has slunk back to London not only because he got a deserved tongue-lashing, but also because he found his infernal missing cravat pin."

Clara stepped up to the shooting line. I retreated to the waiting line, the quiver slung over my shoulder.

"Belinda thinks we've invited a thief to Bathvale Abbey, which is why she's insisting on summoning Sir Randall." Clara nocked an arrow, her stance all wrong, at least according to what my brothers had drilled into me.

"A missing mourning locket is unsettling." So was Clara's form, which would earn her a badly bruised wrist or elbow. "Might I suggest you rotate your elbow straight, Miss Putnam?"

"Clara, please," she said, correcting her error. "Sir Randall will be quite popular with the ladies." She pulled the bowstring back to a point well shy of her chin. "Sir Randall is a frequent dinner guest."

"You don't care for Sir Randall?"

Her arrow didn't go far, landing in the grass barely halfway to the target. "Oh dear. This is harder than it looks."

"You've never wielded a bow before?" I thought back to our

school days, when all the young ladies had been instructed not in the effective use of the bow, but rather, on the hazards archery posed to one's wardrobe. Perhaps the archery lessons had transpired during one of Clara's periodic absences from school.

"I haven't attempted this since I was a child," she said. "You give it a try."

"Very well. Tell me more about Sir Randall."

"I suppose you would call him Belinda's gallant, or a gallant at large. I don't begrudge my sister a diversion—Lord Bathvale is not exactly overflowing with affection—but Sir Randall is a bit too convinced of his own charms."

"Stand back at the yellow line," I said, nocking an arrow. I was of average size, so the bow was easy for me to handle. I drew the arrow back, my body recalling many hours of practice. I let fly and felt a frisson of satisfaction when the arrow smacked solidly into the center of the target.

"Lady Violet, we must change your name to Diana."

"I pulled right," I said, "which is why the arrow isn't quite on center. Shall you try again?" Or would she tell me what really bothered her about Sir Randall?

"I'll learn from your example," Clara said. "Dunkeld has deigned to grace us with his presence. He's tormenting the ladies by wearing his native Scottish dress too."

Sebastian had joined the group on the terrace, and he wore a kilt. If he was trying to deflect the attentions of the single women, his strategy was sadly ineffective. Much like well-aimed arrows, Miss Peasedale, her mother, Mrs. Albright, and Mrs. Bonaventure were all on their feet, offering the marquess effusive greetings.

"You'd think they were starving crows," Clara said, "and he the last bread crumb."

"He cannot help his station." I nocked a second arrow, determined to correct my previous error. "Your sister would not have invited him if he were any old Scottish colonel." Though Sebastian, to be fair, would rather have been any old Scottish colonel.

My second arrow was closer to the center by an inch. Still not where I wanted it.

"You are quite good at this, Lady Violet."

"My brothers are better. I don't suppose anybody searched Lord Hempley's luggage before he was allowed to leave the premises?" I glanced over my shoulder to make certain Clara was at least as far back as the waiting line.

"You think he might have nicked a few baubles and then set up a hue and cry? Are we to spend the next week discovering more of his larceny and blaming one another for it?"

My third arrow landed dead center. "Stranger thefts have happened. If he was late to the initial buffet, he would have had an opportunity to search several rooms for valuables. Any servant discovering his lordship in the wrong room could have been put off with a tale about lost bearings and new surrounds."

I took up the quiver of arrows at Clara's feet. My theory, tossed out as a casual possibility, appealed to me more strongly the longer I considered it. Summoning the magistrate had likely been discussed among the men last night, hence Hempley's scarpering this morning.

"But would Hempley be clever enough to conduct such a ruse?" Clara asked. "To rob his fellow guests by daylight, complain loudly of being victimized himself, then accost you, all for the purpose of having an excuse to leave in high dudgeon?"

"He could have left in high dudgeon without accosting me," I said, walking with Clara toward the terrace. Lady Bathvale had joined her guests, Thaddeus Baxter providing her escort. Where was Bathvale, and were he and his wife truly feuding?

"Or perhaps," Clara said, "Hempley already knew he was leaving in the morning, so why not trifle with a widow before quitting the scene?" Her tone was bitter, making me wonder if somebody had trifled with Clara—or declined to trifle with her.

None of my business. Lord Bathvale had also joined the assemblage on the terrace, a tall, fair-haired fellow at his side.

"And there is our Sir Randall," I said, though we were still some distance away.

"How can you tell?"

"Dunkeld looks angry enough to call him out on the spot," I replied. "You must escort me to Sir Randall, before the marquess can get himself arrested for assaulting the king's man."

CHAPTER SEVEN

Archery was far more interesting when one held the bow than when one sat beneath an awning some yards away, pretending to be entertained by competitors who were more accurate with verbal barbs than physical arrows.

"I am getting too old for this," Mrs. Bonaventure said, taking the seat beside mine. She was a tallish, well-formed blonde with pretty blue eyes and a languid air. "House parties should be limited to one week. A day or two to recover from traveling, another day or two to choose a flirt, a few days to enjoy flirting, and a day to pack and make any necessary farewells."

The Baxters were captaining opposing teams, Lord Bathvale and Sir Randall were officiating, and Sebastian was putting all the other marksmen to shame. The ladies had apparently given up flirting, for the gentlemen had become intent on their archery.

"If the weather is disobliging," I replied, "one needs a fortnight to get in a week's worth of scheduled entertainments. Oh dear. Miss Peasedale's skill must lie in other directions."

Her arrow went wide of even the safety zones and clattered onto a walkway that led toward the deer park.

"To hear Mrs. Peasedale tell it, the fair Fredericka excels at bagging Scottish marquesses. Why is it the sight of some men's knees sets me all aflutter, but the same joints on another man interest me not at all?"

Sebastian's knees were not particularly impressive, but each one was situated between a heavily muscled thigh and an equally sculpted calf.

"I am not a connoisseur of knees myself. I do favor a witty conversationalist."

The rotation of competitors came to an end. Lord Bathvale called for bows to be put down so the footmen could retrieve the arrows from the targets, and the team captains called for a refreshment break.

"You've been widowed... what? Two years?" Mrs. Bonaventure asked. "Give it another year or two, and you'll be evaluating knees along with the rest of us. Dunkeld is so very virile, he wouldn't have to say a word, and I'd be happy to spend an entire evening in his company."

The marquess had also been at various times a loyal brother, a dutiful son, a conscientious officer, and a decent person. In another year or two, would I lose sight of those qualities in any man while I ogled his knees? I hoped not.

"He likes birds," I said, though I'd forgotten this about Sebastian until I'd opened my mouth. "He had an uncle who could imitate birds, and Dunkeld knows many of their songs by heart."

Mrs. Bonaventure regarded me in some puzzlement. "Birds, you say?"

"Lord Dunkeld is acquainted with my brothers. I've known him for ages." My brothers knew Sebastian well. My youngest brother—Felix—considered him a good friend. They'd bought their colors at the same time and served under some of the same officers.

"Then maybe you can tell me why Dunkeld regards Sir Randall like the personification of a foul miasma. One doesn't want to offend the guest of honor, but Sir Randall has a fine pair of knees too." She smiled and waved at Mrs. Peasedale as if they were long-lost friends.

"I don't know the specific source of their animosity, but I gather they fell out of favor with one another while at public school. Matters deteriorated further when they served in Spain." Felix had mentioned that much in one of his rare letters.

"And years later, they are still very much out of favor with one another. One wonders if Lady Bathvale knew that when she summoned her pet magistrate."

What an unkind creature Mrs. Bonaventure was. "If my mourning locket had gone missing, I'd appreciate having somebody on hand who knows how to make a thorough search of the premises."

"Do you truly think Helene's mourning locket has gone missing—in the actual sense?"

"I have no reason to doubt her word, ma'am."

"Well, she couldn't be upstaged by Little Miss Lost Earbobs, could she?"

The final round of competitors was assembling at the waiting line, and not a moment too soon. I was seriously considering feigning a megrim, for both Lady Bathvale and Clara would recall that I was prone to such afflictions and lend credence to my exit.

I refrained. I was superstitious about false illnesses. She who pleaded a headache for her own convenience was asking providence to strike her down with a megrim in truth at the worst possible time. I took up my fan, for the day was growing warm.

"The result for anybody accused of taking either the earbobs or the locket could be very unpleasant, Mrs. Bonaventure. I hope the people invited to this house party regard transportation or hanging as serious matters."

"They don't," she said, unpinning her straw hat and shaking out her curls. Her coiffure was that half-undone creation that took hours to achieve and looked like it would come down completely in the next five minutes. "Their own hanging or transportation would of course be worthy of comment, but what this crowd takes seriously is gossip, matrimony, and *recreation*. I hope I haven't shocked you." She treated me to the same sunny smile she'd fired at Mrs. Peasedale.

A smile that gave no hint of grief or sorrow.

"I have four brothers, Mrs. Bonaventure, and my husband was not one to shelter me from life's more risqué discussions." St. Sevier, bless his sense of timing, waved at me from his place at the waiting line. He was shooting well, though not obnoxiously so.

Sebastian, by contrast, was apparently trying to make some obscure masculine point for Sir Randall's benefit.

"You think I am shallow, mean, and silly," Mrs. Bonaventure said. "I daresay you're right, but I am not stupid."

"Ma'am, I haven't known you long enough to form any impression of you worth repeating. You are lingering here with me for some purpose other than to avoid the afternoon sun."

"I do like to watch men being athletic."

She apparently like to do more than watch. "And?"

"And I'm waiting for the rest of the ladies to stop fluttering their fans at Sir Randall. Then I can discreetly let him know that in addition to looking for Helene's locket and a pair of earbobs, he'd best keep an eye out for my favorite silver necklace. My grandmother gave it to me when I made my come out. I have the matching bracelet and earbobs, and I don't care what anybody says about blondes looking better in gold, I will miss that necklace."

"You don't want to let Lord and Lady Bathvale know of the missing jewelry?" And why tell me?

"When I can instead confide in Sir Randall? I'm sure he'll advise them of my misfortune. Perhaps it's time you lost something too, Lady Violet."

I was losing my patience by the moment. "When did you notice your necklace was missing?"

"After breakfast. I'd set it out for my maid to polish so I could wear it at dinner tonight. When I came back from strolling by the lake with Mr. Thaddeus Baxter, my maid was polishing the bracelet. She hadn't realized I'd also set out the necklace, because it was gone."

"I am very sorry to hear this. I suggest you tell Sir Randall at the first opportunity."

She put her hat back on, tying the ribbons in a loose bow beneath her chin. "Being a widow gets easier, you know. The first affair is like getting back on the horse after a bad fall. A vulgar analogy, but any woman who's ever taken a tumble understands the comparison. The first affair, or first encounter, feels so portentous and significant, but then you're staring at the bed hangings, realizing it wasn't of any great moment at all, and you can have as many encounters as you please if you're careful. You might cry a bit, because it's yet another one of those I-really-am-a-widow moments, but if you chose well, it was a pleasant encounter, and that helps a little."

More than I ever wanted to know, but doubtless a useful perspective. "How long?" I asked.

"Five damned years." She adjusted her fichu so the silk frothed about her décolletage. "Soon to be six. My husband died of a lung fever caught while riding to hounds in the Midlands. Came home to me half dead, and two weeks later, I was a widow."

"I'm sorry. You must have loved him very much."

"I still do." She rose gracefully and hallooed at Miss Waltham, who'd proved to be the standout talent among the lady archers.

Mrs. Bonaventure's recitation—if true—eliminated Lord Hempley as the thief, unless, of course, the missing necklace was the work of a second thief inspired by Hempley's example. I rubbed at my temples, feeling the beginnings of a true headache, which was most unfair considering I'd refrained from claiming a false one.

I ladled myself some punch and drifted into the house, wanting solitude to ponder my conversation with Mrs. Bonaventure. She was a deceptive woman, feigning ennui to mask old heartache, but had she truly lost that necklace, or was she simply doing her part to keep up with Little Miss Lost Earbobs?

～

We were to have another buffet for the evening meal, followed by cards. I was sorely tempted to take a tray in my room.

"Best not, ma'am," Lucy said, pouring me a cup of tea. "That lot of idlers will talk about you behind your back, and Monsieur St. Sevier will worry about you."

"He's merely a friend, Lucy." Was that all I wanted him to be? Despite myself, I could not get Mrs. Bonaventure's remarks out of my head. *The first affair is like getting back on the horse...*

"Sir Randall is apparently a friend to both Lord and Lady Bathvale," Lucy said, giving one of my shawls a shake and refolding it over the back of a chair. "I had it from the third footman, who's sweet on Miss Clara Putnam's lady's maid."

The tea was weak and none too hot, but it was still tea. "Sir Randall is here to help locate the missing jewelry."

"Yours is all accounted for, my lady, and if I leave your rooms, I note the counter on the lock first."

My apartment, being in the family wing, was in the oldest part of the house. English locksmiths of previous eras had developed clever mechanisms that displayed how many times a lock had been set or opened, and one of those locks adorned my door. The detailing in the metal plate that displayed that total number was so minute that I'd missed it until Lucy had pointed it out to me.

Better still, the counter could not be reset except with a special key, which only a butler or housekeeper was likely to have. Several other guest rooms had such locks, including St. Sevier's and Dunkeld's. I had told St. Sevier about his lock that afternoon, but Sebastian had been too busy strutting about in his kilt for me to speak with him privately.

"Keep monitoring the lock, Lucy, and I shall do likewise. Can we do something uncomplicated with my hair tonight? A coronet and a few flowers, maybe?"

Lucy laid out an evening gown of brown velvet. "Have you a headache coming on, my lady?"

"I hope not. Why do you ask?"

"Because when you request the simpler styles, you often end up with a megrim. I can't decide if plain styles give you a megrim, or if you ask for the uncomplicated coiffure because a megrim is already sneaking up on you."

Again, I did not have a true headache—yet—but neither was I in good spirits. "The thefts, or misplacements, have cast a pall on this house party. Some guests are apparently titillated to think we've a criminal in our midst. I confess I find the whole business tiring."

Nonetheless, I donned my brown velvet dress, collected the requisite shawl, fan, and gloves, and sat patiently while Lucy twisted my hair into a chignon secured with pearl netting. Around my neck I wore a simple strand of pearls, which might make me look dowdy, but I honestly did not care.

I wasn't in the mood for anything showier than pearls.

"You look a treat, ma'am," Lucy said, twitching at my shawl. "Shall I walk with you to the stairs?"

I wanted her company, which was silly. I was no longer a new widow—Mrs. Bonaventure was right about that—and I knew my way to the portrait gallery.

"You shall finish tidying up here, then enjoy your own evening as you please. I can see myself to bed, Lucy."

"You're sure, ma'am?"

At home, I usually ended my nights in solitude. All but my fanciest stays tied in front, and I never wore them more than middling snug. I'd become adept at wiggling free of a corset or jumps at the end of the day, and taking down my own hair was the work of a moment.

"I'll be fine," I said. "I'll see you tomorrow, but do check the lock before you leave."

"Of course."

I said a prayer that no headache would find me and left the room. I made it as far as the first turning before Sir Randall emerged from the opposite corridor and made me a polite bow.

"Lady Violet, I thought I spotted you on the terrace this afternoon. May I say you are in quite good looks?"

He was tall, blond, lean, and broad-shouldered. Evening attire showed off his physique, but then, so had the riding attire he'd worn that afternoon. His smile was friendly—only friendly—and he and I had been introduced more than once over the years.

I curtseyed. "Sir Randall. A pleasure to see you. I was just going down to dinner."

"As was I. How was your journey down from Town?"

We chitchatted, something I would have done without effort three years ago, but I was out of practice, or perhaps I no longer saw the point to idle banter.

"What do you make of the missing jewelry?" I asked.

"It is only jewelry that's been taken, isn't it?" he murmured.

That should have been the moment when I informed him about my shawl, but I kept my peace. Sebastian had taken Sir Randall into dislike, and though Sebastian had also apparently taken *me* into dislike, I would exercise caution where Sir Randall was concerned.

And I would be very certain to introduce him to Mrs. Bonaventure too, of course.

~

Sir Randall's presence proved to be a stabilizing influence. Over the next three days, nothing else went missing, save the last remnants of common sense from among the unattached females. Those who weren't flinging themselves at Sebastian took to chasing Sir Randall, and thus for the walk back to Bathvale Abbey after Sunday services, I had St. Sevier to myself.

"Do you still long to return to Town?" he asked when we had sufficient distance from the rest of the group not to be overheard.

"I do, but not for the same reasons I would have listed a week ago."

"I see you out walking with this or that fellow, Violet. You are eating and drinking in moderation, and I suspect you have raided the library of its best treasures. Bathvale Abbey is affording you the pleasures of a country retreat without the bother of imposing on family."

Was *that* why Hugh had encouraged me to attend this gathering? "I like my family."

"But you don't seek their company when your spirits are low, do you?"

When my spirits were truly low, I permitted only Lucy to attend me. "I needed my two years of mourning to sort myself out. Do you miss your brothers?"

He strolled along with me, arm in arm, the picture of gentlemanly composure. "Terribly. The older two served out of patriotism and for the glory of France—which even they knew meant the glory of that bloodthirsty Corsican. Theodore, the youngest, was little more than a boy. As the war dragged on, every able-bodied Frenchman either enlisted or was conscripted. Grandfather should have sent Theo to me, but by then, even getting a letter through was difficult."

Hugh had never confided this much personal history to me before, and yet, he raised more questions than he answered.

"Why were you sent to England?"

"My grandmother was English, and she had the means to insist that my sister and I, as the eldest, be sent to her family. Her reasoning was sound: If Napoleon was ultimately victorious, I could return to France as an adult, liberated from my English abductors. If King George carried the day, I'd already be ensconced among the victors when peace came, having turned my back on the Corsican menace."

"What terrible choices your family faced." And yet, Hugh St. Sevier seemed to be a man at peace.

"Your brother Felix served, if I recall correctly."

"As did Sir Randall, as did Lord Dunkeld."

"That pair." Two words, dripping with Gallic disdain. "They should duel with foils to first blood and be done with whatever divides them. I would patch up the loser, the ladies could be genteelly horrified at the violence—about which they would pretend to know nothing, of course—and we could all get on with our intrigues. I knew something of Dunkeld in Spain. He was a formidable officer. Sir Randall would likely get the worst of the encounter."

We turned up the lane that led to the old Bathvale postern gate, the road petering out to little more than a cart track. A dozen yards ahead, Mrs. Bonaventure was glued to Sir Randall's side, and not far ahead of that couple, Miss Peasedale strolled on the arm of a Baxter.

Where was Sebastian? I hadn't seen him at services, now that I thought back on it, and as the ranking guest, he should have joined Lord Bathvale in the family pew. But then, Clara had also been absent, as had Miss Waltham and one of the Baxters. An excess of whist had been cited in the latter two cases.

"Are you enjoying an intrigue?" I asked, mostly to turn the topic from war, duels, and violence.

St. Sevier leaned near. "Would you be jealous if I were?"

Over the meadow-grass aroma of a summer day, I caught the scent of his shaving soap. Honeysuckle, leavened with some spice that added elegance even to such a lovely fragrance.

"Are you flirting with me, sir?"

"You were supposed to say yes,you would be consumed with envy for the lady lucky enough to frolic with me. I'm a reasonably skilled frolicker. I have a Frenchman's complement of élan and an Englishman's honest appreciation for sensual pleasures."

"And which part of your heritage provides the hubris?"

"Both, which is why our countries could wage war for years on end." He drew me off the track, down a path that led to the stream. "I am also very discreet, in case that matters."

"You are very naughty." And yet, he'd made me smile, made me feel a little naughty myself. "Do you suppose our thief has been subdued by Sir Randall's presence?"

The sound of shallow water burbling over rocks was peaceful, and my friends the tree pipits were flitting about in the branches overhead. Perhaps St. Sevier had been right to send me on this country idyll. Every day revealed a new spot where I could take a book and read away the hours.

"We might never have had a thief," Hugh said. "People misplace small items all the time."

"A widow doesn't usually misplace her mourning locket. It can become as special as her wedding ring."

"And yet,"—he took my hand and held it before him—"you are no longer wearing your ring."

I looked at my hand—my gloves were in my reticule—and had the oddest sense of not recognizing my own appendage. My wedding ring was a part of me, a plain gold band, but also a symbol of my standing as a former wife and of the loyalty that Frederick had shown me even when he couldn't muster fidelity. I typically wore both my wedding band and engagement ring when in company, and my wedding band even when at home.

Freddie had wanted me to have two rings, though some women didn't wear even one.

"I take off my rings at night," I said. "I put them on my vanity before I brush out my braid so the settings don't catch in my hair."

"Your maid does not brush your hair?"

"Some nights she does, but other nights I don't want Lucy to wait up for me. She's usually awake to dress me in the morning, and today I overslept. I all but dashed down to breakfast, and when I returned to my room, Lucy had to hurry with my toilet to see me ready in time for services."

"Were you in too much of a hurry to put on your wedding ring?"

"My rings weren't on the vanity. I know exactly where I left them —where I always leave them, on top of my jewelry box—and they weren't there." Had they been there when I went down to breakfast? I was almost certain they had been.

Almost.

Hugh kissed my fingers and let me go. "Could Lucy have put them away?"

"I don't know." I headed up the path, intent on resolving that question. St. Sevier accompanied me back to the Abbey and waited in my sitting room while I rifled my jewelry box and personal effects for the missing jewelry. Not by so much as a raised eyebrow did his demeanor suggest that the loss of my rings surprised him.

"Gone?" he asked.

"Apparently so."

"Shall I fetch Sir Randall for you?" St. Sevier's tone was so polite as to approach diffidence. I was learning to see past the Gallic savoir faire, the physician's detachment, and even the gentlemanly manners.

"You don't want to." And I did not want to bring the situation to Sir Randall's attention either. "Why not?"

"Because Dunkeld was not at services, and Sir Randall will seize upon that fact to cast suspicion on the Scotsman. Dunkeld is a peer, he has no need to filch baubles, and he has done nothing to deserve suspicion. Nonetheless, I do not trust the scruples of the average English magistrate when he arrives at a crime scene bearing an obvious grudge."

"Neither do I, but I treasured those rings."

St. Sevier looked like he was about to, for once, offer me a rejoinder that was less than suave and sophisticated. Instead, he bowed. "You may trust my discretion until such time as you choose to disclose the situation. Dunkeld should be warned."

If I knew anything for an utter certainty, it was that Sebastian had not taken my rings. "Thank you."

St. Sevier gave the room a final perusal, as if attempting to ascertain the source of an off odor, then left me in solitude. I checked the counter on the lock, but without Lucy to consult, the fact that the number was advanced by three since I'd gone to bed last night meant little.

I had changed out of my walking dress and into a day dress and was repinning my hair when the oddest thought interrupted my mental list of possible suspects. Had St. Sevier led me down to the stream out of sight of the other guests in order to *kiss me*?

Would I have allowed that, and if not, *why not*?

~

"Whatever benighted imp conceived of the scavenger hunt as a diversion should be consigned to the pit for all eternity." Sebastian stalked along at my side, looking as grumpy as he sounded. His cravat was less than pristine, the pin a half-inch off-center, and his boots were in need of a shine.

"Just think," I said, "you have the rest of the Sabbath to contemplate tomorrow's penance. If you have been a particularly naughty boy, you will be assigned to my team, and I can send you and Mrs. Bonaventure in search of a robin's egg."

He plucked a stick from the middle of the path and hurled it into the hedgerow. "Even you, Violet, could not be so cruel."

"Even *I*? What is that supposed to mean?"

He gave me a sidewise look that suggested scorn and something else. Hurt?

"The season is too advanced for *anybody* to find a robin's egg," he said. "The task would be pointless."

We came to the stile that led to the grassy meadow. Sebastian offered me a hand, though I was more than capable of mounting three steps unaided.

"You have grown thick-witted in service to your king, Dunkeld. The object of searching for a robin's egg is not to find the egg, but to have an opportunity to wander far afield in the company—"

I fell silent and backed down the steps. "The bench is occupied." I took Sebastian by the elbow and dragged him away from the stile, which was rather like trying to drag a plow horse away from his oats.

"Occupied? By whom?"

"Lady Bathvale and Sir Randall. Keep your voice down."

"Considering that you were lecturing me in tones fit to reach the back pews at St. Paul's, I hardly see the point in skulking about. They are neighbors, and though I don't trust Sir Randall any farther than I could throw a piano, a quiet chat on a Sunday afternoon is hardly scandalous."

I waited until we'd gone some distance in the direction of the lake to speak. "Why didn't they notice us? We were having our usual cheerful bicker, and neither Sir Randall nor Lady Bathvale even heard our approach. They were tête-à-tête, if you take my meaning."

"Assign them to look for robin's eggs, why don't you? Give Sir Rascal a leg up on whatever mischief he's planning."

About twenty yards on, the lake stretched out from the shore, a placid expanse mirroring the summer-blue sky. Because today was the Sabbath, and neither work nor frivolity was to be encouraged, no group activity other than the outing to services had been planned. Lady Bathvale had mentioned at luncheon, however, that the lists of objects to be retrieved in tomorrow's scavenger hunt were available in the library.

The table had been deserted within twenty minutes.

My stroll to the lake had two purposes. First, to learn where the bed of blooming water lilies might be, because a water lily blossom was one of the more obscure items on the scavenger list. Second, I wanted to know why Sebastian hadn't attended services. The quiet meadow had struck me as a good place to have a private chat.

Lady Bathvale and Sir Randall had apparently reached the same conclusion.

"Why don't you care for Sir Randall?" I asked. "He seems tolerable, if a bit impressed with himself."

"He's very impressed with himself. Don't turn your back on him, Violet."

For Sebastian, that was tantamount to cursing the man in the village square. "I might need to consult Sir Randall regarding the missing items."

"No, you might not. They are not *your* missing items, this is not *your* house party. Stay out of it."

"Why weren't you at services this morning, Dunkeld?"

He kept right on walking as if I hadn't spoken.

"Sebastian?"

"You call me Sebastian when you want to scold me. I overslept."

"Why?"

He came to a halt on the shore of the lake. "I was tired, Violet. Marching across Spain was not half so taxing as enduring the company at this house party."

Had Mrs. Bonaventure kept him up half the night, and if so, what business was that of mine? "My wedding and engagement rings are missing, and before you ask, no, I did not misplace them."

He was like the surface of the lake—entirely still. "Your *wedding ring* has been stolen?"

"And my engagement ring. Frederick liked to give me jewelry, but those are the only pieces I value. Once, about a year ago, my engagement ring snagged on a woolen blanket. If I hadn't awakened, I might have torn the stone from the setting. Until that happened, I didn't take them off except to bathe."

Sebastian looked out over the water as somebody in a punt pushed off from the dock a quarter of the way around the lake.

"I do not care for this," Sebastian said softly. "A mourning locket, now a wedding ring. This thief is not merely greedy, he is cruel."

"Or she is."

One corner of his mouth quirked. "If you think I can provide any of the ladies an alibi for last night, I am sorry to disappoint you. I was out looking for Upjohn."

"Has he quit so soon?"

The punt was occupied by a single individual, a female. She pulled at the oars as if familiar with the task and was soon making for the middle of the lake.

"He has not quit, but I believe he walks in his sleep. St. Sevier said disturbances of sleep can follow a head injury, though your physician friend didn't specifically mention sleepwalking. Upjohn was not waiting for me after dinner, which didn't particularly bother me, but as I was preparing for bed, I saw him—or who I thought was him—crossing the formal courtyard."

The moon would be full at the end of the week, when the

concluding ball was to be held, meaning after moonrise, a fair amount of light was to be had.

"You aren't sure it was Upjohn?"

"He says not. I got down to the courtyard and trailed whoever it was across the lawn to the stables, but I found nobody. I checked every stall, the harness rooms, and the saddle rooms. Whoever it was did not want to be found."

The lady in the little boat had reached the center of the lake, which seemed to be her destination. She took up her oars and reclined in the boat, a large parasol providing her shade.

"You're sure it was a man you saw, my lord?"

"A woman can wear trousers and a jacket, and Upjohn is shorter than many men, but the walk looked masculine—purposeful, confident, not cautious. Have you told Sir Randall about your wedding ring?"

"I have not. Is that boat taking on water?"

Sebastian tossed a pebble into the lake just as the lady boater sat bolt upright. She scrambled to fix the oars into their locks and began pulling hard for the dock, but her vessel was unseaworthy.

"The water is twelve feet deep out that far," Sebastian said, yanking off one boot, then the other. "The bloody fool will never make it back to the dock."

I helped him peel free of his coat, then he raced out to the end of the jetty and launched himself in a clean dive into the lake. The boat was all but capsized and the woman who'd taken it out, despite her competent rowing, didn't know enough about handling small craft on water.

She ought to have flipped the boat, trapping air beneath it so she could cling to the gunwale until Sebastian could reach her. Instead, she kept stroking ineffectually with the oars while yelling for help.

I knew how to swim. With four brothers to teach me, and four brothers to compete with, I'd become proficient in the water before the age of eight, much to my mother's shock and horror.

Few proper ladies had had the eccentric upbringing I'd had, and

the creature screaming frantically from the lake was clearly too terrified to save herself. Then too, she wore petticoats, boots, spencer, and
bonnet... None of which she had the sense to remove.

She flailed about until the boat went down, then she too dipped
below the surface. I began to pray, the same, useless prayer every
person in desperate straits prays.

"Please, oh please... Please, please..."

Sebastian dove where the boat had gone down, and for an eternity under the pretty blue sky, I held my breath with him until he
rose, his arm lashed around the lady's neck.

"Thank God." Thank God and Sebastian's athleticism and
determination. His progress was not toward the dock, but rather,
toward the shore where I stood, a slightly shorter distance than the
dock. He had to be tiring, but he swam on until he reached shallow
water.

The lady was capable of stumbling to shore on her own, though
her sodden skirts hampered her progress. At first, I thought the ship-
wreck survivor was none other than my hostess, but no...

"Clara!" I called. "Clara, this way!" Foolish of me, as Sebastian
was leading her by the hand while she stumbled, righted herself, and
slogged on.

"You poor dear," I said when Sebastian helped her up the bank.
"You poor, poor dear." I tucked my shawl about her, then draped
Sebastian's coat over her shoulders, though the day was mild. "Say
something, please. I was terrified for you. Petrified, and if Sebastian
hadn't..."

He stood beside Clara, his sodden clothes plastered to his frame.

"Lord Dunkeld," Clara said, "thank you. I'd be at the bottom of
the lake with my boat if you hadn't saved me. I should have realized
the boat wasn't sound, but we're to have a regatta on Wednesday, and
I naturally assumed the boats were in good condition."

She was pale, soaking wet, and clutching Sebastian's coat in a
desperate grip.

"Come," I said, wrapping an arm around Clara's waist. "We will get you back to the Abbey before you can take a chill. What a dreadful accident, but how fortunate that Sebastian was on hand."

Clara gave me a wan smile, and yet... it was a smile. I had twice referred to a marquess by his given name, and despite the near tragedy, Clara had wits enough to notice that.

Sebastian gathered up his boots and walked with us as far as the Abbey's back terrace. Clara passed him his coat and watched him go when he bowed in parting and ducked in through a side door.

"He lacks charm, but never have I been so grateful for a man's strength," she said.

"You will be even more grateful for a hot bath. I hope Lord Bathvale intends to have every single boat on the property inspected before Wednesday's regatta."

She shivered, drawing my now-damp shawl around her. "But that's just it, Lady Violet. Bathvale had the boats inspected before the first guest arrived. The boats were all repainted and repaired last week, because the regatta isn't the only occasion guests might enjoy being on the water."

Now I felt like shivering. "I suppose you'd best let Sir Randall know of your mishap."

If it *was* a mishap.

CHAPTER EIGHT

"Did your nocturnal searching ever bear fruit?" I asked Sebastian as we chose a shaded table on the terrace. "You said Upjohn wasn't in the stables." The scavenger hunt was due to begin in an hour, and Sir Randall had asked to speak with us privately before that great frolic ensued.

"Saturday night, I have no idea where he got off to. Last night, he wandered out to the orchard, compelled by a memory of being on picket duty. He said he liked standing watch because it was mostly a matter of napping and trusting the horses to alert him to the presence of trouble."

"And Saturday night, he told you he hadn't been in the stables. Where had he been?"

Sebastian pulled out a chair for me, the wrought iron scraping against the flagstones. He did so with a militant gleam in his eye, as if he thought I'd make a fuss over even so small a courtesy. Had I been fifteen, I might have.

"Thank you, my lord."

He took the seat beside me so we both faced out across the sunny terrace. "Upjohn was in my dressing closet when I returned from my search. The hour was well past midnight, and there he was, dozing in a chair, ready to take my boots and see me off to bed."

"He's not working out, is he?" I felt for the man. If not for this house party, where all was commotion and new faces, he'd have had a chance to settle into Sebastian's London household. Here, he was doubtless disoriented and without close friends.

Rather like a new widow.

"He's had less than a fortnight to learn his duties, Violet. Give the man a chance."

That was a mild rebuke, considering that Sebastian had a protective streak as wide as the North Sea.

"You dread this discussion with Sir Randall, don't you?" I asked.

"'Dread' is too mild a word for the bottomless loathing I hold toward the brave knight."

"I'm to be the referee in this conversation?" I was familiar with the role. Not only was I the only female among five siblings, I was also the only female among fourteen paternal cousins. If the Crown had any sense, which lately it did not, I would have been given a senior post in the diplomatic corps.

"Don't even try to referee, Violet. Sir Randall will be on his best behavior around you, and I will refrain from calling him out."

"You cannot call him out. You are a peer, while he is a mere magistrate with a lowly knighthood."

Sebastian's smile was bleak. "I *can* call him out, but he would have to refuse the challenge on the grounds of my status, wouldn't he?"

Sebastian was stubborn, pigheaded, determined, and occasionally hard-hearted, but he was not petty. He could hold a grudge for an imagined wrong, though—witness his odd testiness toward me. Was Sir Randall the butt of a similar resentment?

"Why would you embarrass Sir Randall needlessly?" I asked. "It's not like you to waste your time in stupid games."

"Isn't it?" He lounged back in his chair, putting me in mind of a great cat contemplating whether to hunt in the forest or the field. "I saw Sir Randall order a boy of fourteen hanged for stealing. In the military, such matters are handled with breathtaking dispatch, but do you know how long it takes a slight lad to die on the end of a rope?"

The pictures that tale conjured were horrible. "Too long."

"I shot the poor boy after he'd literally been twisting in the breeze for ten minutes. Sir Randall tried to have me court-martialed for interfering with military justice, but what I was witnessing was a condemned child needlessly tortured."

Sebastian spoke mildly, as if reciting the news from his sister's latest letter.

"But surely stealing or looting or whatever the boy was engaged in was a serious offense?" Everything under English law, from poaching a few pheasants to stealing a single spoon, was a serious offense, and the punishment for more than two hundred different infractions was death.

"The boy was engaged in the great crime of illiteracy. He could not read. His captain had jotted down three items to be retrieved from the locked stores—pepper, sheets, and some ramekin bowls, God knows what for. The boy was too proud to ask for help deciphering the words. He was found in possession of a pepperbox pistol, shot, and a ramrod. Somebody had been stealing ammunition, and an example was made of a terrified, ignorant Scottish lad."

"Or was that Scottish lad the thief?"

"At the drumhead court martial, the boy offered Sir Randall the list as proof that he was merely executing an order for his captain. The chaplain testified that the boy barely knew his letters, much less how to read. The captain, a viscount's spare, had nothing to say for his own private, other than that he'd given his subordinate the list and the keys to the storehouse."

"The captain was English?"

"A school chum of Sir Randall's. The thefts of ammunition continued after the boy's murder."

～

The morning was still a pretty, English summer morning. Off in the distance, a cowbell tinkled, and a soft breeze sent the potted salvia gently bobbing in their urns. Sebastian's recitation left me physically sick, to know a child had been put to death, and a terrible death, for the sake of making an example.

Worse yet was the brutal mercy Sebastian had felt compelled to extend to the condemned.

"Sir Randall would tell you," Sebastian went on, "that in times of war, harsh measures are sometimes necessary to ensure discipline in the ranks. He'd say the youth could just as easily have fallen to an enemy bullet. If the boy was innocent, his death helped restore order; if he was guilty, then his execution was necessitated by justice."

Like most self-serving tripe, that reasoning rested on a foundation of illogic. "The ranks were not in disarray, were they? Nobody acquired a firmer grasp of the rules for having seen that child die."

"The men always grumbled, but the military is exquisitely designed to protect the interests of those in a position to buy their commissions, and to do so at the expense of those taking the king's shilling of necessity. Here comes the brave knight now."

Sebastian rose, as manners required, while I wanted to slink off and consider what manner of justice rewarded a murderer with a knighthood—if Sebastian's version of the facts was accurate. That conclusion was hard to support, given the smiling, polite man who sat down at the table with us.

"Unfortunate business yesterday at the lake," Sir Randall said. "But then, unfortunate business seems to plague this gathering. Lady Violet, what can you tell me about Miss Clara Putnam's mishap?"

"Not much," I replied. "Lord Dunkeld was good enough to escort me to the lake so I might spy out where water lilies are blooming. One white blossom is on the list for today's scavenger hunt. We'd just arrived at the shore when Miss Putnam climbed into her boat and began rowing for the center of the lake. By the time she reached the middle, her boat was sinking."

Sir Randall turned a politely curious expression on Sebastian. "Anything to add, my lord?"

"Her ladyship noticed the boat was sinking before I did. I cannot say if the leak started the moment the boat was put into the water, or if the trouble began only as Miss Putnam reached the center of the lake."

A snippet of conversation with Clara came back to me. "She said every one of the boats was recently repainted and inspected."

"Samuel himself confirmed that fact," Sir Randall said. "I cannot like this. A few trinkets going missing is troublesome, while stealing a widow's mourning locket has an obvious element of malice about it. Sabotaging a boat and putting a young woman's life in jeopardy escalates malice to attempted murder. What I cannot for the life of me deduce is the motive behind these occurrences."

"You are making prodigious assumptions on very little evidence," Sebastian said quietly.

"My lord, with all due respect, the boats had recently been inspected. Somebody had to have tampered with Miss Putnam's boat between then and when she decided to enjoy some time on the lake. What if you hadn't been there? What if some less athletic fellow had been escorting her ladyship? These people are my neighbors, and I am determined to get to the bottom of the crimes threatening their peace."

"Say what you've come to say," Sebastian replied, "for you apparently aren't interested in gathering much evidence."

"MacHeath, I wouldn't be talking to you at all but for the need to investigate these crimes. What else would you have me do?"

MacHeath? Was Sir Randall being deliberately rude by neglecting to use Sebastian's title, or was the magistrate's composure imperiled by this quiet chat?

"Have you questioned whoever put the boat into the water for Miss Putnam?" Sebastian asked. "She's fit, I'll grant you, but fit enough to carry a craft from the boathouse to the dock? Have you raised the boat from the middle of the lake? The water can't be more than twelve feet deep, and Bathvale could see the lake partially drained to make retrieving the boat easier. If he starts now, the water level will be substantially lower by morning."

Sir Randall sent me an apologetic smile: *Such an unreasonable man, this presuming Scot.*

"That is an excellent idea," I said. "I wish I'd thought of it. If the boat has been tampered with, then we will know for a certainty that Miss Putnam's mishap was not an accident." I affixed my Guileless Empty-headed Female smile to my face and beamed at Sir Randall.

He'd apparently withstood such artillery before, because he returned fire with a Patient Gentlemanly Wince.

"I see little benefit in raising a boat that's been submerged for a day. Who knows what the currents have done to disturb evidence of tampering or to create the fiction of such evidence at this point? I want facts, not speculation, and it is a fact that your man Upjohn has been seen wandering at odd hours."

Sebastian's gaze narrowed ominously.

"Sir Randall," I said, "this is a *house party*. Wandering at all hours is practically the agenda for those attending. I do believe Upjohn has developed a friendly acquaintance with my maid, Lucy Hewitt. I warn you against questioning her too closely regarding that situation, for she will spare you no detail whatsoever, regardless of who might be within earshot."

Sebastian regarded me as if I'd offered to sing a few arias for the company after the scavenger hunt, while Sir Randall's wince had become a carefully blank expression.

"My lady, your frankness does you credit." He managed to imply that my frankness appalled him. "I agree with you that house parties can be highly *social* affairs, but perhaps you are unaware that this Upjohn person was recently the subject of unkind talk regarding an incident in London involving..."

He looked to Sebastian, as if that sufficed to indicate all manner of wrongs and who was responsible for them.

"The poor man was set upon most cruelly," I said. "I was

there when he stumbled into Mrs. Robertson's gallery, barely able to stand because he'd been beaten so badly and robbed of the very clothes on his back. It's a wonder he survived, and now you imply that his brush with death has inspired him to purloin jewelry and sabotage boats? On the basis of what logic and to what purpose?"

"Yes," Sebastian said. "To what possible purpose? His wages are generous, he's now attached to a titled household, and he would not have known where the boathouse was, much less which boat Miss Putnam would choose for her outing."

"You have inspected all of the other boats, Sir Randall?" I added. "Please say you did."

"Samuel is responsible for inspecting the boats. He grew up on this estate. He knows the equipment, the staff, and the lake. He assured me those boats were sound last week, and he's reinspecting the lot again this afternoon."

"Isn't it more likely," I said, "if the boat was sabotaged somehow, that the objective was to create awkwardness at the regatta rather than to harm Miss Putnam? The goal of the thefts seems to be to embarrass Lord and Lady Bathvale, to cast a pall over the house party. A boat sinking before all the guests would accomplish that end at a time when many strong swimmers were on hand to give aid to the shipwrecked."

"Excellent point," Sebastian said. "If we're to attribute all the mischief to a single perpetrator, then disruption and embarrassment create a logical connection between every occurrence. Attempted murder, however, makes no sense at all."

"Fortunately," Sir Randall said, "I am an experienced investigator. I know better than to cease my inquiries when the first convenient explanation comes to hand. I'd like to question this Upjohn fellow."

"Why?" I asked. "His memory is dodgy as a result of blows to the head, and Monsieur St. Sevier, the physician who treated him for those injuries, is among the guests. He can tell you quite plainly that

Upjohn had a lucky escape, but that his recollections are not to be relied upon."

Sir Randall's mouth opened, then closed. The brave knight looked puzzled. "Upjohn isn't a reliable witness?"

"If his memory is unsound, as the physician himself would tell you, the man cannot speak in his own defense," Sebastian said. "Though why you'd accuse him alone of all the domestics, guests, and staff on the property defies logic."

Sir Randall gazed off across the terrace as Lady Bathvale emerged from the house. She was in the company of a Baxter—I could not tell which one—and she'd brought with her two footmen, who set out trays under the white canopy. More footmen with more trays followed, because of course a scavenger hunt would require that guests be fortified with food and drink, though breakfast had been but two hours ago.

"My lord," Sir Randall said, sounding like a barrister at his closing oration, "if you have theories as to *why* somebody seeks to disrupt the gathering, I would honestly like to hear them. Somebody is stealing items of value. Now it appears somebody—possibly the same person—has tampered with a boat, a more serious matter. I am at a loss, and while I am curious about your wandering valet, I rule nobody out as a suspect. *Nobody,* regardless of rank, means, or title."

Sir Randall was either very brave or very foolish to accuse Sebastian himself of wrongdoing.

"If you'll excuse me." Sebastian rose and bowed to me. "I will leave you to your speculations, Sir Randall. My lady, best of luck with the hunt." On that clever note, Sebastian took himself down into the garden. I lost sight of him as he strode behind a privet hedge.

Sir Randall's smile was pained. "You must not think too badly of MacHeath—Lord Dunkeld, rather."

I thought rather highly of Sebastian, despite his bouts of surliness. "Oh?"

"He has reason to wish me ill, good reason, and I've wondered if that's not a motive for making me look like a fool. He could nick baubles from the other guests and create a problem I'm supposed to solve. He's a peer of the realm now, and he'd be tried and acquitted in the Lords, and I'd never be able to show my face in Society again."

Men and their fanciful nonsense. "Why would a marquess risk scandal, if not ruin, merely to disgrace one obscure rural magistrate?"

"Fair question. Shall we stretch our legs?"

Sir Randall wanted privacy for this discussion, in other words, and I wanted to move—not that I was intent on trailing Sebastian, of course. I took Sir Randall's arm, and we descended into the garden.

"You and Lord Dunkeld served together on the Peninsula, did you not?"

"We did, in the most general sense. I was military police. He was commissioned. Our paths crossed and not happily."

The fountains in the garden splashed to life, the sound of cascading water blending with the chatter of the guests assembling on the terrace.

"Would that unhappiness explain a rather complicated plot on his lordship's part all these years later?" I asked.

"Yes. Dunkeld plays the stubborn, hot-headed Scot when it suits him, but he's shrewd and patient when he wants to be. A man like that can wait years for his revenge, and when he takes it, he will be thorough. He was a brilliant tactician. Wellington noticed that right off. Why besiege a town with shells and sappers when you could slip one little old woman through the postern gait with enough laxative herbs to poison the whole well?"

Oh, Sebastian. Shrewd indeed. "And you believe Dunkeld would steal jewelry and sabotage a boat to make you look foolish?" Though how would Sebastian have known that Sir Randall was the king's man in these surrounds, much less known he'd be summoned over missing jewelry?

Sir Randall plucked a pink rose from a bed blooming against a low wall and passed me the flower. "When I was new to my duties with the military, I was too zealous. Too anxious to show all those wealthy officers from titled families that a mere squire's son could make a meaningful contribution to the war effort. Somebody was stealing ammunition and selling it—to the enemy, to the locals who had to defend themselves against deserters from both armies. If I could solve that mystery, I would be the hero of the day. I thought I had found my culprit."

"You were wrong?"

"At the time, I thought I was making the right choice. In hindsight, I must admit to uncertainty. The thief was found with a weapon and powder, as well as with the keys to the storehouse. His commanding officer testified that he'd sent the fellow there to procure entirely different items. One should not accuse a man of a capital offense if his guilt is less than certain, should one?"

No, *one* should not, and even more so if the suspect was an illiterate boy unlikely to have the guile necessary to sell contraband. If the youth had been a born schemer, he would have procured both the items he'd been sent to retrieve *and* the contraband, keeping only the former in plain sight.

Sir Randall had been the hotheaded and stubborn party. "What can you do to make amends?"

"Military justice is swift and severe, ma'am. The accused was convicted. All these years later, I can make no amends."

The dinner gong sounded three times, the signal to assemble on the terrace. I did not want to go hunting for robins' eggs or blooming water lilies. I wanted to hunt a thief whose games were growing nasty.

"If you cannot make amends," I said, "the least you can do is refrain from making more unjust accusations. Upjohn has no motive, he's barely able to function in his position with Dunkeld, and engaging in a successful spree of larceny would be much more likely from a disgruntled housemaid who knows this house from pantries to attics. Did you know I found one such maid rummaging through my effects?"

I explained about the woman who'd given me the false name Haines and that she'd had dark hair. I further indicated that my shawl had gone missing and turned up in the library shortly thereafter. The very last truth I would divulge was Sebastian's involvement in that situation, and I also refrained from mentioning my missing rings.

"My lady, why haven't you disclosed this to me sooner?"

"Because I cannot prove anything was stolen, and I do not make careless accusations. Whatever guilt you carry because you caused the death of an innocent soldier cannot be expiated by causing more innocent deaths. Nobody should be hanged for purloining a shawl when I have six others that serve just as well."

"I cannot agree," he said, gaze on the laughing, chatting crowd on the terrace. "Unless punishment is swift and severe, the lower orders and those of a criminal bent will take every advantage. Justice must be unflinching and vigilant."

"Hundreds of years of unflinching, vigilant justice have only provided us the ghoulish spectacle of public hangings at which the pickpockets and purse robbers ply their trades. Your theory wants evidentiary support, while the lower orders want a decent meal, honest wages, and a safe place to sleep."

I had gone too far, applying logic to a situation that Sir Randall's plodding mental powers were determined to drag into the shadows of male conceit. My brothers would have howled with laughter at Sir Randall's consternation, but offending the magistrate was rank foolishness—stubborn and hotheaded of me even.

"I have watched for this maid calling herself Haines," I said. "Contrary to her story, I have not seen her again in my corridor. I would know her at sight, particularly without her mobcap."

"You are saying I should search the maids' quarters," Sir Randall muttered, pacing before the roses. "I had thought to do that after I finished searching the guest quarters."

Truly the Almighty had been parsimonious when doling out powers of deduction to the magistrate.

I twirled the little rose stem between my gloved fingers. "Sir Randall, if I had stolen several easily identifiable articles, would I, as a guest, keep them in the one location bound to incriminate me, or would I secret them someplace bound to incriminate another?"

"Lady Bathvale raised the same argument with me when I told her I had begun my search. My response remains the same: An investigation proceeds by thorough, detailed examination of the evidence. If a guest is our thief, then the only area that guest can control of a certainty is his or her quarters. Then too, wherever the goods are recovered, those victimized will be pleased to have their personal effects restored to them, even if a thief cannot be arrested."

That was a valid point, though searching the guest rooms wasn't likely to turn up anything related to the thefts.

"The solution is simple," Sir Randall said, making another pass before the roses. "I will have Lady Bathvale line up the chambermaids, and you can identify this so-called Haines person."

Subtlety was apparently also not in Sir Randall's gift. "Might we do so in a manner that obscures the point of the inspection?"

"How so?"

"Domestics take pride in their work, Sir Randall. If you make it clear that the maids have come under suspicion, they will take it amiss. You will also make it easier for the thief to cast false lures in the direction of a maid to confuse the evidence."

The gong sounded again. I was growing to hate that wretched noise.

"What do you propose, my lady?"

"Lady Bathvale can have the kitchen set out a midday tea for the chambermaids tomorrow, a thank-you for their extra work during the house party. While the guests are occupied with the afternoon's activities, I will pop in on the maids, ostensibly to find my own lady's maid, Hewitt. If the woman I found in my rooms is among the housemaids, I'll see her and have Hewitt inquire as to her true name and occupation."

"And if she's not among the maids?"

"Then a lot of hardworking women will have had a few biscuits and ten minutes to rest their feet."

He came to a halt, his hands clasped behind his back. "I will put this to Lady Bathvale. The only flaw I can see in this notion is that you will miss part of the day's diversions."

"I will bear up under that sorrow, I assure you."

He needed a moment to catch the irony in my words, then he smiled and offered his arm. "This party means a lot to Lady Bathvale. She has been a long time adjusting to country life, and I daresay Lord Bathvale has not made the way smoother for her. We'll sort out this little contretemps with the jewelry and get that behind us."

Us? Who was *us*? Given how raptly Sir Randall and Lady Bathvale had been engaged with each other the previous day, I wasn't sure I wanted to know the answer.

Sir Randall parted from me on the terrace. I made a display of sniffing at the pink rose, though it hadn't much fragrance. I had finished crossing the terrace when Sebastian fell in beside me.

"Are you dodging off, Lady Violet?"

Yes. "Finding a vase for this humble blossom." I twirled the stem again gently and got pricked on the finger through my glove. "Ouch."

Sebastian produced a linen handkerchief. "I don't suppose your friend St. Sevier knows how to swim?"

"I can ask him." I took off my glove, passed him the rose, and wrapped my finger in Sebastian's handkerchief. "I am quite a good swimmer, you know."

"I do know, but you are also a lady, and no matter how much you bat your eyes at me, plead, or insist, you are not helping me raise that boat."

"Don't flatter yourself, my lord. My days of pleading with a man for any reason whatsoever are long past." I left him on the terrace holding the thorny little rose. I had no intention of returning out of doors until the teams had been chosen and were off on their quests.

CHAPTER NINE

My first objective upon escaping the scavenger hunt was to search Sebastian's rooms. He was concerned for his valet, but if Sir Randall had a score to settle with Sebastian—*and he assuredly did*—then the marquess himself could come under suspicion.

I wasn't about to let that happen.

Sebastian's effects were noteworthy for two qualities. First, everything in his dressing closet was arranged with painful neatness, from the wardrobe and clothes press to the boots and shoes lined up in tidy pairs along one wall. The room bore the scents of leather and starch, with an undernote of Sebastian's sandalwood and cedar shaving soap.

The second quality was good taste. Even as a boy, Sebastian had been something of a sybarite. He would rather have had one exquisitely tailored shirt than a half-dozen serviceable items of indifferent fit and workmanship.

Of Upjohn, I found no evidence. The dressing closet had a single chair—a place to sit when donning or removing shoes—but no cot for the valet to sleep upon.

Perhaps that was for the best.

I used a hairpin to pick the lock on Sebastian's jewelry box—a lady always had a hairpin handy—and peeked and poked only long enough to assure myself none of the missing items had been stashed inside. The night table by his bed bore only a pair of reading glasses and a few coins. Inside the drawer, I spotted a journal.

"Don't you dare," I said to myself, closing the drawer without touching the journal. The vanity was similarly without incriminating evidence, and a cursory examination of the rest of the room—bed hangings, curtains, beneath the bed, carpets, and window casement—revealed all to be in order.

I searched my own rooms next, finding nothing out of place. I considered embarking on a search of other guest rooms, starting with those victimized by the supposed thief. Miss Waltham, Mrs. Albright, and Mrs. Bonaventure were all shrewd enough to avoid suspicion by painting themselves as victims, but then, wouldn't they also be shrewd enough not to keep the stolen goods in their very guest rooms? I assumed they would be.

"St. Sevier," I muttered. He, too, would make a credible suspect, having a reason to resent the entire English aristocracy.

The place I truly wanted to search was the maids' quarters, but the female domestics were likely housed on the same floor as the kitchen. With the cooks and housekeeper to keep a watchful eye on them, the maids would also enjoy the warmth of the kitchen in winter and the ground floor's coolness in summer.

The footmen, poor fellows, were usually housed up under the eaves. I dared not venture into their quarters, though perhaps Sebastian or St. Sevier could.

St. Sevier's quarters also bore a faint echo of his scent—gardenias or honeysuckle, I could never decide exactly which. Whereas Sebastian's rooms had been painfully neat, St. Sevier's looked as if he'd been living in his apartment for some time. A wineglass with a half inch of claret in it sat on the mantel. A pair of slippers at an odd angle lay to the side of the reading chair. A smoking jacket lined in blue satin had been tossed over the back of the chair, and a bound volume of French poetry lay facedown on a hassock.

The urge to tidy was nearly overwhelming, which was odd. My own quarters were neat enough, but I was by no means a woman who must control a space by ordering all to suit my whims. St. Sevier's jewelry box was a fine, smooth walnut creation with a fleur-de-lis carved into the top.

"Another man with good taste."

But apparently without much vanity. Hugh's jewelry case was nearly empty.

"I keep most of the better items rolled up in my clean stockings." Hugh lounged in the doorway, though I'd not heard him open the door. How long had he been observing me?

"My lady," he went on, "I am surprised to find you here. Do I dare hope you are in the mood to frolic?" He watched me as if he expected me to brandish a weapon and flee out the window and down the drainpipe.

I closed the jewelry box after satisfying myself that it held no stolen goods. "I am making sure Sir Randall's planned search of the guest rooms holds no unfortunate surprises. I searched Dunkeld's quarters as well, because Sir Randall is suspicious of Upjohn."

Hugh lounged against the doorjamb, arms crossed. "Forgive me if my question is out of order, but might you not have simply warned me to have a look myself? Another look?"

Was he angry? Amused? I could not tell. "Yes, I might have warned you, but I learned of Sir Randall's intention less than an hour ago, and I did not want to waste this opportunity to investigate. I have not yet searched your bedroom."

He pushed away from the doorjamb, took me by the wrist, and led me into the bedroom. The bed was draped with blue velvet hangings, and the rest of the room was done in burgundy and cream. My own chamber was smaller, and Hugh's had a better view of the back terrace.

"Let's have a look, shall we?" he asked, strolling to the far side of the bed.

I had not been in a bedroom with a man since my husband's

death, and the impropriety of the situation—or the novelty?—scattered my thoughts.

"Violet," Hugh said, lifting his chin in the direction of the dressing closet. "A quick perusal of my wardrobe would be helpful. I'll take the bureau." He set about opening and closing drawers as if searching bedrooms with awkward widows was another one of the many diversions on the house party schedule.

I retreated to the dressing closet, my cheeks warm for no earthly reason. Hugh's informality was evident here as well. A morning jacket hung from the wardrobe door. A hairbrush sat on a pink-upholstered chair. His riding boots stood in the corner, though one had been fitted with a boot tree, while the other curled over at an angle, the second boot tree nowhere to be seen.

I had to touch his clothing to examine the wardrobe, and that presumption felt horrendously intimate when he himself was in the next room making a racket. His clothing was, like Sebastian's, in the first stare of fashion, but less severe. A bit more lace on a cuff, several colors threaded into the embroidery of his waistcoats. He was not a peacock, but he was stylish.

"Find anything interesting?" He sauntered into the dressing closet, making me very aware of just how small the room was.

"You cut a dash," I said, "but you are not as careful of your boots as an Englishman would be."

"I do not engage in blood sport. Those boots are merely for riding, not for impressing the rest of the first flight in the hunt field. Have you established my innocence to your satisfaction, my lady?"

"Don't be like that," I said, closing his wardrobe. "Don't be cross. You are as vulnerable as Sebastian and Upjohn are. Everybody is a potential victim of whoever seeks to ruin this house party. I've searched my own apartment and warned Lucy to keep a sharp eye out as well."

I brushed past him, and such were the confines that we could not help but touch. He appeared to ignore the contact, while I endured a bolt of awareness. Hugh was a handsome, intelligent man whom I esteemed and trusted. He'd offered to frolic with me—perhaps half in jest?—and I...

Was tempted.

He would make *getting back on the horse* enjoyable, and he'd be discreet. Was that what I wanted, or would a romp with St. Sevier ruin a friendship for the sake of an experiment in enlightened widowhood? Would intimacies leave me lonelier than ever and feeling pathetic and desperate?

Or would I feel comforted? *Satisfied?*

"You are frowning," he said, following me from the dressing closet. "Thinking to conduct another search?" His smile suggested his person was available for that undertaking.

"I'd like to search the maids' quarters, but if I show myself belowstairs for no reason, Lady Bathvale, if not her good friend Sir Randall, will soon get word of that."

"Then what are we to do with this gift of free time and privacy?" St. Sevier asked, stepping closer. "What would you like to do?"

I honestly wanted to kiss him. Not to kiss him, but to *be* kissed by him and learn if his attentions suited me. When I'd been at school, one of the grooms had initiated me into the wonders of the stolen kiss, except that Simon's version of a kiss was a nibbling, groaning business that had nearly provoked me to laughter the first time I'd ducked behind the saddle room door with him. His technique had not improved with practice—he'd become louder and more nibbly—and I'd been relieved when he'd taken a post at a nearby manor house.

I had dragooned Sebastian into kissing practice a time or two, though I recall those occasions descending into laughter on his part and mortification on my own.

I had not kissed many men, in other words, and only with my husband had I allowed my kisses to become passionate. Would I enjoy kissing Hugh?

"Violet." He stepped closer, smiling down at me. "If you could see your expression. You are either plotting to steal the crown jewels, or you have stolen them and are deciding whether to confide in me."

Delicately put. I tried an experimental lean against him. He was tall and solid, but not as tall or as solid as Sebastian. Why I would compare him to Sebastian rather than to Freddie was a puzzle.

"How are you?" St. Sevier asked, looping an arm around my waist and propping his chin on my crown. "Still ready to leave the premises without looking back?"

"I am concerned. If Sir Randall is to solve the thefts, he will soon run out of time." I pulled back enough to study Hugh, whose countenance was for once devoid of the faint insouciance he wore so well.

"Time is precious," he said. "Time with you is especially precious."

His words pleased me and surprised me, though he'd probably said them to any number of women. "Thank you."

He was watching my mouth, probably waiting for me to kiss him first. Hugh would do that, he'd be that considerate and patient. He would need to know that I was choosing the next step for myself, not merely enduring activities in which I had only a passing interest.

Get on with it. Get back on the horse and get past this. He will be charming and lighthearted, and he won't make odd noises, nibble excessively, or expect too much.

"Violet?" He drew his finger along the curve of my jaw.

I turned my face into his palm, and a movement on the terrace below caught my eye. A group had gathered, and something about postures and positioning suggested it was not a happy group.

"What is going on?" I murmured.

Sir Randall stood amid a circle of guests, Lord Bathvale at his side. Sebastian faced them, and Upjohn stood near him, eyes downcast.

"Bloody hell," Hugh muttered. "Sir Randall is doubtless stirring the pot."

"Let's go." I ducked past Hugh and marched for the door. "If Sir Randall arrests Upjohn on the strength of anything other than hard evidence, and lots of it, Dunkeld will call him out, and bedamned to the *Code Duello*."

~

St. Sevier and I emerged onto the terrace through a door from the music parlor. This put me at the back of the crowd, where I had no intention of remaining. I wiggled between the Baxters, then sidled around Mrs. Bonaventure, until I was at the front of the group, watching a muscle leap in Sebastian's jaw.

Not good. Not good at all.

"My lord, I must insist," Sir Randall said. "This man was caught in possession of stolen goods, and he cannot account for his where-abouts at critical points since arriving at Bathvale Abbey."

"Then question him further," Sebastian said. "Finish your snooping and question the rest of the guests, but don't arrest him because Hempley's cravat pin showed up in a dormitory shared by six footmen."

Oh dear.

"Not merely in a dormitory," Sir Randall retorted. "In the drawer of *his* night table."

Upjohn made matters worse by staring at the flagstones, head hung in what looked very like shame.

I took the place beside him. "In fact," I said, "the night table was not Upjohn's. It was merely beside the bed he's using when he isn't waiting up for his lordship. Anybody, particularly any man, could easily have put that cravat pin in that drawer. Hempley's own valet doubtless had access to that room and might well have left the evidence behind to incriminate another."

"Madam," Sir Randall began, "with all due respect—"

"Upjohn is the ideal victim for such a scheme," I went on, going toe-to-toe with the magistrate. "As you well know, and as the staff here has remarked to me, he's new to his livery, is recovering from severe blows to the head, and has nobody to vouch for him."

I could not say what prompted me to confront Sir Randall, much less so publicly. Perhaps I'd spent too many years being talked over and interrupted by the men in my family, perhaps I'd wearied of a widow's invisibility. Maybe I'd overtaxed myself, spending more than a week among strangers far from my familiar surrounds.

Or perhaps seeing Sebastian again had reminded me of the confident, outspoken girl I had once been.

Lady Bathvale stood pale and silent near her husband, whose scowl called to mind the wrath of Zeus. Clara held her sister's hand, as if an armed highwayman rather than one annoyed woman argued with Sir Randall.

"Upjohn has no motive to steal from strangers," I said, "and every motive to be on his best behavior. If you accuse him merely on the basis of his humble station, then the same limited means can be attributed to every domestic on the property. Those employed at Bathvale Abbey know the premises far better than Upjohn does. They know which guests are assigned to what rooms and when the entertainments are scheduled. They are familiar with the routines and personalities of the house staff and residents. Upjohn has none of those advantages, and yet, you regard *him alone* with suspicion."

I was prepared to launch into another recitation regarding the maid who was *not* named Haines when Lord Bathvale stepped closer.

"That will be quite enough, madam." His lordship glowered at me, the wrong tactic if his intention was to cow me into silence.

Sir Randall had chosen this very public situation to confront the suspect, probably because he did not trust himself to prevail against Sebastian privately. Respect for the king's man made the presence of witnesses—spectators, more like—a shrewd choice. And now, I would be held responsible for "causing a scene."

I had not *caused* this scene—Sir Randall had—and I could make him regret that choice.

"Sir Randall," I went on, refusing to so much as glance at Lord Bathvale, "I have personally acquainted you with facts that point suspicion at a party other than Upjohn. You propose to make an arrest before even investigating that avenue. You have no explanation for why only Lord Hempley's cravat pin, of all the missing items, was found in that drawer. If Mrs. Albright's locket turns up in the nursery, will you arrest the children? If a pair of earbobs are found in the stables, will you arrest the horses?"

Bertie Baxter was trying not to smirk. Mrs. Bonaventure was grinning outright. Pamela Albright's mouth was hanging open.

And I was not half finished.

"Lady Violet has a point," Miss Waltham said hesitantly. "If I were to steal a small item, I would not be so foolish as to keep it in a drawer beside my bed, particularly not if I shared sleeping quarters with five other people."

"Any schoolboy would have more brains than that," Bertie Baxter offered. "In fact, schoolboys are notorious for leaving contraband where it will incriminate others. I daresay schoolgirls have discovered the same diversion."

The first gong sounded for luncheon, and I had the sense that the crowd was ready to disperse, an indication that Sir Randall's decision to arrest Upjohn lacked support among the guests.

"Sir Randall," Lord Bathvale said, "is the authority appointed to keep the peace in this corner of the realm. If in his opinion this man,"—he swept Upjohn with a contemptuous glance—"poses a threat to my guests and my household, then Sir Randall's authority will be respected."

St. Sevier had found a place at Sebastian's side, though I hadn't seen him move. The two men were in a whispered consultation as Lord Bathvale held forth, and it was St. Sevier who spoke up when I would have commenced shouting at Lord Bathvale.

"If I might interject a word," St. Sevier said, all sweet reason. "As a medical professional, I can confirm that a severe beating will often leave gaps in a man's memory, and Mr. Upjohn was indeed brutally assaulted. I am concerned that incarceration under inhospitable conditions will impede Mr. Upjohn's recovery. Might we strike a compromise in the name of Christian charity, common sense, and respect for law and order? Confine him to a private room for the present, allowing his recovery to progress, while containing any threat he might pose. Continue the investigation and see where matters stand in a few days' time."

I hated that compromise. It implied that Upjohn—slight, harmless, blameless—was the culprit. I was about to make my opinion known when I caught Sebastian's eye.

He regarded me steadily, conveying a sense of warning and also of shared purpose. He'd clearly put St. Sevier up to intervening, and coming from the only medical expert on hand, St. Sevier's opinion would be hard to gainsay.

Clever. Even in my anger, I could see the cleverness of Sebastian's strategy.

"One does not want to act too hastily," Lady Bathvale said, aiming her comment at her husband. "Nor does one want to be uncharitable toward those recovering from serious injuries."

They, too, communicated in a dialect of subtle glances and nuances of expression.

"Sir Randall?" Lord Bathvale said. "If I confine this man to a private room, will that suit your purposes?"

Lady Bathvale's gaze went to the magistrate, whom she had insisted on involving in her house party. "We have plenty of unoccupied rooms."

"I can manage without my valet for a few days," Sebastian said. "Upjohn can doubtless use some peace and quiet and a bit of rest."

People were drifting away from the back of the crowd, more interested in food than in this petty drama, and yet, for Upjohn, the stakes had become life or death. If he was arrested, if he was bound over for the assizes, his chances of being acquitted were minuscule. He faced transportation at best and hanging very possibly, assuming he survived the contagion rampant in England's fine jails.

"Very well," Sir Randall said. "This fellow will be kept confined until I can either exonerate him or bring him to justice."

Exoneration of the innocent *was* justice. I was about to share that truth with Sir Randall and his scowling lordship when a slight pressure on my palm distracted me.

Sebastian had discreetly, briefly squeezed my hand.

"If that's settled," Clara said, *much* too brightly, "let's see what's for lunch, shall we? I vow all this haring about the grounds has left me famished." She slipped her arm through Lady Bathvale's and led a procession from the terrace into the house. Upjohn sent Sebastian one bewildered look, then shuffled off between Sir Randall and Lord Bathvale.

"Well done," Mrs. Bonaventure murmured as she passed me. "I cannot abide a bully."

Miss Waltham gave me a little wave as she took Bertie Baxter's arm.

St. Sevier kissed my cheek and then offered to escort Pamela Albright, and soon I was alone on the terrace with Sebastian.

"Not here," he said when I would have launched into a rant about incompetent magistrates and pompous earls.

"Then where? I will not be silenced, Dunkeld. Not on a matter of this much import."

Something furious and determined in my tone must have caught his ear. "Violet, are you all right?"

Now that Upjohn had been granted a measure of temporary safety, I was nearly lightheaded with relief, though I was also unaccountably rattled.

"I want to pummel Sir Randall."

"He needs pummeling." Sebastian was smiling at me, the charming, crooked grin I hadn't seen from him in years. "You made a good start on that thankless task."

"I must not cry." I hadn't meant to say any such thing. "I must not descend into profanity either. I would like to. Very much."

Sebastian gestured in the direction of the steps that led down to the garden. "I enjoy your cursing. You have a talent for it. Let's find someplace where you can air your vocabulary in private."

I took his arm, not because manners required it, but because I honestly needed his support.

~

The garden was peaceful, also in plain view of the house. I wanted privacy to settle my nerves, and retreating to my room held no appeal. The vanquished retreated, and I was not vanquished in any sense. To the contrary, I was more determined than ever to get to the bottom of the thefts.

"What did you mean?" Sebastian asked as we turned from the garden onto the path to the lake. "You said you gave Sir Randall another avenue to investigate."

"The maid in my room who lied about her name. Sir Randall will arrange an opportunity for me to see the housemaids at an impromptu mid-afternoon tea offered in appreciation for their hard work. If I spot the liar with dark hair, I'll point her out to Lucy, who can unearth her true name."

"Which proves nothing. With Sir Randall bumbling about, casting suspicion elsewhere won't be enough to preserve Upjohn from being bound over for the quarter sessions."

Such a pretty day to have such a gloomy conversation. The sun slanted benevolently through the stately oaks. The lake shone placid and blue in the distance. The pervasive quiet of the English country-side should have settled my nerves, but that tonic was slow to take effect.

"I have wondered about something," I said, slipping my hand around Sebastian's arm. "Did Clara put her own boat into the water? I'm trying to recall, and I can't. If a boatman was on the scene, why didn't he make an effort to rescue a woman at risk of drowning?"

"If there was a boatman on duty, perhaps he couldn't swim. Not everybody can."

"We have too many questions, my lord, and not enough answers. Why was only Lord Hempley's pin found? I searched your rooms, you know."

"Did you really?" Sebastian sounded merely curious when I'd expected indignation.

"I searched my own as well. I don't want any more stolen items showing up where they are hard to explain."

"What did you find, Violet?"

"In your room? Nothing of any interest. You are surpassingly tidy."

"No evidence of all the lovers who've been bouncing on my sheets?"

I shoved him rather than concede the point. "You will be relieved to know my rooms were similarly in order."

We came to the stile, and I chose the quiet meadow over the lake. I wanted to have a good look at the situation at the boathouse, but not until I was calmer. Confronting Sir Randall had upset me beyond the normal frustration of dealing with male pigheadedness. I needed to discern why that was and what to do about that.

"You still have nearly two dozen or so guest rooms yet to search," Sebastian said, handing me up the steps.

I paused on the top step, which put me a foot or so higher than Sebastian. "Sir Randall will be thorough and methodical. He ought to search the maids' quarters, but that would insult Lord and Lady Bathvale, so the guests will be eliminated from suspicion first. I don't suppose you could take on the challenge of searching the maids' quarters?"

"Your lady's maid would be a better choice for that challenge, if she's willing to bear the risk."

"I'm not willing to ask it of her. Lucy won't be tried in the Lords and acquitted if she's accused of theft. Sir Randall bears no love for you at all, Sebastian." And that gave me a chill, because Sebastian had ever been one to minimize risks to his own person. He wasn't arrogant in this regard, so much as he was hopelessly blind.

We took the wooden bench, which at this hour sat in full sun. I hadn't brought a parasol, nor was I wearing a bonnet. The sun felt good on my face, a rare pleasure for a lady.

"You'll get freckles," Sebastian said as I tipped my chin up and closed my eyes.

"Why don't men get freckles? One sees the occasional redheaded fellow with freckles, but you marched all over sunny Spain. I daresay you carried no parasol, and there's not a freckle to be found on your person."

He stretched an arm along the top of the bench and leaned back. "Your mind, Violet, is the most unpredictable place. Thank you for standing up for my valet."

A thank-you from Sebastian did more to restore my mood than all the fresh air and bucolic peace in the shire.

"He should have stood at attention," I said. "A martyr bravely facing injustice. That hangdog air all but reeks of guilt. We must search the rest of his belongings."

"That would take about thirty seconds. He has one change of clothes, an old army jacket that's too big for him, a pair of ill-fitting boots—the best I could do on short notice—and a Bible given to him by my butler. Sir Randall has doubtless already inspected the lot."

And so, apparently, had Sebastian. "Can you recall anything at all about the person you saw crossing the terrace on Saturday night?"

He was silent for a moment, while my mind seized on a cheering thought: At the Robertsons' ball, Sebastian had been nearly rude to me. His animosity had been an invisible cloak draped over his broad shoulders and swirling about him with every movement.

We had not regained the easy camaraderie of our youth, but neither were we at daggers drawn. That gave me hope both for our future dealings and for solving the mystery before us.

"All I recall about the person crossing the terrace was that they wore trousers and a jacket, and knew exactly where they were going. They carried no lantern, nor did they need one."

"Build?"

"Trim, neither overly tall nor stout. The stride was brisk and energetic. They had a purpose and a destination."

Not much to go on. "A purpose such as sabotaging a boat?"

"Or enjoying a cigar in the garden, meeting a lover, walking off a fit of wind. Thank you for searching my rooms, Violet."

Two thank-yous in one conversation. Why did that please me so? "You are welcome." I felt compelled to offer Sebastian something in exchange for his graciousness, and all I had of value was the truth. "I didn't want to come to this gathering. I've been rather a hermit since Freddie died."

"I know. Your family worried for you." Sebastian scooped up three round, smooth rocks and began to juggle them. "Felix and I keep in touch. Your father was on the point of ordering you to quit Town and return to Derwent Hall. I advised against it."

To learn that my father and brothers had been discussing me behind my back provoked an old, tired anger.

"They mean well. Whenever they meddle, belittle, and interfere, they mean well. As far as I'm concerned, they can wallpaper hell with their dratted good intentions."

"Precisely my point to Felix." Sebastian caught all three rocks and tossed them to the ground. "A widow's sole consolation is her independence, and if your family threatened yours, you could make them regret it."

"Endlessly, I assure you. When did this exchange take place?"

"Felix is a faithful correspondent. I hear from him at least once a quarter, but his concern for you has been a regular feature of his letters for the past year and a half. You did not come out of full mourning as he'd hoped you would."

I was not a faithful correspondent where my brothers were concerned, but Felix would receive a missive from me before the week was out.

"Widowhood has been an adjustment," I said. "Freddie had flaws, as did I—as do I. I was reconciling myself to our mutual imper-fections, though the process was far from complete."

"He was decent to you?" Sebastian posed the question quietly, though I sensed that my answer mattered to him.

"He was a hopeless tomcat and a worse flirt. I failed to give him sons, and I think that made his proclivities all the worse. He never reproached me for my failure. Not by a word, silence, or even a glance. He provided well for me both as his wife and as his widow—very well—and he never once embarrassed me in public. Freddie was funny to the point of irreverence, and he taught me to put my family in their place when they tried to intrude on my business. 'To perdition with the lot of them,' he'd say. I needed to hear that, to learn to say it."

I apparently needed to learn to say it more loudly.

"If your marriage was happy, then I'm glad for you." That sounded like a concession, but to what and why?

"My marriage had its positive qualities, though I needed a few years to appreciate them." The infidelity had been a source of sorrow and rage, then resignation. I told myself that intimate pleasures were simply of less moment to Freddie than they were to me. That explanation had been cold comfort on the nights when he'd failed to come home. But then he'd show up at the breakfast table, smiling blandly, and I'd swallow my discontent with my morning tea.

Most of the time.

"Perhaps the lack of children was not your fault, Violet."

Few men would have offered even that much comment. "The fault was mine, of that there can be no doubt." I had not admitted that to anybody, and why should I? Childlessness was always laid at the feet of the wife, and in this case, justly so.

"I'm sorry. You wanted children."

He would recall that. As a girl, I had often bleated forth about having a big family of my own someday, mostly girl children if divine providence had any compassion. I would spend all of my days doting on my offspring and making my home a pleasant place to grow up.

Ye gods, I'd been a lonely girl. That insight landed amid the day's other revelations, to be stored away for later consideration.

"Maybe that's why Upjohn's situation bothers me so," I said. "He's alone in the world. Doubtless, he has family in some distant shire, but he's among strangers here, and I cannot bear to see anybody without allies in adversity."

"He has me," Sebastian said. "I'm not sure I'll be able to do him any good, given Sir Randall's antipathy toward me."

"Keep a close eye on your quarters," I said. "Sir Randall will make a thorough inspection, I'm sure of that. I also ventured into St. Sevier's rooms, in an abundance of caution."

"Intrepid of you." Said mildly—too mildly.

"Hugh St. Sevier has been a good friend to me." And he was apparently willing to be even more, but what did I want where he was concerned?

Sebastian rose and paced off along the trail that ran parallel to the wall. Hoofed stock had made that path, a little track packed hard by decades, if not centuries, of use.

"I know I will offend you with my next remarks," he said, "but I offer them in the spirit of the friendship we once enjoyed."

Sebastian appeared honestly troubled, though on him the result also resembled annoyance. "Stop sounding dire and speak your piece."

"On the terrace just now, I'm sure every guest's attention was riveted by Sir Randall's histrionics, but I happened to glance up. In St. Sevier's window, I saw you in his embrace, as plain as the buttons on the Regent's waistcoats."

"My *dear* marquess," I began, shooting to my feet. "If you presume to think for one instant—"

Sebastian caught me with a hand on each of my arms. "Violet, hold your tongue. St. Sevier seems a decent sort—more than decent. His efforts as a physician on behalf of wounded soldiers, regardless of nationality, are the stuff of legends. If he's your choice for a frolic or a friendship, for *anything*, that is not my business, but have a care for your reputation *and his*. The mood of this gathering has turned predatory. For the love of God, *be careful*."

Had Sebastian shouted, lectured, or threatened, I might have stood up to him as I had to Sir Randall, but Sebastian was genuinely worried for me. And—more to the point—he was right. To embrace

Hugh in a bedroom window amid a house full of gossip and intrigue had been rank folly.

"I will be more careful, I promise you, but St. Sevier is truly a friend. He all but dared me to accept this invitation because I was growing reclusive. My brother's tattling was accurate in that regard, though if Felix tells similar tales in future, I will disown him. St. Sevier opined that I needed to challenge myself with unfamiliar surrounds and new faces, so here I am. He worries for me, and given my behavior toward Sir Randall, perhaps he should."

"Fine way to worry for you," Sebastian said, stepping back. "Accosting you where anybody might see the spectacle."

That sounded more like the Sebastian I knew and resented. I preferred the gentleman who offered me a private word of caution to the testy marquess.

"We should get back to the house, or we'll miss luncheon entirely," I said. "Are you involved in the rehearsals?" A portion of the afternoon was reserved for preparation of various amateur scenes to be enacted for the company on Thursday evening.

"I declined that honor, thank you very much. My guess is Sir Randall has as well, the better to continue his snooping."

"I am no sort of thespian. Let's have a look at the boathouse, shall we?"

CHAPTER TEN

The endless tromping about I was doing at Bathvale Abbey was improving my appetite and my sleep. In London, I had servants whose hard work allowed me to remain behind the walls of my home. Here, I might send Lucy to the kitchen for a tea tray, but otherwise, I was required to get up and move.

"Is your afternoon free?" St. Sevier asked me when I'd finished my third sandwich of cloved ham and cheddar.

"I have not attached myself to a theatrical group," I said, pushing the last strawberry about on my plate. This was the largest specimen, plump and bright red. I had abruptly lost my appetite for it as self-consciousness eclipsed pleasure in the food.

St. Sevier had embraced me in his bedroom, touched my face, and made it plain I was welcome to explore his person intimately.

"Neither have I volunteered to make a fool of myself for the entertainment of the other guests." St. Sevier took the place beside me on the love seat. Lunch had been a cold buffet served in the gallery, and guests were spread out over the music room, parlor, and terrace. I'd chosen to remain in the library rather than subject my complexion to another midday encounter with the sun.

"I made a mistake with you earlier." I put the plate aside, knowing a footman would happily devour the strawberry.

"No, you did not. If your behavior is to rise to the level of the I-made-a-mistake speech, you must first have something of substance to make the speech about. Friends can be affectionate with one another, Violet."

His tone was bland, his expression merely bored, but I had the sense that was a performance. A lady didn't rebuke a man for familiarities without encountering his pride.

"The mistake," I said, "was in enjoying your embrace before a bedroom window."

He took the strawberry from my plate and popped it into his mouth. "You *enjoyed* our embrace?" he asked when he'd dispatched the stolen fruit.

"We were observed." The only other people in the library were the footmen cleaning up after the buffet. They would eat well, and for that I was glad. In the tradition of their calling, they were being run off their feet.

"We were observed by Lord Dunkeld?" St. Sevier asked.

"Do I have no privacy at this blasted gathering?"

"Not enough, apparently. You and the marquess rambled off toward the lake after you pinned Sir Randall's ears back, and Dunkeld escorted you to the buffet."

Miss Waltham had claimed Sebastian's company for lunch, and that suited me, because I wanted time to think. But for the occasional greeting, the other guests had granted my wish to be left in peace.

"Hence, you conclude Dunkeld was the one who saw us."

"He's an astute man, Violet. The Scots would call him canny. He will keep his mouth shut, but your point is well taken. I was indiscreet to display my regard for you before a bedroom window. I do apologize, and I will not make that mistake again."

A pretty speech, but I detected no real hint of remorse in it. "Do you know how to swim?"

"*Comme un poisson.* When I was sent to my grandmother's

people as a lad, I devised a plan to run away and swim the Channel to France. Instead, I learned that exercise can tame all manner of unruly emotions."

This house party was reminding me of the same lesson, though being raised in the country, I should not have had to review that curriculum in adulthood.

"Lord Dunkeld would like to raise Miss Putnam's boat. Sir Randall was unwilling to do that, but I think the craft might yield useful evidence."

"I went to the lake for a swim last night. Cold water settles the humors, you know. I'd be happy if the marquess sought to join me on a similar excursion at some point. Let's tell him that, shall we?"

Sebastian approached across the library, Miss Waltham nowhere to be seen. He offered us a bow. "My lady, St. Sevier. I thought to enjoy a constitutional after my meal and hoped that Lady Violet might join me."

"To the boathouse?" St. Sevier asked, rising. "I was planning on strolling out that way myself."

Next, they'd decide I needed a nap while they went off to poke into dark corners without me. "I'll fetch my bonnet and parasol and meet you both on the back terrace in five minutes."

I left the gentlemen eyeing each other. Sebastian doubtless planned to scold Hugh for that scene in the window. His lordship had no right to intrude in such a manner, but really, Hugh and I had been very foolish. Very.

And not foolish enough?

I put that question aside and fetched the requisite articles from my room. Lucy was nowhere to be seen, and I hoped she was off enjoying herself. Bathvale Abbey itself wasn't a particularly welcoming or commodious dwelling—too big, too drafty, too formal— but the grounds were lovely, and the weather was delightful. Perhaps Lucy had needed a respite from life in London as much as I had.

Sebastian and Hugh were discussing some bill to regulate the hours of tailors' apprentices when I gained the back terrace. They politely bickered all the way through the garden until I put an end to their argument.

"That will do, gentlemen. Let us focus on the matter at hand."

"The thefts," St. Sevier said.

"Location of the remaining stolen items," Sebastian added.

"Upjohn's impending conviction," I said. "Sir Randall's pride is involved now. What common sense he has is likely insufficient to see justice served. Upjohn has no motive to steal, and Sir Randall hasn't even established that Upjohn had the opportunity."d

We went through the sequence of events. When was each item likely purloined? Who had the opportunity to steal it? We could not exonerate Upjohn on that basis because Sebastian was largely ignorant of his valet's whereabouts.

"He shows up in the morning to lay out my clothing and make up my room. He is available to me when it's time to change for dinner or retire for the night—usually—but for much of the day and the night, he's not underfoot."

"He should be resting as much as his duties allow," St. Sevier said. "Recovery from a head injury can take weeks, and for some, the process is never entirely complete."

We ambled along the path, which was becoming familiar to me. With the meadow beyond the stone wall to the left, the park to the right, and the lake through the trees up ahead, the way was peaceful and pretty.

"St. Sevier is quite a competent swimmer," I said when our conversation had reached a melancholy lull. "*As am I.*"

"Wednesday night," Sebastian said, glancing at the canopy overhead. "Nobody will be out here after the regatta. They'll all be taking cool baths and retiring early."

"Wednesday night suits," St. Sevier replied.

How convenient for them. "I'll arrange my schedule accordingly."

A beat of silence went by as Sebastian came to a halt. Hugh was the first to recover. "We'll need somebody to stand watch."

The menfolk regarded each other like whist partners across the table after a long evening of serious play. I wasn't supposed to know what agreements they were silently reaching, but a woman awash in male relations grasped only too well what those looks presaged.

"I'm glad that's settled," I said, twirling my parasol. "Wednesday, let's say midnight."

Sebastian resumed walking. "Very well. Midnight."

The boathouse revealed little. The square-backed leisure punts were kept inside, propped upright against the wall. Sleeker versions, such as those used for crew, were arranged across rafters, and several triangular sails, affixed to portable masts, hung down from those same rafters.

"All very neat," I said, though the place had a musty smell. "Not very secure."

Two little craft bobbed gently next to the dock. The boats were tethered to cleats by single lines.

"Could you get one of those boats out of the water?" Sebastian asked as we stood on the shore.

I thought for a moment as St. Sevier tossed pebbles one by one into the water from the end of the dock. He looked lonely out there, the breeze riffling his hair.

Lonely and handsome in a melancholy Gallic way.

"I would tow the boat along the dock by the rope affixed to the prow. When I'd dragged it into the shallows, I'd use the rope to haul it up onto the shore. From there, I could wrestle it against the bench and invert it over my head, though it might be quite heavy. The distance to the boathouse isn't great, though, and if I had to, I could drag the boat over the grass for most of the way."

"And you could reverse that sequence to put the particular boat you favored into the water."

St. Sevier skipped a rock toward the middle of the lake. The stone bounced four times before sinking into the water.

"But who would have known that Clara would come out here alone to go boating?"

"I doubt Clara was material to the plan," Sebastian replied.

"These boats only hold one or two people. Somebody was bound to get a drenching at the regatta at least, and the house party would be further disrupted as a result."

Hugh dusted his hands and strolled back toward us along the dock.

"We are back to motive," I said. "Who is doing this, and why? Nobody needs an amber cravat pin, a pair of earrings, or a mourning locket."

"People need money," Sebastian replied. "I notice you did not mention your rings."

I hadn't, had I? Nor did I particularly miss the feel of them on my finger. They made wearing gloves more complicated, and both rings had become somewhat loose in recent months.

"I want to find them," I said. "They have more sentimental value than anything else, though my engagement ring is likely worth a pretty penny." Freddie had put on a show as the smitten swain, and I had fallen for it. The engagement ring had been an expensive prop in that little pantomime.

St. Sevier joined us on the grassy bank. "Are we finished here? Anybody had access to these boats, and if we wanted to sabotage the lot of them, we could do that right now."

"How?" I asked. The boats seemed sound enough to me, but then, I was no sort of sailor.

Sebastian took my parasol, opened it, and handed it back to me. "A small boat can simply be turned upside down between uses to ensure any bilge water drains or dries out, but these boats are a tad more sophisticated."

"In what way?" I asked. They all seemed like rudimentary vessels. Wooden, with three benches—fore, amidships, and aft—for cushions, and flat boards laid over the ribs in an open pattern to make the bottom of the interior smooth and dry.

"They are designed to be propped up on their flat stern," Sebastian said. "They have a bilge plug. You whack that out with a mallet, tip the prow of the boat up, and the water all runs out the drain."

"So if somebody loosened the plug on Clara's boat, it might well have come out when she'd been rowing for a few minutes."

"Or," St. Sevier said, "a clever saboteur would make the drain plug look snugly in place, though it in fact could dislodge as it grew damp. In the alternative, a truly dedicated malcontent would not be so obvious as to tamper with the drain plug. He or she would remove caulking that makes the boat watertight."

"Wouldn't that require some time to accomplish?" I knew how to swim, but I knew nothing about shipbuilding.

"Not necessarily," Sebastian said. "Tar grows brittle with age, which is why seagoing vessels must be recaulked with pitch and hemp regularly. A sharp knife and twenty minutes would be enough to see one of these little boats made unsafe."

"We have company," I murmured.

Samuel strode up the path. He wasn't in livery, something I had noticed previously. Like a butler, he wore his own clothes, a sober dark suit that fitted him well.

"Samuel, good day," I said. "Are you here to make another inspection?"

"I am, my lady, and then I'm to lock up the boathouse." He brandished a large key and a friendly smile. "I can come back later if you're of a mind to take out a punt."

Any lock opened with so crude an implement would be easy to pick. "No, thank you," I said. "We'll have enough of that sort of excitement tomorrow, I'm sure." Though I would be peeking in on the chambermaids' tea. "I did have a question for you, Samuel."

"Ma'am?"

"Two questions, actually. Might you tell us where Mr. Upjohn has been confined? Dr. St. Sevier would like to have a look in on his patient."

All domestics learned to hide their emotions of necessity, but in Samuel, the talent was imperfect.

A shadow dimmed his smile. "I'm not supposed to bruit that about, ma'am. For the prisoner's safety."

He was surely quoting one of Sir Randall's bloviations, and he apparently knew it for the clumsy pretense it was.

"I am a physician," St. Sevier said. "Trained in Edinburgh, tempered in battle. Do you suggest I am a threat to my patient, young man?"

Oh, how French he sounded, how ready to take offense.

"No, sir. Perhaps I could have a private chat with you at some point in the near future?"

"The marquess and I will just be going," I said, taking Sebastian's arm. "But one other question, first, Samuel."

"Of course, my lady." He dreaded my question, though. That much was evident as he tapped the handle of the heavy key against his palm.

"Did Lord Hempley's valet occupy the bed Upjohn was using?"

Both Sebastian and St. Sevier had adopted the demeanor of men humoring a woman's harmless eccentricity. Sebastian studied the lake. St. Sevier wore a patient smile.

And to think we'd all three eschewed the amateur theatricals.

"The footmen and valets aren't particular, ma'am. When they are finally dismissed for the night, they take any available bunk, if you know what I mean. When Hempley's valet departed, and I left that bed free in the dormitory, Upjohn took it. The bed closest to the window is always to be preferred this time of year."

"You had to give up your own room for Hempley's man?" I asked.

"Hempley was set to make a fuss. His guest room had no dressing closet—had an enormous wardrobe, though—and he didn't want his valet making a pallet in his room. A place had to be found for the man. The footmen's dormitory didn't meet with his lordship's approval, so I offered my room. It's quite nice, and that spiked his lordship's guns."

All of this was offered with an air of cheerful good humor toward the crotchets of the Quality, but it raised troubling questions. Had Upjohn slipped out that window, for example?

Sebastian left off perusing the lake. "If my lady is finished keeping this good fellow from his appointed rounds, might we return to the house?"

"Let's do, but I'm of a mind to find a blooming water lily first." The scavenger hunters' best efforts had failed to discover that treasure. "Samuel, have you any idea where I might look?"

"Of course. If you follow the shore path around to the west, you'll see a side path that leads down to the ladies' cove. It's not really a cove, but it's out of view of the house, if you take my meaning. Her ladyship and Miss Clara have declared it off-limits to the menfolk. Just past that path, about twenty yards on, you'll find a patch of lilies along the shore."

"Thank you." I trundled off at Sebastian's side, to all appearances the docile guest with her handsome escort. We left St. Sevier to further interrogate poor Samuel.

I'd found answers, but not the ones I'd been anticipating.

~

Arguing with Sebastian was invigorating. We'd spent many a youthful hour in debate, and unlike my brothers, who were always ready to dismiss both my observations and my reasoning, Sebastian engaged me in verbal battle and gave no quarter.

"Samuel had been using that bed, my lord. He as much as admitted it."

Sebastian set a maddeningly relaxed pace, when I was in the mood to march. "You're saying Samuel had an opportunity to plant the cravat pin?"

"No. Well, yes, he did, but more to the point, the pin might have been placed there to incriminate Samuel."

"Your imagination, *my lady*, would conjure unicorns from cart ponies."

Unicorns and cart ponies were related, not simply because both were equines, but because both inspired the affections of young children.

"You will allow, *my lord*, that Samuel had a motive to steal the pin."

Sebastian steered me down a side path that led in the direction of the lake. "Because the valet made him give up his private room? In the first place, Hempley was the impetus for that change, and in the second, do you honestly think Samuel would risk criminal prosecution for so petty a slight?"

The way was narrower, barely wide enough for two to walk abreast, and the undergrowth brushed at my skirts. Sebastian fell back half a step so we approximated the promenade posture of dancing couples. This was fortunate, because I caught my toe on a disobliging rock, barked my shin on the protruding limb of a downed tree, and would have ended up on my hands and knees but for Sebastian's strong arm.

"Heedless and headlong," he muttered, keeping a firm grasp around my waist. "You would have made a convincing cavalryman."

I righted myself and batted at my skirts, though my shin smarted terribly. "Better that than heedless and arrogant." As a girl, I'd often accused him of those shortcomings.

Sebastian's glower became a smile. "I have missed you. I haven't wanted to, but how typical of you, to thwart my ambitions even in so small a thing."

I might have snapped off another retort, referring to the appalling infrequency with which Sebastian had obliged my convenience, but here we were, on an errand of my choosing, when he ought to have been playing Perseus to some fair maid's Andromeda.

Or bouncing on the sheets with Mrs. Bonaventure.

"I've missed you too." My mouth and my dignity had not consulted each other before I'd made that admission. "And I worried for you."

If I'd had any sense, I would have patted his chest and sailed off down the path, smarting shin be damned, but such sadness came into his eyes, such wistfulness, that I was blinking back memories of years spent searching the casualty lists from the Peninsula, thanking heaven that Sebastian's name was nowhere to be found.

"Come," he said, taking me by the wrist. "Let's have a look at the ladies' cove."

I limped after him, and he ignored that awkwardness. I walked off the pain in the grand English tradition, and we were soon at the shore of the lake again.

"Pretty," I said.

"Secluded." Sebastian let go of my wrist and strode to the edge of the water. "A trysting place."

Bathvale Abbey was full of such places, so why didn't the estate arouse any affection in me? I found a long stick and plunged one end into the water.

"This is a swimming hole," I concluded, for my stick hadn't touched bottom. "One could bathe here."

The ideal swimming hole had at least one bank bordered by rocks, and the ladies' cove met that criterion. One could get into and out of the water without risking muddy feet. One could dangle one's feet in the water from a perch that wouldn't leave grass stains on one's shift. One could even dive...

"Clara Putnam can swim," I said. "I know she can." Images from my school days came to mind, of moonlit outings to the pond of an abandoned mill. We girls had considered ourselves quite daring as we'd paddled about on the occasional hot evening. Clara had come along once or twice, while her older sister had kept to the path of prudence and enjoyed a good night's sleep instead.

"Hard to swim wearing skirts, corset, and petticoats." Sebastian said, peering into the water. "Trout might like this place."

"Hard to swim, not impossible in summer-weight fabrics. Not impossible to tread water anyway. If she can swim, then that incident on the lake wasn't really so dangerous, was it?"

He straightened and considered me. "If her boat was sabotaged— a fact yet to be established—and if that person knew she could swim

—another fact yet to be established—then the incident was still plenty dangerous. What makes you think she can swim?"

I started up the path and explained how I *knew* Clara could manage in the water.

Sebastian followed, again at the barest amble when I wanted to dash. "Splashing around in a pond," he said, "with a half-dozen friends right at hand to fish you out might not be very dangerous. In the middle of a lake, wearing stays and skirts, with nobody near and a boat sinking in the immediate vicinity, is a far riskier situation."

I wasn't so sure. Fashions were changing, but my attire still allowed me significant freedom of movement, and summer day dresses were seldom fashioned from heavy velvets or wools. Most ladies favored jumps in the country, or only light stays for all but the most formal occasions.

"You are missing the point," I said when we were once again wandering the main path. "Very few of the guests would know that Clara can swim. Myself and Lady Bathvale, perhaps, or some of the oldest staff at the Abbey, but not the guests."

We resumed our progress around the lake, though now I regretted my itinerary. The circumference was greater than it appeared, and the path both rose and fell along the shoreline. A folly set on a rise opposite the picnic woods marked the halfway point, and I fixed upon that as my interim destination.

"I still cannot see that this trivia about Lady Clara being able to swim makes a difference," Sebastian said. "If the motive was merely to embarrass Miss Putnam, few were on hand to see it. If the motive was to kill her, then only you and her sister are exonerated, for you would not have attempted to drown her if you wished to end her life."

Motive again, that complicated, necessary, elusive element to any well-solved mystery.

"You are exonerated as well," I said. "You did rescue the lady." And what an impressive figure he had made, dripping wet, muscular chest heaving, clothes plastered to his frame.

The direction of my thoughts surprised me. Sebastian was handsome in a dark-haired, uncharming sort of way. He lacked friendliness or warmth, or some quality that made good looks the stuff of social success. He was Scottish, which many a proper Englishwoman considered to be a barbaric heritage—did that make him more attractive or less?—but he was careful to comport himself properly under all circumstances.

Why shouldn't I appreciate that he was well formed and in good health? He was also intelligent and honorable, and he didn't ruin a quiet walk in nature with ceaseless chatter.

Another thought popped into my mind. "If the object of sinking the boat was to add another embarrassing incident to the thefts, then Lady Bathvale and I become the primary suspects."

"Because you knew the accident was unlikely to be fatal, but, firstly, how could you know a guest able to swim would take *that* boat out, and secondly, why should you or our hostess try to ruin the house party?"

"Somebody is apparently bent on that goal." And Sebastian had a point: Any guest could have taken out any boat, but the other boats had all been pronounced sound.

"Does Samuel remind you of anyone, Violet?"

"He reminds me of a competent first footman." One very confident of his positions, though I also knew what Sebastian meant. Samuel had a knowing quality, a confidence, unusual for one holding his post. "Whose idea was it to traverse this whole blasted path?"

"Yours, apparently. I'm simply your escort. Samuel is unlike any first footman I've met. What first footman have you encountered who's called by his first name? Though is he called Samuel or Samuels? As a surname, Samuels is more likely."

I dropped Sebastian's arm to start up the long rise to the folly. "Samuel. He introduced himself to me thus, and the travelogue inscription I saw also bore the name Samuel, no *s*. He doesn't wear livery."

"And Sir Randall hasn't arrested him for that? Surely the end of days is nigh."

Sebastian had taken the side of the path closest to the lake, which was gentlemanly of him—also overly trusting.

"I could push you straight into the lake, *my lord*."

"I can swim too, *my lady*, and in my surprise at your discourtesy, I might inadvertently pull you in after me. In that event, your competence in the water would be a very great blessing, would it not?"

I *had* missed him. He didn't treat me like a porcelain shepherdess to be waltzed around the room then returned to the mantel of his choosing. He didn't approach me the way the ever-pleasant Baxters did, as if I hadn't a brain in my head and must be smiled at incessantly, like an elderly eccentric or tired child.

"What have you missed about me?" I asked.

"Your ability to keep quiet. Somebody's in the folly."

The building was a temple in miniature. Hexagonal with open arches for the sides. Steps led up from the shore path, so the folly rose a good ten feet above the trail and perhaps thirty feet above the lake. A chestnut gelding stood with a hip cocked at the foot of the steps, suggesting the horse had been tied long enough to have settled in for a nap. A gray mare, smaller, her eyes half closed, stood beside the gelding.

"A pair of somebodies," I said as a woman's voice rose in anger. The breeze snatched the words away, and because the unhappy couple gazed out over the lake, we remained unseen amid the trees lining the path. "We should not eavesdrop."

"Our host and hostess should not air their differences in so public a location."

The earl's hands were linked behind his back, though for a man beholding his ancestral home in all its bucolic splendor, he looked more like a soldier awaiting the lash than lord of all he surveyed. Lady Bathvale spoke from his side, gesturing across the lake, then pacing the width of the folly behind him.

"Maybe her ladyship wants him to retrieve that sunken boat," I suggested.

Sebastian held up a hand to shade his eyes. "Is that her ladyship?

Miss Putnam has a slightly more robust figure than her sister, and I do believe that is not her ladyship."

I squinted, and upon closer examination, Sebastian was right. "Why would Clara deliver a dressing down to his lordship?" For she most assuredly was. The tongue-lashing she'd given Samuel was tame compared to this ranting and pacing.

"Maybe she perceives the connection you are about to point out. Samuel inspected the boats before the mishap, and he's still being trusted to inspect them after his efforts proved inadequate. Samuel also had an opportunity to place Hempley's cravat pin in the footmen's dormitory."

I turned and walked back the way we'd come. "Families quarrel. That is none of our business, and the boathouse is not secure no matter who inspects it. I could pick the padlock on the doors with a hairpin." Or a combination of a hairpin and a hatpin.

"Do fancy finishing schools now teach young ladies how to pick locks?"

I did shove Sebastian, harder than I ought. "They teach us to flatter all gentlemen all the time, also to always have a hatpin on our persons. Gentlemen cannot be trusted to know the difference between flattery and invitation in the first place. In the second, sometimes a lady needs to pick a lock." And for this skill, I had Felix to thank. He'd shut me into the saddle room one too many times when my brothers were intent on riding off without me.

Sebastian was apparently willing to concede my point regarding the utility of hatpins. A pair of greenish-gold birds swooped before us, then flitted aloft, where they commenced a high-pitched, chirrupy song that carried out over the lake.

"Wood warblers," Sebastian said. "I defy anybody to sleep through that song." He did something with his thumb and index finger set against the corners of his lips, imitating the warblers with uncanny accuracy.

The birds paused in their trilling, then resumed their song.

"We used birdcalls as signals during the war," he said. "Seemed profane to me, but the French never caught on."

"I nearly hated you for buying for your colors."

"My uncle did hate me and pulled every possible string to keep me from seeing battle."

"But you did see battle." Over and over, Sebastian had led his men onto the field, his unit sometimes sustaining frightful casualties. "Upjohn did as well. For six years, he fought when he was told to, risked his life at some officer's command. We cannot allow him to be tried for crimes he didn't commit, Sebastian."

I could not allow that, but who was I—an obscure widow—to allow anything?

"Sir Randall has made it plain that he'll hand Upjohn over to the assizes unless exculpatory evidence shows up. The more I'm seen to meddle, the worse it will go for Upjohn."

How I loathed that reasonable tone from Sebastian. "That is the commanding officer talking, the man who made hard decisions about life and death on a battlefield. This is England, and Upjohn does not deserve to die for the sake of a damned pair of earbobs." I kept my voice down, but the temptation to wave my fists and bellow was strong.

"If he dies, it will be for the principle that stealing is wrong and the king's authority must be respected."

"The king's authority deserves deference, but the dangerous, self-serving mistakes of a pompous bumbler should merit only contempt."

The boathouse came into view, the single antique lock chained around the main doors. The lock was as much a farce as Sir Randall's version of justice was.

Sebastian drew me to a halt with a hand on my arm. "Violet, I am Scottish. The other guests and the magistrate are English. This is their battlefield, and I am an outsider here. I have no authority, no advantage that I can bring to bear that won't do more harm than good where Upjohn is concerned."

I rounded on him in the middle of the path. "You are a *marquess,*

likely the ranking peer in the whole shire. You served with distinc-
tion, and you have enormous wealth. The Sebastian MacHeath I
have always esteemed enormously, the man whose safety I prayed for
nightly, would not back down for the sake of paltry social niceties.
Meddle loudly and relentlessly. Go to Bathvale, get him meddling.
The Baxters have some influence, and—"

I fell silent and nearly despairing. Sebastian might as well have
been carved of the same unyielding stone that formed the massive
edifice of the Abbey.

"Violet, *think*. If I cause that much uproar, I truly will ruin this
house party, won't I? I'll take a few missing pieces of jewelry and
escalate them into a scandal that people still whisper about ten years
hence."

I wanted badly, badly to shout, but sound carried over water, and
Lord Bathvale and Clara might hear me. "I'd rather deal with whispers about a high-handed Scottish marquess than about *another* innocent life ended on the gallows."

Deep beneath my ire, I sensed that Sebastian's warning pointed
to a connection between all of the incidents and the means by which
they'd been carried out. What was so important about ruining a
house party? A frivolous gathering of near strangers had turned all
but deadly, and I had no idea why.

I left Sebastian standing alone on the wooded trail, the birds
chirping overhead and the lake lapping gently at the nearby shore. I
had never been more frustrated, not with my bothersome brothers or
my philandering husband, not with the strictures proper society put
on women of any standing.

I was in an unladylike passion for the first time in years. Perhaps
that's why, when I took the bend in the trail that passed behind the
boathouse, I nearly didn't see Samuel and Mrs. Bonaventure in a
lover's embrace until my presence was all but obvious.

CHAPTER ELEVEN

I simply kept walking, and if, despite their mutual enthusiasms, the couple noticed me, then they should have had a care for their privacy. Mrs. Bonaventure's back was to the wall, and Samuel was pressing his *attentions* upon her. She was all but climbing him, her fingers twined in his hair, one leg wrapped around his flank.

I should have been disgusted or amused. Had I been more of a true lady, I might have convinced myself they were pathetic.

I was pathetically *envious*. Envious of two people who could yield to desire without tearing it into tiny bits of guilt, indecision, and self-reproach. Envious of the animal pleasure that carried them both far from reason and regret. They were healthy adults beholden to nobody, and casual frolics were the reason most people attended these stupid gatherings.

My envy had subsided to something between self-pity and consternation—where was Freddie Belmaine's withdrawn widow, the woman who'd arrived at Bathvale determined to read away two weeks' penance in the country?—when Lady Bathvale and Sir Randall came upon me.

Oh dear. Bad enough if they happened across the couple at the boathouse, but worse yet if Clara and Lord Bathvale were still having a set-to.

"Greetings to you both," I said, curtseying. "The birdsong in these woods is amazing."

Sir Randall peered at me. "And you came out here without an escort the better to enjoy nature?"

Nasty man. "I left the marquess farther up the path. He is something of an amateur ornithologist, and he was in conversation with a pair of wood warblers when I decided I'd had my fill of nature for the day. His lordship's talent with birdcalls is impressive. As for an escort, I do know the way back to the Abbey, and I am capable of walking without a masculine arm to lean on."

Lady Bathvale patted Sir Randall's hand. "Widows can be independent, as can widowers. Let's leave Lady Violet to her solitary rambles, shall we?"

The hostess was ever consigned to the peacekeeping role, and her ladyship managed it with a gracious smile. Sir Randall, having fired off the requisite insult at me, tipped his hat.

"To the boathouse, then," he said.

On a rise in the distance, two riders cantered in the direction of the Abbey, a man on a chestnut and a woman on a smaller gray.

"If you fancy a hack," Lady Bathvale said to me, "we have ladies' mounts among the guest horses. That's Clara on the gray and his lordship with her. They are avid equestrians, and either one could point you to the best bridle paths."

I had been an avid equestrian, before marriage had confined me mostly to London, where keeping a riding horse was an expensive and complicated matter.

"Perhaps tomorrow morning," I replied. "Starting the day in the saddle is one of many pleasures of life in the country." Along with being relieved of one's wedding ring and bearing the insults of arrogant magistrates.

"Ask the grooms for Blossom," Lady Bathvale said. "She is my preferred mount, and a better-trained mare you will not find."

Was anything more annoying than graciousness when one was in a taking? "Thank you so much. That is most kind of you. I'll see you at dinner."

Mrs. Bonaventure and Samuel came up the path, and I felt for a moment as if I'd stumbled into a lost scene from *A Midsummer Night's Dream*. Couples cavorting in all directions, mischief running alongside decorum, intrigue and folly side by side.

And escorts for all who could abide them.

"Mrs. Bonaventure, Samuel. Good day. If you're going back to the Abbey, perhaps you'll allow me to walk with you?"

"Of course," Mrs. Bonaventure said. "Samuel was good enough to help me retrieve my parasol. We'll be happy to have your company."

Lady Bathvale's gaze swept over Samuel, her composure faltering only in so far as her lips thinned, as if she were biting back a rebuke. For a footman to escort a widow in search of a lost item on private grounds was unremarkable. For him to return her ladyship's gaze without a shred of self-consciousness was unexpected.

I took Samuel's free arm and consigned myself to more infernal toddling, though we hadn't gone far before my parasol snagged in a low-hanging branch. Samuel paused to assist me, while Mrs. Bonaventure strolled on a few paces to sniff at some honeysuckle.

"Your discretion," Samuel said quietly, "is appreciated." He separated the lace of my parasol from the leaves of the disobliging birch sapling. "I forgot myself, and I owe you and Mrs. Bonaventure an apology."

The parasol was still serviceable, but to a discerning eye, the snag in the lace was visible. "I do not carry tales, Samuel, but others at this gathering are only too happy to spread slander."

"Don't I know it."

We caught up with Mrs. Bonaventure, who'd plucked a sprig of honeysuckle and tucked it into the top buttonhole of her spencer. I was annoyed with her for jeopardizing a footman's livelihood, but also for tearing off the sprig of flowers. Honeysuckle was a thirsty plant, and the blooms would wilt before she could get them into water.

"You may be about your duties," she said to Samuel. "Lady Violet will keep me company, though I do very much appreciate your assistance."

He bowed correctly, she smiled like a cat who'd spent a happy interval in the company of a cream pot missing its lid. I wanted to bang their heads together, both for cavorting in plain sight and for burdening me with keeping their secret.

"Hold still," I said to Mrs. Bonaventure when Samuel had all but jogged off toward the Abbey. I batted leaves and bracken from the back of the lady's skirt. No grass stains or dirt marred the muslin, though her dress had acquired an interesting set of wrinkles.

"Thank you," she said. "One grows forgetful when enjoying the splendors of nature."

"I don't begrudge you your pleasures, but a first footman can lose his post for a stolen kiss." Samuel hadn't stolen anything—not from Mrs. Bonaventure.

"What a righteous creature you are. If the temperance league recruits you, all of London will soon be teetotaling."

I *amused* her, and I was not in the mood for a merry widow's condescension. "You will see him turned off without a character. I've already come across Clara scolding him mightily, and she has the ear of both her sister and brother-in-law." My defense of Samuel was in part on general principles and in part because I'd seen him with Bathvale's heir.

A man who took the time to humor a little child, a man who clearly had that child's affection, deserved an advocate.

"They'll never turn him off, my lady. He's family."

The nagging sense that Samuel reminded me of somebody fell into place, like a key in a lock. "Family to Lord Bathvale."

Samuel's hair was more reddish, his features less austere, but in his posture, around the mouth and nose, he and Bathvale shared a resemblance.

"A by-blow?" I asked.

"Cousin. Samuel's papa was the younger brother of the previous earl. This family is not exactly abloom with male progeny, so I gather even a by-blow had some value, if he is a by-blow. His father saw him educated and made sure he had a post here. One speculates."

My own family tree had a few such branches. "And his mother?"

"I have not inquired. This time next week, we guests will be scattered to the four winds, and I'll be admiring the beauties of nature somewhere else. What of you? Do you head back to Town, refreshed by your sojourn in the shires?"

I was *not* refreshed. Far from it, and yet, I'd been more physically active in the past week than in the previous ten weeks. I had dusted off old social skills, I had grown not merely piqued but furious, and I had entertained, albeit in a mostly theoretical way, the concept of accepting a man's intimate attentions.

"This house party has been like a tonic," I said. "Unpleasant in some regards, but not without salubrious effects." Would I admit that much to St. Sevier?

"Get back on the horse," Mrs. Bonaventure said as the gardens came into view in all their sunny, formal splendor. They looked barren to me, bleak even, despite the potted salvia and white crushed shells on the geometric paths.

"For all your hacking out," I said, "are you less lonely? Less angry?"

To my surprise, Mrs. Bonaventure appeared to take the question seriously. "Yes, and no. Physical pleasures are fortifying, if undertaken with the right party. In the usual course, nobody touches a widow as a husband does. She recalls the way he leaned close to whisper a quip in polite society, or how even in church, he sat close enough that his thigh touched hers. His assistance into and out of a coach has a certain casual familiarity. Footmen take our hands, but they dare not watch us to ensure we don't trip. A husband watches and chides, though we've been getting in and out of coaches our whole lives."

She was making me miss Freddie, who had had many shortcomings as a spouse. "Why not remarry?"

"Why don't you? You drag the marquess into the woods and emerge without him. The gentleman is supposed to leave a tryst first, you know, to deflect the curious and allow the lady time to compose herself."

Trysting with Sebastian? I mentally batted the notion aside as if it might sting me. "You misapprehend, ma'am. Dunkeld and I are acquaintances of long standing, and he's here ostensibly to begin his search for a marchioness." Though, had he made *any* progress toward that objective?

"Maybe you are the party misapprehending, my lady. Dunkeld is the pick of the lot, and beneath all that hauteur, I suspect he'd be an attentive spouse." She gave the word *attentive* a brush of innuendo, and I was reminded of Sebastian, sopping wet, no coat or boots...

I had harbored a tendresse for Sebastian as a schoolgirl, but then I'd left the schoolroom, he'd gone off to war, and Freddie Belmaine's proposal had put an end to tendresses and other foolishness.

"I have a parasol to mend," I said. "Thank you for your company."

She curtseyed, and that formal gesture reminded me of the truth of her words: Widows drifted about, doting on nieces and nephews, taking the arm of a brother or cousin, but in some vital, human way, we were consigned to the scrap heap of life.

And I was not thriving on that scrap heap, not content to remain there, trying to bloom amid the orts and leavings of others' joys.

I watched Mrs. Bonaventure glide across the garden, graceful as a sylph. For all her cavorting, I'd never seen a woman with a greater air of loneliness. Perhaps Freddie had done me a favor by being part ideal husband and part raging disappointment. I missed him, but not like that.

Never like that.

Sebastian disturbed my melancholy reverie, and I was more glad to see him than I ought to have been. Freddie's reaction when I started a quarrel was to leave the house and stay out all night. Sebastian marched up to me, a battle light in his blue eyes.

"This house party cannot end soon enough," he said, "but you have a point. Upjohn's fate should not be decided by default for the sake of anybody's social convenience. Will you search Sir Randall's room, or will I?"

~

I had Sebastian to thank for determining where the magistrate's room lay and providence to thank for the fact that Sir Randall's lock was not of the counting variety. My hatpin was sufficient for the challenge of easing the door open, though waiting half of Tuesday for an opportunity to use it drove me nigh barmy.

"A very fine apartment," Sebastian murmured, drawing the door quietly closed behind us. The sitting room was large and commodious, with a writing desk near the window. A French door led out to a balcony, and the fireplace was faced with pink marble. The mantel, side tables, and windowsills showed not a speck of dust, and fresh red roses graced the sideboard.

"An honored guest," I said, taking a sniff of the roses. They were more for show than scent, but still... my room lacked flowers, as did Sebastian's and St. Sevier's, though the Bathvale conservatory was half the size of the ballroom, and the cutting gardens were enormous.

"Where would Sir Randall put something he didn't want even his valet to see?" Sebastian asked.

"Where would *you* put such items?" I wasn't here to find contraband. I was searching more for Sir Randall himself. What sort of evidence would he think sufficient to exonerate Upjohn? What might sway his concept of justice in Upjohn's favor?

"I'll take the bedroom," I said, crossing the parlor.

The bedroom was similarly splendid, boasting another marble fireplace that shared a chimney with the one in the sitting room, an enormous canopied bed, thick carpets, a japanned dressing screen, a vanity with a sparkling mirror, and a cheval mirror in the corner. The French door was covered with lacy drapery that must have taken an age to tat.

The entire room was painfully well ordered, from the perfectly smooth coverlet, to the cravats hanging at precise intervals over the dressing screen, to the brushes and bottles on the vanity, neat as a cook's knife drawer. On instinct, I lifted a pillow from the side of the bed closest to the windows.

Nothing.

The other side yielded an interesting find—a lady's fichu. The lace was delicate and abundant. This was not a scrap intended to call attention to a woman's cleavage. This article would lend modesty to a dress cut a bit too daringly for daytime. Mrs. Bonaventure was partial to fichus, but then, I could not see her trifling with Sir Randall.

I had not envisioned her trifling with a footman either, though.

I lifted the material to my nose and detected a faint fragrance, too faint to place. Neroli, perhaps, a scent nearly as common as lavender. The white of the lace suggested a younger woman, but not conclusively. I had a half-dozen white or ivory fichus, and I was courting the decrepitude of five-and-twenty years.

Sebastian appeared at my side, silent as a shadow. "Somebody's coming."

A soft scraping at the lock on the parlor door and a muted voice confirmed that we were to be discovered. I stashed the lace back under the pillow and smoothed the coverlet.

"The balcony," I whispered.

We slipped from the bedroom onto the balcony, which, fortunately for us, looked out over a deserted side garden. *Un*fortunately, the windows were wide enough that the balcony offered little in the way of a hiding place.

Sebastian took me by the hand, pushed me into the far corner, and bundled himself right up against me. The proximity startled me, even though it was necessary for concealment. Had I not just seen another couple in nearly the same posture, I might have exercised greater restraint over my imagination, but then again... my imagination had a will of its own.

Sebastian's scent up close was luscious. Cedar lurked beneath hints of sandalwood and cinnamon. The fragrance was complicated, like the man, and confirmed for me that I dealt with a mature adult male, not the somewhat difficult, dear youth of my girlhood.

Sebastian's form was that of a man in his prime. He was warm, lean, lithe, and large enough that I was entirely shielded from view. His strength was evident both in the security of his embrace and in the supple muscles of his back.

At some point, I had slid my hands around his waist and tucked close of necessity.

Voices—plural—carried from inside, the first of them male.

"Himself can be a right tyrant about the smallest detail," the man said. "He were particular as a lad, but going to war turned him up ridiculous. If I wanted to drive him daft, all I'd have to do is put his boots beside the bed, the right and left on the wrong sides of each other. I could set him off for days that easily. What are we looking for?"

Sir Randall's own valet was aiding in the search, regardless of its objective. Disorder in the ranks, indeed.

"A scarf," said a woman. "A plain white lace scarf. Madam could not ask her own lady's maid to search for it, because that one would tattle the news to the whole household. I can be trusted to keep me mouth shut."

The sound of a door opening followed, perhaps the wardrobe. "Maybe our thief took that scarf," the man said. "He'll look a treat in lace and earbobs. Nothing in here, and I would know. Look behind the privacy screen."

If I risked leaning a few inches to the left, I could see a corner of the bedroom beyond Sebastian's shoulder, and that corner revealed the back of a woman's skirts. Plain skirts that told me little.

"I recognize her voice," I whispered.

Sebastian pressed a finger to my lips and wrapped his hand

around the back of my head. The search went on inside the bedroom, while I endured an internal sense of mayhem—and the most intimate proximity to a man that I'd experienced in years.

This was *Sebastian*. We did not particularly like each other, at least not in recent years, and yet, his embrace felt wonderful. His strength was abundant, and his hold on me was confident, unlike St. Sevier's delicate advances.

And he was all male. Body parts I'd consigned to my own mental scrap heap—my breasts, my womb, my mouth, my *fingertips*—came to life with inconvenient awareness that a healthy, vigorous, unattached male was plastered to me in a posture usually reserved for lovers.

I ought to have been mortified. I was instead intrigued. Sebastian would have found my mental flights hilarious—or would he?

"It's not here," the man said. "Himself isn't likely to keep a memento of a lady's favors—too ungentlemanly of him. She probably left it in the conservatory or the stables. Don't suppose you'd like help looking for it there?"

His tone was flirtatious. A laugh followed. The lady moved so her skirts momentarily hiked a bit higher. I saw sturdy half boots, the left heel heavily scuffed.

"She was certain he'd have it," the woman said. "But she's been certain of all manner of things, and this house of nutters has proved her wrong. To the stables, my good man, and we can have a look in on the conservatory too."

"Oh, the Quality." The sound of kissing followed. "The lengths we travel to keep them happy."

The pair of them decamped, and I sagged against Sebastian. "That was the maid who isn't Haines," I said. "We should follow them."

"*I* will follow them," he retorted, stepping back. "You will for once pretend to be a demure widow who likes to read books and talk to her cat."

I loved to read books and frequently talked to my cats. "Your cravat is wrinkled." I smoothed the folds of his linen and drew the lace edging flat against his shirt. "You will prowl around looking half tumbled, and the guests will conclude it was you who met Mrs. Bonaventure for a tryst at the boathouse."

He took my hands in his. "Cease fussing me. Mrs. Bonaventure was trysting? With Sir Randall?"

"With Samuel. He is apparently related to Lord Bathvale."

"Interesting, but not likely relevant to our inquiry." He led me from the balcony, then went first out into the corridor. I followed, and we strolled along, a pair of guests without a direction. Our path took us past windows that looked out over the stables, a stately two-story U-shaped edifice of the same gray stone as the house.

"Lord Bathvale returns," Sebastian said, "with Miss Putnam."

His lordship assisted Clara from her horse, his manner more perfunctory than gallant. "They are still not in charity with each other," I observed, "though Lady Bathvale says they ride out together often."

"Bathvale is a cold fish. I get the sense he's hosting this house party under duress."

"As do I, but you must away to the conservatory. Find out who that maid is and who Sir Randall's lady love is."

"While you do what?"

"Have a lie-down," I answered honestly. "All this hiking about has left me fatigued."

"Violet, promise me you will be careful." Sebastian looked as if he might say more, which I could not allow him to do. My emotions were in a muddle, my body had become that of a wanton stranger, and I needed peace and quiet to think.

"Careful no longer has much appeal, my lord. I carefully obeyed my father when he chose a spouse for me. I carefully contorted myself into the role of Frederick's charming wife while my husband cavorted with dollymops and *grandes horizontales*. I carefully observed the mourning rituals demanded by polite society, and what do I have to show for it? A lack of freckles and a lack of confidence in my own worth. That is no sort of bargain, and I am finished pretending otherwise."

The daft man was smiling at me. "Your *father* chose Belmaine?"

What had that ancient history to do with anything? "I hardly knew Freddie prior to our engagement, and that was doubtless by design. That my brothers did not warn me regarding Freddie's nature is a source of ongoing resentment. Go chase down that maid, please, and promise *me* you'll be careful."

Sebastian stalked up to me, brushed a kiss to my cheek, and glowered down at me. "I am always careful. Until dinner."

He marched away, and—ye goddesses, the fresh country air must have made me demented—I enjoyed the view of his retreating form.

～

Dinner was interminable, though Bertie Baxter's efforts to charm Miss Waltham yielded some entertainment. I had been unable to nap that afternoon, my mind whirling with unanswered questions. Fatigue made the meal a test of my endurance. From either end of the table, Lord and Lady Bathvale radiated gracious hospitality. In his lordship's case, the effect was tempered by formality, in her ladyship's, by what I suspected was weariness.

Clara became a beacon of gaiety, a role she fulfilled more naturally than I would have anticipated. The more she directed conversation and matched Bertie quip for quip, the cooler Lord Bathvale's demeanor grew and the less her ladyship said anything at all.

Family squabbles were the worst.

St. Sevier seemed to be getting along well with Mrs. Bonaventure *and* with Mrs. Albright, while Sebastian appeared to be making a polite effort with Miss Peasedale.

"For a Scot," Thaddeus Baxter said, "the marquess isn't a bad sort." He refilled my wineglass, though I'd barely drunk half.

"For an Englishman, you aren't either," I replied. "Do you fear his lordship will charm the fair Miss Peasedale?" I'd meant to tease with that comment, but the poor young fellow's gaze turned despairing.

"Miss Peasedale is the last woman who should be dragged into the Highlands to shiver away her days in some drafty castle. She's delicate, and he's..."

Sebastian was *not* delicate. "He's not making much headway with her, Mr. Baxter." More accurate to say that Miss Peasedale wasn't making much headway with Sebastian.

"How can you tell?" Such hope lay in that question, such vulnerability.

"They are both attending to their food, aren't they? When one is smitten, the food barely earns any notice. He has glanced twice at the clock on the mantel, and so has she."

St. Sevier had also noted the time more than once, as had I.

Lady Bathvale chose then to signal that the women would withdraw for tea, and not a moment too soon. I made my excuses to my hostess and went up to my room rather than join the hens gabbling over their scandal broth. Lucy was waiting for me, and she'd laid out the clothes I'd asked her to.

"I hate to see you put this dress on again," she said. "I almost didn't pack it."

A lady traveled with at least one set of mourning attire. Elderly relations, parents, and even siblings could expire without notice, and when one was truly burdened with grief, the deference shown those wearing black was helpful.

"I consider it bad luck not to pack some mourning clothes," I said. "Like pretending to have a headache can dare one to start. Haul the dratted weeds around with us, and we'll be spared having to use them."

The attire Lucy had laid out was a simple walking dress. The waist was higher than current fashion, and the only ornamentation was blackwork embroidery on the collar and cuffs.

"You won't let me go with you?" Lucy asked, doing up the

buttons in back. The buttons were cloth-covered rather than jet, the better to avoid reflecting even the smallest sliver of light.

"You are to remain far from any taint of mischief, Lucy, the long-suffering lady's maid to an occasionally outspoken widow."

"The staff here," Lucy said, stepping back. "They are not a happy lot. Lady Bathvale has been planning this house party for ages, and she's run them ragged with silly details. Red salvia or blue on the front terrace, or some of both? A string quartet or a piano trio for the final ball? She settled on a six-piece ensemble, but only after Lord Bathvale put his foot down a fortnight before the guests were to arrive. Told her there would be no ball if she couldn't make up her damned mind. If you sit, I can redo your hair."

"Why *have* a house party at all if you can't enjoy the whole business?" I asked, taking the vanity stool. "Why go to all the trouble and expense?" If Lady Bathvale had daughters ready to make their come outs, then lavish entertaining would have made more sense.

"A neglected wife will have her revenge." Lucy drew the pins from my hair, working with brisk efficiency.

"You think Lady Bathvale is neglected?"

"She's certainly not doted upon, is she? The maids say his lordship never trifles with the help, but he doesn't trouble his wife either."

When husband and wife had separate bedrooms, the staff was in a position to notice such private matters.

"Perhaps they're trying to space their children. They have their heir, and a woman's body needs time to recover from childbed." Though they did not have their spare, did they? Lord Bathvale struck me as a man who'd want at least one spare and preferably three.

"All I know is, I will be glad to get back to London," Lucy said, drawing the brush through my hair. "Nobody in this household seems content, and now poor Upjohn has been locked away like a crook."

"But nothing else has gone missing since his incarceration. One braid, please, and tie it off with black ribbon."

Lucy did as asked, and I was soon ready for my outing. A black shawl completed my ensemble, for I hadn't brought a black cloak.

"I don't like this place," Lucy said, "but I do like to see you regaining some of your old fire. You were beginning to scare me, staring off into space for half the afternoon, troubling over letters that should have taken you a quarter hour to write. Getting old before your time."

Not old, precisely, but... I thought of what I'd overheard from Sir Randall's valet and what I'd seen in the magistrate's room. Cravats hung just so, bottles arranged in order of height on the vanity, footwear assembled with ruthless precision.

A person who kept his effects that tightly organized sought control over a daunting world, one that had thrown him too many unpleasant surprises. He was in some way fragile, as widows could be fragile. Sir Randall would need absolute proof that Upjohn *could not* have committed the thefts.

Proof I did not have. Yet.

"Off to bed with you now," I said to Lucy. "I don't know how long I'll be gone."

She checked the corridor for me, and then I was out the door and down the stairs, half expecting to run into Sebastian or St. Sevier as I crossed the terrace. I traveled the path to the lake by the light of a rising moon not quite full, shadows shifting with the night breeze. I approached the boathouse to the low murmur of male voices, both of which I recognized.

"You're better off taking a punt out to the middle of the lake," I said. "That way, you can conserve your energy for the actual diving."

St. Sevier emerged from the gloom. He was unclothed from the waist up, his flesh pale against the darkness. "I told you she'd be here."

Sebastian, similarly half naked, joined him. "We told you we'd raise the boat tomorrow night."

"I know what you told me, and I know the sooner we examine the evidence the better. Putting the task off for another day makes no sense when time grows so short; therefore, you were dissembling for the sake of sparing yourselves my involvement."

St. Sevier tried for a winsome smile. "We were sparing you the inconvenience of this outing, *cherie*."

I smiled back when I wanted to kick him. "By lying to me. How very considerate, *mon cher*."

"We're sorry," Sebastian muttered. "We are abjectly sorry for thinking to leave you safe and cozy in your sitting room instead of risking the night air and worse. Now, does my lady prefer that St. Sevier and I waste further time groveling, or shall we be about our business?"

"You may grovel later," I allowed. "A two-man racing punt has been stored in the rafters, if I recall correctly. That will have you to the center of the lake in no time."

If I live to be a decrepit old woman, I will never forget the picture those two men made, pulling at their oars, their punt skimming over the silvery expanse of water. The lake lapped gently at the shore as a breeze brought me the tangy scent of the woods and the softer fragrance of grassy summer pastures. Muscles ripped under moon-light, and as the boat drew toward the center of the lake, I beheld a scene of ghostly male splendor.

Sebastian and St. Sevier had apparently decided that only one man would go into the water at a time, and I held my breath as Sebastian dove from the boat.

He came up an eternity later, then dove again. How he could see anything baffled me. Down he went at least a half-dozen more times, while St. Sevier remained sitting in the boat, a lonely figure drifting in the moonlight.

Sebastian surfaced again, and the men spoke quietly. St. Sevier pulled him into the boat, then manned the oars.

Giving up so soon? Not possible. "You found Clara's boat," I said as they carried the punt from the dock to the boathouse.

"I did," Sebastian said. "Bilge plug is stuck tight, but the caulking where the side and the bottom join has been gouged free. The boat would have leaked from the moment it was put into the water, but slowly, between the floorboards and the ribbing, so Clara would not have noticed at first."

They returned the punt to the rafters and replaced the padlock on the doors. St. Sevier tossed a blanket over Sebastian's shoulders—dark wool—and the men collected their boots.

"So the boat was definitely sabotaged," I said. "And had the occupant been somebody else—Miss Peasedale, Miss Waltham, perhaps both—the result could have been far more serious."

St. Sevier retrieved a shirt from a bench near the dock. "The result could have been death. While I applaud the need to free Mr. Upjohn from Sir Randall's custody, determining who would wreak such mischief on a boat under lock and key has become equally important."

The regatta was tomorrow, and I, for one, was glad I would not be participating in it.

CHAPTER TWELVE

The maids' tea was served in what was referred to as the back terrace gallery, not to be confused with the portrait gallery or the front terrace gallery. The terrace galleries ran on either side of the ballroom, and the "back" terrace opened onto the informal courtyard. Maids and footmen alike had been readying that area for the weekend's ball, and thus serving tea for the maids there afforded them a minimal respite from their labors.

"The footmen nearly revolted," Lucy said, passing me a cinnamon bun on a plain white plate. "They are to have their tea tomorrow, while those of you who survive the rigors of today's regatta rehearse your dramas."

"Rehearse our farces," I said. "Go mingle, be agreeable, complain about me."

"As if," she sniffed, flouncing off to take her place in the buffet line.

I watched from between the fronds of enormous potted ferns, feeling that farce had, indeed, gained a hold of my afternoon. I had a book with me, should I need to pretend a reason for lurking all on my own, nobody to keep me company except a statue of Hermes. His winged feet sported a few chips, hence the abundant greenery to hide his wounds.

In all honesty, I did not mind missing some of the regatta to bide with a slightly damaged god.

The maids had been chattering and milling about the food for the past twenty minutes, but I had yet to spot my quarry. I studied faces, closed my eyes the better to listen to voices, and then busied myself peering at bootheels.

Lucy occasionally tossed a glance in my direction, waiting for my signal. I was to cough into my handkerchief if I saw the woman I sought, and Lucy would know to sidle over to my lurking place. Not a very sophisticated plan.

My cinnamon bun was stale, likely left over from yesterday's breakfast for the guests. The maids looked a bit frazzled. An apron was streaked with dust here, a cap slightly askew there, but they were a healthy lot, with plenty of energy for socializing when the opportunity arose.

When the housekeeper joined the group, the women snatched a final biscuit or quarter sandwich, drained their teacups, and took up their dusters, brooms, buckets, and mops. The entire gathering had lasted less than forty-five minutes and had apparently been for naught.

Lucy wafted past me, deep in conversation with a woman of mature years and ample dimensions. The older woman's cap was more extravagantly adorned with lace than was the typical maid's, and her demeanor was that of an authority.

My guess was that she was Clara or Lady Bathvale's personal maid, probably from a family that had been serving at the Abbey for generations.

The informal courtyard went quiet, except for the maids tasked with cleaning up after the tea. Sir Randall came up the steps from the garden, his bootheels rapping smartly against the flagstones.

"Well? Did this considerable expense and inconvenience to the household yield any great news, my lady?"

He had nowhere to strut about in the fern-choked alcove, and I felt reluctantly sorry for him. He clearly pined for a woman not his own, he was badly fumbling the riddle of the thefts, and he had to humor a blasted female determined to deprive him of his culprit of choice.

"We are making progress," I said, rising. "I have ascertained that the woman who dissembled about her identity was *not* a chambermaid attached to this house. She was likely familiar enough with the house to toss out the name of a chambermaid, but she could well be in the employ of a guest."

Sir Randall held an anemic fern aside for me to pass, leaving a shower of dead bits of fronds on the floor. "Now you'll want to inspect all of the guests' maids? I really must object, my lady, and quite firmly."

Sir Randall doubtless undertook all tasks *quite firmly*, which was no substitute for executing a job *quite competently*.

"I will simply go looking for Lucy when the servants take their next meal and probably spy the trespasser in the servants' hall before sundown."

We moved in the direction of the garden, though I'd had my fill of time spent at the lake. From the top of the garden steps, I could see the water shimmering blue in the distance, the folly sticking up amid the trees on the far shore. A trio of punts skimmed across the surface, and the occasional shout came to me on the afternoon breeze.

Somewhere in the house, Upjohn was likely gazing out a window, awaiting a fate he'd done nothing to deserve. My passing sympathy for Sir Randall ebbed on that thought.

"I must ask you," Sir Randall said, "to have done with your poking and prying. What does it matter, if a guest's maid got lost and ended up in the wrong room? Of course she'd spin a Banbury tale rather than admit her error. You are making much out of nothing because you cannot accept that the dodgy fellow already under arrest is the guilty party."

He would have harangued me all the way to the lake, but I

stopped at the bottom of the steps. "What if you're wrong, Sir Randall? What if Upjohn, who had no motive and no more opportunity than any other servant, isn't our thief?"

"Then wiser heads than ours will sort that out at the quarter sessions in September, won't they?"

"You've already decided to have him bound over? Without taking any testimony? Without hearing from a single witness? You will see him jailed among the lowest of the low, exposed to all manner of illness, put on short rations at best, when he's still trying to recover from a crime nobody has bothered to consider, much less solve?"

Sir Randall stared past my shoulder, as if he could will himself back to the lake like a schoolboy longing to fly out a window. Who or what drew him that strongly to a silly boating party?

"My lady, I know you regard me as both unfeeling and unbending, but I am a magistrate and former soldier. I have a sense of these matters that someone of your genteel disposition cannot claim. Upjohn is being well cared for, and he's not protesting his innocence in my hearing."

"Because he cannot," I retorted. "His recollections are jumbled, and one cannot prove actions in the negative. All you know is that a cravat pin was found in a drawer in a dormitory frequented by at least a half-dozen men all similarly situated to Upjohn. The first footman had the use of that very bed earlier in the week, and I doubt you've even questioned him."

Sir Randall paced away from me, and I thought he was to do me the very great discourtesy of simply leaving the conversation without replying, but no. He executed a parade turn and came marching back.

"Lord and Lady Bathvale are my neighbors. I consider them friends and esteem them highly. All her ladyship wanted was to host a pleasant country entertainment. She's been immured here for years because Bathvale venerates this damned pile, and her ladyship is loyal. Bathvale finally relented and permitted this, her first major entertainment beyond a hunt ball or spring fête. Is it too much to ask that you mind your own business for the few days remaining of this interminable gathering? Can you do that, please?"

I ascended halfway up the steps before replying. "Did Monsieur St. Sevier tell you about the boat?" We had decided that Hugh was the best party to convey that information, which he'd *happened upon* while enjoying a late-night swim.

"A leaky punt is hardly a great revelation, Lady Violet. This is the country. The air takes a toll as seasons change and temperatures fluctuate."

"Samuel inspected every boat last week. The caulking on Miss Putnam's craft had been gouged free. Either Samuel didn't see what was obvious, or somebody damaged that boat once the guests arrived."

Sir Randall came back up the steps so he once again had an advantage of height. "Samuel is human. He could well miss some minor damage, and Miss Clara came to no harm. I respect that you seek to ensure justice is done, but that is *my job*. Continue to interfere with my investigation, and I will be forced to take stern measures."

Oh, he ought not to have spoken to me in the tone of a disappointed nanny trying to shame a small charge into contrition.

I climbed to the top of the steps. "I can't see that you're investigating much of anything. You might have nosed through a few guest rooms, but other than the cravat pin, which was all but lying in plain sight, have you recovered any of the other items?"

He flushed, he huffed, he stared at the treetops in the distance. "For your information, I have searched *every* guest room. I have searched the public rooms and even had a go at the attics and lumber rooms. I've been through the pantries and maids' quarters and stables. If it would dissuade you from your infernal prying, I'd search the very crypts, but even that degree of thoroughness is unlikely to placate your stubbornness. I will wish you good day, Lady Violet, and remind you in parting that interfering with the king's man is a chargeable offense."

He stalked off, while I subsided onto the steps. His diligence both surprised and pleased me—less searching for me to do—and gave me much to consider.

∽

"If I ever hold a house party," I said, "my guests will engage in adult entertainments rather than occupy themselves with the pastimes of children."

St. Sevier poured me another half glass of wine. "Blind man's bluff is not to your taste?"

On the lawn before us, a sunburned Thaddeus Baxter waved his hands through the air, Miss Waltham's fichu having been commandeered to cover his eyes. Miss Peasedale helpfully shrieked at nothing, and Mr. Baxter turned his flailing in her direction.

"This game might be a diversion for children," I said, "but for adults it's an excuse to grope and be groped, to stumble into another person most clumsily, and otherwise engage in flirtation disguised as buffoonery."

"Are you disgusted or jealous, my lady?"

I was wondering where Sebastian had got off to and if St. Sevier had drawn the duty of minding me for the morning lest I discover Sebastian at his task.

"I am bored," I said. "With the exception of present company, these people are not my friends, nor are they likely to become my friends." Mrs. Bonaventure intrigued me, as a coaching accident intrigued me. I might be tempted to gawk and linger, but I would ride on past as swiftly as possible.

"The marquess is your friend, *Violette*. You drive that poor man daft."

Hugh smiled at his wine, the thought of Sebastian's alleged torment inspiring a purely masculine humor. Not gloating, but affection for the human condition.

"His lordship and I might have been friends once," I conceded, "but our paths diverged years ago. He's intent on finding a wife now. He allows my assistance regarding this situation with Upjohn because a woman has access and insights a man does not."

I could also argue with Sir Randall without entirely losing my temper—so far—or calling him out.

"Do your old friends typically offer you marriage?" Hugh put his question so casually, between one sip of wine and the next, that I at first didn't grasp the substance of his query.

When I did, I nearly choked on my drink. "I *beg* your pardon?"

Fortunately, even Mrs. Albright was laughing and clapping at Mr. Baxter's gyrations, while Miss Peasedale giggled uproariously, and Bertie Baxter quacked at his brother like a hysterical duck.

"I beg your pardon?" I repeated, more softly. "Sebas—*his lordship*, has not offered me marriage. I am the last woman he'd offer for."

"Quite the contrary, I believe you were the first woman he considered courting, and I gather the only one so far. Dunkeld was sure you knew."

"*When* did he seek to court me? *Why?* A marquess can look much higher than the widowed daughter of an earl. He would *never—*" Except that Sebastian hadn't always been a marquess, had he? He'd once upon a time been a dear, thoughtful youth, who—for no *apparent* reason—had decided to thwart his uncle and ride off to war.

That behavior would have suited a proud young man denied permission to court a lady he esteemed.

"Perhaps you should ask him those questions, hmm?" Hugh took another languid sip of unremarkable wine while I reeled in shock.

"Dunkeld told you this?"

"After a few late-night brandies, as we attempted to puzzle out what the hell is going on at this lovely party."

English profanity sounded better with a French accent. "I will kill my father, and my brothers." For all four of them likely knew that Sebastian had sought permission to court me. "Slow, agonizing death is too good for them."

The indifferent wine and too many stale biscuits had unsettled my digestion, and frustration—or sleepless nights—were giving me the beginnings of a headache. Now St. Sevier had casually delivered a cataclysmic shock to my private reality.

Thaddeus Baxter wasn't the only fool flailing around blindfolded.

"Violet, please do not be angry," Hugh said. "I am a great believer in honesty, and I did not think I could keep such a truth from you. Not in good faith."

"I am not angry with you." I was impressed with his integrity, in fact, also confused by it. "I do believe I should go up to my room for a bit." Solitude had become a craving in the past half hour, and a dull throbbing had begun at the base of my neck. That Sebastian had sought to *court me*, doubtless years ago, was more of a revelation than I could endure amid the laughing, clapping strangers with whom I was rusticating.

"Forgot your hatpin?" St. Sevier asked, all innocence.

"Misplaced my sanity. Sir Randall threatened to arrest me if I couldn't stand idly by while he sends an innocent man to perdition."

"He is the magistrate."

"And that makes him God?" I'd spoken too sharply, but the contrast between Upjohn locked in some dusty garret and the inanity on the lawn before me, between Mrs. Bonaventure urging me to get back on the horse and a youthful Sebastian asking leave to court an equally innocent version of me...

Between Sir Randall claiming to diligently search the entire house and insisting that he already had his villain in hand...

"Sir Randall knows Upjohn is innocent," I said.

Hugh stopped pretending to drink his wine. "I beg your pardon?"

"Sir Randall claims he's searched every guest room, every pantry, the attics, the maids' rooms, the public rooms, and even the stables... He has looked and looked and looked, ostensibly to recover the locket and the earbobs, but that's not the reason. He's continuing his investigation because he doesn't want to be made a fool of."

"Nobody enjoys humiliation."

I rose, compelled by my whirling thoughts to move. "If Upjohn were guilty, then a suggestion from him about where Sir Randall might look for the other items would constitute cooperating with the king's man without admitting further guilt. That could only help Upjohn's situation, and Sir Randall would emphasize such a point to his prisoner."

Hugh stood as well, as a gentleman must. "Upjohn cannot cooperate, because he has no idea where the stolen goods are." He took my hand, placed it on his arm, and bent near, as if sharing a risqué comment. "If you are seen pelting into the house, you will draw notice."

I felt as if my head would burst, figuratively and literally, for the throbbing had escalated to my temple and was no longer dull. Some great insight was trying to struggle into my awareness, some connection between facts and observations.

"I have a headache," I said. "If you would see me to my room, please."

"Of course." He set a decorous pace for the French doors that led to the library. "Too much sun can have unpleasant results, and—"

A child burst forth from the house, his little legs churning, his smile joyous.

"The heir has escaped again," I said, standing aside as the boy scampered past. Samuel came next, bearing a kite, followed by a nurserymaid with flushed cheeks.

"I'm not sure this is a good idea," she said, trotting after the footman. "Not with guests on the lawn and the master and mistress entertaining."

"Nonsense." Samuel caught sight of us and paused, his free hand held out to the boy. "Master Owen, we must greet your guests."

The little fellow skipped over and flung a bow at us. "Good day! I'm Owen. Samuel and I are to fly my kite. Sissy could not come because she is too little. Nanny is too old, so Hartles brought me down. Would you like to watch?"

Samuel ruffled the boy's hair. "Her ladyship and Monsieur have better things to do, lad. I bet we'll find a lively breeze in the pasture near the postern gate."

The maid, Hartles, cast an anxious glance toward the game of blind man's bluff. If Lord Bathvale had spotted the escapee, he gave no sign of it. He was seated between Clara and Lady Bathvale and failing utterly to look amused at the antics of the younger guests.

Clara, for her part, scowled thunderously in our direction. Lady Bathvale leaned past his lordship to whisper to her sister, and Clara resumed watching the spectacle on the grass.

Family squabbles, I thought, though I would have an all-out war with my papa if I learned that he'd turned aside Sebastian's interest in me without even consulting me. All those years ago, I'd been a gormless girl, but even that girl deserved to be heard on so serious a matter as a suitor for her hand.

"Enjoy your outing," I said to the child as he all but dragged Samuel across the terrace.

"Why is it," St. Sevier said quietly, "English children are uniformly adorable, but the adult version of the same specimen is so often insufferable?"

His comment inspired me to look once again at Lord Bathvale, who now also watched the boy and the footman. His lordship, a notably stoic man, looked positively bleak. What manner of father could behold such a darling child, much less his only begotten son, with anything other than rejoicing?

I had been denied the joy of motherhood, and Bathvale's reaction bothered me. Perhaps his lordship wanted more children, and her ladyship was unwilling to cooperate.

"They are a puzzling family, aren't they?" I said, setting out for the door. "They have all of this,"—I waved a hand at the Abbey —"and yet, they are not happy. Stables, conservatory, an entire wing of guest rooms, two courtyards, a dozen public rooms..." I crossed into the library, and a new thought arrived there with me. "Hugh, nobody has searched the family's private quarters."

He closed the door behind us. "You cannot be serious. You

cannot possibly, in a thousand flights of English stubbornness, be seri-ous. I promised Dunkeld—"

I barreled on, my conviction growing by the instant. "We've elim-inated every other possibility. The servants' quarters, the guest rooms, the rooms frequented by both. The only area where Sir Randall would not dare to peek is the family's private wing.

"A family member would have access to the boathouse," I went on as we left the library, "though I have no earthly idea why Lord or Lady Bathvale would bother ruining one of their own boats."

"Perhaps the objective was to humiliate Miss Clara?" St. Sevier suggested. "She got a good soaking for her troubles, and her ladyship would have known that Miss Clara can swim."

Sebastian and St. Sevier had apparently been discussing the situ-ation, though not with me.

"That makes little sense, St. Sevier. Why would Lady Bathvale spend months importuning her husband to host this gathering and then use it to humiliate her own sister?"

We started up the stairs, the house having the empty feel of a large dwelling in the late morning. The climb was made more difficult because I was battling a headache. Evasive maneuvers were pointless at this stage. I was in for pounding misery, just when I most needed my wits about me.

"Perhaps Lord Bathvale doesn't care for Miss Clara," St. Sevier suggested, "or perhaps the leaky boat was intended to embarrass Samuel."

At the top of the steps, we could turn left into the guest wing, or right into the family apartments.

"Clara does not care for Samuel," I said slowly. "But then, I suspect the sentiment is mutual." Did she resent his family connec-tion? His place in the household was apparently more than poor rela-tion from the wrong side of the blankets.

"Do you even know where the family apartments are?" St. Sevier asked.

"Lady Bathvale asked me to have a look at the sleeping arrangements, so I've seen a plan of the whole house." But where to start? "What if you take Lord Bathvale's apartment, and I take her ladyship's?"

I started off down the corridor, which was carpeted. Between that, and today's festivities on the lawn along the opposite side of the house, the quiet became pronounced.

"If either one of us is discovered searching alone," St. Sevier said, "we have no alibi. If we are found searching together..."

"Then we are a naughty couple who sought the use of the most private rooms in the house for our trysting. The excuse is flimsy. Let's hope we don't have to use it. Her ladyship's chamber should be here." The door was carved with a swan, and Lord Bathvale's rooms were next door.

St. Sevier pushed the door open. "After you."

I preceded him into the room, an elegant chamber done up in rich claret and cream velvets with dashes of blue in the carpet and pillow embroidery. The fireplace was large and spotless. Fresh roses graced a table by the window. Whatever else was true, Lady Bathvale enjoyed a commodious apartment.

The bedroom was equally lovely, though here the color scheme was flipped. Blue and ivory dominated, and a deep red hue was used for accents.

"What are we looking for?" St. Sevier said.

"I don't know. Clues, insights, missing items, hints... That's odd." The shawl draped over the dressing screen was one I'd seen on Clara. She'd worn it the first night of the house party. The pattern was an unusual blend of scarlet, orange, and yellow, like a bouquet of brilliant flowers. A garment easily noticed and not soon forgotten. Also not particularly flattering to her coloring.

"Perhaps Clara left this here," I said, running a hand over the shawl as St. Sevier sat at her ladyship's writing desk. I went to the wardrobe and opened both doors. The dresses before me were familiar, but I needed a moment to grasp why they bothered me.

"I made a mistake," I said. "This is not Lady Bathvale's chamber at all. This is Clara's suite."

Hugh began opening and closing drawers. "Are you sure?"

Sisters, especially twins, sometimes borrowed clothing from each other freely. Clara and Lady Bathvale never had, that I knew of.

"The map of the house that Lady Bathvale showed me last week was clear," I said. "These rooms are for the lady of the house, though the wardrobe holds Clara's dresses. If we wanted to be certain, the jewelry box would tell the tale." I crossed to the vanity and opened the jewelry box. The very first item I spotted had me sinking to the vanity stool. "St. Sevier, please come here. Now."

He was at my side in an instant. "Mon Dieu," he murmured, peering over my shoulder. "This will be very difficult for Miss Putnam to explain."

~

My wedding ring and engagement ring shared a small velvet-lined compartment with a pair of pearl earbobs and a mourning locket.

"Clara either stole the jewelry, or she knows who did."

"You do not believe she came upon the jewelry and is trying to discover who the thief is herself?" St. Sevier asked.

"No." I wasn't sure what Clara's scheme was, or why she'd undertaken it, but I did not want to be discovered in her room. "Let's leave this for now."

St. Sevier considered me, his expression troubled. "You will leave your rings?"

"For now." They were a symbol of who I'd been. I wasn't sure they mattered all that much to who I had become.

Voices sounded in the corridor. I closed the lid of the jewelry box and considered diving under the bed, but St. Sevier took me by the wrist and slipped out onto the balcony with me.

"This is becoming a habit," I whispered as he silently closed the door after us. I hauled back on his hand, because while one of the voices was Clara's, the other was also familiar to me.

St. Sevier tugged on my wrist.

I shook my head.

Clara had moved into her bedroom. "I must rest. I absolutely must rest if I'm not to expire before the regatta. What on earth do you suppose Samuel was about, hauling Owen across the garden for all the guests to see?"

"I'm sure I don't know, ma'am. Shall I take down your hair?"

"Yes, please, and then have a raspberry cordial sent up. I vow this house party has been the most trying ten days of my life, which is saying a great deal. I hope her ladyship has learned her lesson."

Whatever was Clara going on about?

St. Sevier tugged on my hand again, less gently. He pointed to his left. The balcony we were on abutted that of the neighboring suite. The two were separated by a partial divider of iron scrollwork, but that divider was in actuality a gate.

"Lord Bathvale's suite is next to this one," I whispered as Clara maundered on about aching feet and Sir Randall's infernal war stories.

"Ma'am," the maid said, "I did hear that Sir Randall has been searching the premises. He's making a proper job of the search too, according to Marple."

"He'll not dare to poke his nose into the family wing, not to search for missing trinkets in any case. Be off with you, Jessup, and mind you, don't forget my cordial. My digestion has been most bilious, and the cordial is the only remedy that works."

"Yes, ma'am."

Jessup. The maid's name was Jessup.

"Violet," St. Sevier murmured, "I beg you, we must go."

I allowed him to lead me across to the next balcony, and we slipped out of Lord Bathvale's rooms not two seconds before the man himself rounded the end of the corridor.

He regarded us, a pair of mature, unattached houseguests all but holding hands in the broad light of day. "Admiring the door carvings, I presume?"

"The lintels," I said. "Grinling Gibbons's work, if I'm not mistaken? I know he was very active at Petworth, but I hadn't realized he'd also taken commissions for the Abbey. Or perhaps one of his students did those carvings?"

His lordship's brows rose. "Gibbons himself," he said. "He'd stop at the Abbey on the way to and from Petworth. My favorite is the lintel over the armory, right across from the nursery."

I aimed a bright smile at St. Sevier, though my headache had reached the abandon-all-hope stage. "To the armory, monsieur. We can't miss the best of the lot, can we?"

"Of course not, your ladyship." He offered his arm, and we toddled off down the corridor.

"Keep walking," he murmured, "and I hope to hell you know where the nursery is."

As it happened, I did, but we ran into Lady Bathvale before we reached our destination, and I was reduced to rhapsodizing at length over the craftsmanship of the Abbey's lintels.

～

"You are an idiot of the first water," Sebastian said, setting a brisk pace up the back staircase. "A fool, a gudgeon, a ninnyhammer, and a dunderpate."

"You left out clodpole," St. Sevier said from my other side.

"And you are no better, *Doctor*," Sebastian declared when we'd reached the landing. "I fault you for having put her ladyship's reputation at risk not once, but twice. Lurking on balconies is for fools."

"And marquesses," I muttered over the pounding in my head. "Both of you, hush."

I'd barely remained sentient during luncheon. Miss Waltham had delivered Hamlet's soliloquy wearing what had to be a lampshade on her head, claiming that rehearsal was the secret to a convincing performance.

Sir Randall and Mrs. Albright had traded dialogue from a scene from *Twelfth Night* barely recognizable for all its mangled lines. The climax of the meal had been the sunburned Baxters prancing about the dining room in bedsheet togas and declaiming their plan to destroy the city of Iolcus in revenge for King Pelias's treachery.

Revenge figured prominently in several other presentations, and now my head was taking revenge upon me.

I'd asked Sebastian to escort me up the back stairs because I wanted the cool and the quiet, and the hope of a lie-down. Missing trinkets, sabotaged boats, a servant wrongly accused... None of it made sense, but Upjohn would be bound over on Monday if I could not sort out the puzzle pieces before then.

"What sort of physician," Sebastian said, pausing on the landing, "escorts a woman with a pounding megrim down to luncheon?"

"My lady, have you a megrim?" St. Sevier asked.

"Of course she does," Sebastian retorted. "You can see it in her eyes. Dragging a widow still in the throes of grief to this infernal farce of a house party was harebrained, self-serving, and—"

I stepped between them and put a hand on each of two fine male chests. "Cease, the pair of you. I go where I please, I do as I please. I am no longer in the throes of grief. My headaches always pass, and we should be focused on determining why a wealthy young woman, one enjoying every luxury in her sister's home, is stealing trinkets."

"More than trinkets," Sebastian retorted at the same time St. Sevier said, "She stole your rings, *my lady*."

They were angry, and on my behalf. I was ashamed to say their ire gratified me, because I was angry as well—also puzzled—but a woman's anger was an impotent thing... "I was furious with Sir Randall, and he nearly walked away from me."

"What are you wittering on about?" Sebastian asked, peering out the window.

"A woman's anger." Anger could be a motive for theft, and this

house party was full of angry women. Mrs. Albright's furious determination to see her daughter well wed. Miss Waltham's aggressive
piety, which masked an angry need to be noticed and approved of.
Mrs. Bonaventure's ire at the fate that deprived her of the only man
she'd ever loved, and Lady Bathvale's quiet resentment of life at a
polite distance from her spouse.

"And then there's Clara." I stepped away and pressed my back
against the cold stone of the landing. We were in an older part of
the Abbey, one overlooking the stables and carriage house, a fit
view for the back stairs. "What does Clara have to be angry
about?"

"Does a spinster with a fortune need a reason to be angry?" St.
Sevier asked. "If the Putnam money isn't enough to lure even a
fortune hunter to her side, she must be very disagreeable upon closer
acquaintance. She is not a happy woman."

A sound intruded into the echoing quiet of the vast stone stair-
well, carriage wheels on crushed shells. My headache amplified and
sometimes distorted sounds, and I heard the carriage pulling up as if
it were directly beneath the window.

"Is somebody arriving in the middle of the afternoon?" I asked,
joining Sebastian at the window.

The coach was small and plain, a country household's convenience for traveling to services on a rainy Sunday, not an elegant
Town vehicle.

"Nobody important," Sebastian said.

"Somebody's leaving," St. Sevier added, "or being forced to
leave."

Two stout footmen escorted a third man between them. Two
other men flanked the footmen, and the Baxters, still attired in their
togas, brought up the rear.

"That's Sir Randall on the left," I said, a queasy feeling twining
through my headache. "I know his strut."

"And that is my man Upjohn being paraded off to God knows
where." Sebastian was off down the steps like an arrow from a cross-

bow, St. Sevier after him. I had no choice but to follow, lest they tear into Sir Randall before I had the opportunity.

We reached the foot of the steps and dashed through a side garden to arrive at the carriage just as Upjohn was being thrust inside.

"What, may I ask, are you doing with my patient?" St. Sevier asked, his tone lethally polite.

"He's my prisoner," Sir Randall countered. "He's being moved to a secure location to await trial at the assizes."

Lord Bathvale took the place at Sir Randall's elbow. "My lord, St. Sevier, I applaud your concern for a mere domestic and a former soldier, but the needs of justice must take precedence. Sir Randall's authority is not to be thwarted."

One of the footmen was Samuel, who looked exceedingly uncomfortable with the whole business. Anybody in service could be accused of anything at any time, and only an employer's loyalty stood between the servant and a grim fate.

The Baxters were trying to affect the stoic disinterest of the legendary Romans and failing miserably. Their presence assured that this whole blasted business would be common knowledge throughout London by Monday night.

Assuming they didn't pen express letters for posting in the morning.

And yet, it was the presence of the Baxters—Castor and Pollux in the day's earlier rehearsals—that set my mind off on a fruitful line of reasoning. Bathvale Abbey housed two sisters, one titled, one staring at ignominious spinsterdom, much as Pollux had been immortal, while his half-sibling Castor had been human.

Lord Bathvale was titled, while his cousin Samuel was reduced to toadying to the needs of his supposed betters, and yet, Clara felt at liberty to remonstrate at length with both men, the peer and the servant.

Her bedroom—not Lady Bathvale's—connected to his lordship's.

"You have been very naughty," I said to Lord Bathvale. "Very naughty indeed. Unless you want me expounding on the details of your transgressions right here and now, you will turn loose of that man."

"Heed her, my lord," Sebastian said. "Or I will see to it that you and your pet magistrate both regret your folly."

"Leaving me," St. Sevier said, "to patch up what's left of you, though a physician's lowly skill won't be sufficient to repair the damage an angry marquess can do to a man's fortune and standing, much less that of his family."

They were a lovely pair, the Frenchman and the Scot, and when my head stopped pounding and I had seen Bathvale and his household held accountable for threatening an innocent, I was sure the memory of Sebastian's and St. Sevier's loyalty would cheer me considerably.

Sir Randall remained silent, which I attributed to an animal's instinct for self-preservation, rather than a gentleman's latent store of honor.

"Let him go," Lord Bathvale said. "If I hear a word of this—"

I stepped up to him. "Enough. You will summon Miss Putnam and her ladyship to Miss Putnam's sitting room. Samuel, you will join us, and to the Misters Baxter, all I can say is, unless you want it bruited about that you both are cursed with chubby knees, you will keep your mouths shut."

"And puffy ankles," St. Sevier said, peering at their sandaled feet. "Not a healthy sign in young men. Perhaps dropsy runs in your families, or a fondness for hard liquor?"

They stalked off, and Sir Randall would have gone with them, but Sebastian clamped a hand on his sleeve. "Oh, no. The brave knight doesn't get to slink away without admitting his sins. Not this time. Upjohn, you are free to await me in my rooms, and if anyone tries to bother you further, I will press charges to the full extent of the law."

Had Sebastian puzzled out the mystery, or was his show of force based solely on faith in my deductive skills? I suspected the latter, more cause for gloating at another time. St. Sevier escorted me back into the house. Lord Bathvale sent the remaining footmen to notify the ladies, and we were soon assembled in Clara's sitting room.

"Well, this is cozy," Clara said, settling herself into a reading chair. She exuded the malicious good cheer of somebody who expects to watch a public whipping. Lady Bathvale, by contrast, appeared worried. Neither woman approached his lordship, while Sir Randall took the place by her ladyship's chair.

"Sir Randall," I said, "if you would be good enough to fetch Miss Putnam's jewelry box."

"What have my sister-in-law's gewgaws to do with this whole business?" Bathvale's tone held a note of anxiety beneath his indignation.

I almost felt sorry for him, but then I thought of Upjohn, helpless to defend himself, being spirited away for the convenience of a lot of prancing aristocrats with nothing better to do than play stupid games.

"I care nothing for your sister-in-law's gewgaws," I said as Sir Randall returned with the carved wooden box. "It's my wedding ring that concerns me. Sir Randall, if you open the box, you will find in the top right-hand compartment two rings. The inscription on the gold band says, 'Love always, Fred.' If you look closely, you will see that the ring was resized. Originally, that inscription said, 'Love always, Freddie,' but the jeweler had to be clever about how the metal was cut. His name is Morris Newton, and his shop is on Ludgate Hill. He will testify that the ring in Clara's box is mine, as will I."

"I found your silly rings," Clara said, trying for a dismissive smile. "I did not want to get Jessup in trouble, but it was she—"

"No, it was not Jessup," I retorted. "Jessup snooped about, informing me her name was Haines when I inquired, and she might have moved my shawl without my permission, but she did not have an opportunity to steal my rings. You, however, did. You did not come down to breakfast before Sunday services, claiming fatigue. Fatigue had nothing to do with it. When I went up to my rooms after breakfast to change for services, my rings were gone. Jessup, by contrast, was doubtless attending Sunday prayers in the servants' hall."

"Jessup was at prayers," Samuel said. "She wouldn't dare miss Sunday prayers. None of us would."

"Of all the company," I went on, "only Clara was late to the initial buffet, as if she sought to make an entrance in her colorful, expensive shawl. I thought it a little sad at the time that a younger sister would attempt to upstage her elder, but that late arrival allowed you to snatch a few items from the guest rooms nearest the family wing."

Lord Bathvale had sunk into a chair, Sir Randall was staring at the ceiling. Lady Bathvale regarded her sister, consternation giving way to fury.

"Clara, how could you? All I asked for was a bit of diversion, two weeks to enjoy the fiction that I actually mean something in this household. You begrudge me even that?"

"She begrudges everybody everything," Samuel said bitterly. He opened the jewelry box and fished out my rings, holding them out to me. "She stole your ring, but disdained to accept mine."

"Please show those rings to Sir Randall," I said.

"So I came across your rings," Clara said, twitching at her skirts as Sir Randall peered at the inscription on my wedding band. "I would have returned them."

"No, you would not. In addition to Mrs. Albright's locket and Miss Waltham's earbobs, I recognized in your jewelry box a bracelet you stole from me when we were at school. You've been nicking things for years, haven't you? The headmistress would send you down when your larceny got out of hand, and you'd be back the next term, all smiles, recovered from your *indisposition*."

"A girlish prank," Sir Randall said, passing Lord Bathvale my rings. "I will not trouble myself to arrest—"

"Shut your mouth." Sebastian spoke softly, when I would have shouted.

"And keep it shut," St. Sevier added. "Her ladyship is not finished."

"Why would a footman," I began, pacing before the hearth, "even a footman connected to the family who believes himself to be legitimate—"

"I am legitimate," Samuel interjected.

"Think to offer for an heiress?" I went on. "Why, when his offer has been rejected, doesn't he remove himself to some other position?"

Samuel plucked my rings from Bathvale's hand and again held them out to me. "Clara knows exactly why I will not leave the Abbey."

I gestured for Samuel to put the rings on the low table between the chairs occupied by Lady Bathvale and her sister. "Because Owen is your son," I said, "yours and Clara's, and you will not abandon your child."

Lord Bathvale began swearing. Lady Bathvale stared at the rings.

"This is none of your affair," Clara said, rising from her seat. "None of it. Take your damned rings, your handsome bully boys, and your wild notions and leave."

"You even speak as if you have the running of the household," I said, "but then, you now occupy the lord of the manor's bed, don't you?"

Clara settled back into her chair, her expression mulish.

Lady Bathvale rubbed her forehead wearily. "Tell them the rest of it, and then perhaps I'll be the one to leave this place."

"You cannot leave." That from Bathvale, who had much, much to answer for. "We've had this discussion over and over, and you both agreed to it. We all agreed."

"Samuel agreed to allow his son to be raised as the heir to the Bathvale title," I said. "And what of Owen's sister? To whom does she belong?"

"Not to me." Lady Bathvale aimed a disdainful glance at her husband. "His lordship realized there was at least one fertile female in the family, and he wanted a spare the way I crave freedom from the prison my life has become. Clara made it easy for him, and the next thing I knew, another child was on the way."

If there was a victim here—besides Upjohn—it was Lady Bathvale. "While you were banished to the rooms across the corridor."

"Not banished," her ladyship said, chin coming up. "I refused Bathvale his marital rights. He might have conceived children with both of us, and then what was I to do? Watch the legitimate heir pushed aside because Owen had already been drafted into that role? Besides, I find his lordship's company beyond repugnant, and even he doesn't need a spare badly enough to commit rape."

And what a ringing endorsement of lordly honor that was.

I might have gone on unwrapping the rotten parcel that was domestic life at Bathvale Abbey, but Clara chose then to bolt from her chair, pelting for the door. For a woman in a snug corset and formal evening attire, she moved far too quickly for me to stop her.

CHAPTER THIRTEEN

St. Sevier, by the simple expedient of stepping in front of the door, prevented Clara Putnam from leaving the room.

She whirled away from him and stood alone, her posture suggesting we were to be treated to a schoolgirl tantrum, for which I did not have the patience.

"Sit down, Clara," I snapped. "You were prepared to see an innocent man hanged when your scheme to incriminate Samuel failed."

Lady Bathvale took Sir Randall's hand. The gesture was subtle, but I was certain both Sebastian and St. Sevier noticed.

"Samuel refuses to leave his damned brat," Clara retorted. "I wanted Samuel gone, and ordering him off the property wasn't working. In a moment of inexcusable stupidity, his lordship promised Samuel he'd always be welcome where Owen dwelled."

"I do not turn my back on family," Bathvale said, rising. "Samuel is my cousin. He's acceded to a plan that allows me to safeguard the future of Bathvale and all who dwell here. He offered you an honorable union, which you rejected. This scheme is as much yours as anybody's, and your petty dramas grow tiresome."

"My lord," I asked, "are you the father of Owen's younger sister?"

He and Samuel exchanged glances. "I believe I am," the earl replied.

"You are," Clara muttered. "That one"—she raised her chin in Samuel's direction—"won't listen to me when I say so."

"She could be either of ours," Lord Bathvale said. "Clara taunted me with that claim on other occasions, though Samuel denies it. Regardless, as I have no spare, the succession is far from secure."

My father, awash in male relations and blessed with four sons, had never known this kind of insecurity. A third of all titles granted in the early centuries of the English monarchy had died out within three generations. Vast fortunes went tumbling back into the royal exchequer for want of a legitimate heir, and disasters such as the Black Death saw a significant improvement in royal wealth.

Bathvale was not entirely irrational to put a cousin's by-blow in the place of a son, though he'd been beyond desperate.

"And Samuel's welcome here isn't secure either," I said. "Is it? When Hempley's departure meant Samuel was no longer biding in the footmen's dormitory, that left an incriminating cravat pin lying in the wrong drawer. Rather than retrieve the pin and move it to an innocuous location, Clara allowed Upjohn to be wrongly accused, and you, Sir Randall, had to have known the evidence was flimsy at best."

"I knew no such thing."

"But you suspected," I replied, "because when Clara's boat sank, you made little effort to investigate the cause. You saw her ploys for what they were—efforts to incriminate Samuel."

"That is ridiculous," Clara said. "I nearly drowned."

"No, you did not," Sebastian countered. "You loitered at the dock until her ladyship and I were both on shore, then you rowed out directly before us, where we would see you in difficulties. You know how to swim—don't bother denying it, for her ladyship has *seen* you swimming—and you were able to make treading water look like inept flailing about until I reached you. You were in little danger, but if you'd been able to prove that the boat was tampered with, Samuel would have taken the blame."

"And lest we forget," I added, "you dressed in male attire when you sneaked out to the boathouse Saturday night to damage the boat. You doubtless wore the same trousers Shylock will wear in your little theatrical role. Why do that, unless you're laying a trail of evidence that points to another?"

Lady Bathvale rose, assisted by Sir Randall. "I'm leaving. I am packing my bags tonight, and I don't know if or when I'll return."

"You can't," Lord Bathvale snapped. "You promised."

"I did more than promise. I took vows, as you did, but apparently I was the only one of us to mean them."

"You can't leave me here," Clara called as Lady Bathvale walked toward the door. "Not now, Belinda. Not like this."

Her ladyship pivoted and marched up to Clara. "All my life, *all my life*, you have been a burden upon me. You saw me blamed for your thievery when we were children, you are the reason I had no friends at school, and when I finally, finally escaped into a household of my own, you had to follow me even here, poisoning what could have been a cordial, decent union. I am sorry I could not present my husband with legitimate male issue in the earliest years of that marriage, but you did not have to tempt him, Clara. You did not have to prey on his weakness. Had you married Samuel, your legitimate child would have been the Bathvale heir, and we'd none of us be in this predicament."

"Me? The sole remaining Putnam heiress, *marry a footman?*"

Samuel crossed his arms. "I am a footman by choice, you daft woman. I'm university educated, I speak four languages, I took a first in Latin. My father did not leave me a pauper, though I wish to God he'd bequeathed me more sense than to ever think I could be happy with you."

Her ladyship's comment, about Owen being the rightful heir but for Clara's self-importance, stayed with me. As Samuel's wife, Clara could have been known as mother to the heir, but instead, her public role was that of auntie only.

"What matters here," I said, "are the children. Upjohn has gone free, though an apology to him would be appreciated."

"I'll settle a damned sum on him for life," Lord Bathvale said, "but would somebody please end this infernal house party immediately?"

"Do as you wish." Lady Bathvale twined her hand around Sir Randall's arm. "I am leaving, and I do not care who knows what a selfish, impossible family I am leaving behind."

"I care," I said. "Owen and his sister are blameless. If you swan off now, your nose in the air, then what's to stop Clara from announcing that Owen is her son?"

"I'll kill her," Lord Bathvale said, though his words were those of a frustrated boy, not a murderer. "Or I would. Fortunately, the children have baptismal certificates that nobody will contest."

St. Sevier appeared to find the plaster molding fascinating. "Good to know that Miss Putnam would never breathe a word against her own offspring. Not ever. She merely tried to see Owen's father hanged because he refused to be banished from his own family seat. When her plot failed, she allowed another innocent to be arrested, but never say she'd put her own wishes above the welfare of blameless children."

"Miss Putnam needs to be arrested," Sebastian said. "She stole repeatedly. She also conspired with her maid to steal. She interfered with Sir Randall's investigations, such as they were, and she failed to give evidence that would have exonerated another. Sir Randall, you were quick to accuse Upjohn on far less evidence than you have against Miss Putnam."

"Look in the jewelry box," I said. "Earbobs, a mourning locket, and the bracelet my late mother gave me when I put up my hair. It's inscribed too. I've no doubt you will find other contraband Miss Putnam has collected over the years."

Clara didn't dash for the door this time. She instead brandished a handkerchief, dabbing at the corners of her eyes. "You cannot arrest me. I am the mother of two small children."

Every man in the room likely wanted to see her arrested and led away in disgrace, but that I could not allow. "I'd like a word with the marquess in private," I said. "I'm sure Monsieur St. Sevier will be happy to keep the rest of you company for a few moments while Lord Dunkeld and I confer."

I had no authority over the miscreants and criminals in the room, but Sebastian's status was sufficient to ensure that they'd at least consider the arrangement I had in mind. St. Sevier opened the door and bowed me through, and Sebastian followed me into the corridor.

"Violet, I have not the least idea what you're planning," Sebastian said, "but I know I won't like it."

"You'll hate it, but it's the best I can come up with when my head's in a muddle." I explained my proposal as succinctly as I could.

Sebastian swore colorfully in three languages. The Gaelic was beyond me, but I followed the French and the English well enough to know that I'd been right: He hated my scheme. I wasted precious minutes arguing with him, during which verbal altercation he raised several good points.

When Sebastian and I returned to the parlor, all eyes were upon me. I would have one chance to convince these fools that they had a means of extricating themselves from this most imbecilic of coils. If they decided not to heed my suggestion, then Owen and his sister would likely be revealed as bastards before polite society and to blazes with what the baptismal documents said.

"You are right," I began, addressing Lady Bathvale. "You must remove yourself from Bathvale Abbey and never dwell here again."

Clara began to weep, until Lord Bathvale told her to hush.

"Go on," Sir Randall said, "and be quick about it. My coach is waiting to take her ladyship wherever she wishes to go."

～

"You tell me to be quick, Sir Randall, when your haste to miscarry justice for the convenience of your neighbors could have cost an innocent man his life. We'll start with you, then. You will resign as magistrate and leave the post to others going forward."

"Say you agree," Lady Bathvale murmured. "The sooner you agree, the sooner I can depart from this house."

Sir Randall patted her hand. "I agree. Never wanted the damned job anyway."

Oh, *of course* he hadn't. "As for you, Clara," I went on, "you will sign a witnessed confession admitting to the theft of the missing items, but the signature you will append to it is that of Belinda, Lady Bathvale."

His lordship's brows rose. "I beg your pardon? My countess is many things, but she is not a thief."

"No, you are the one stealing children here, aren't you, sir? What I propose is that you allow Belinda to leave and take up her sister's identity. Clara will remain, assuming the role and reality of Belinda, Countess of Bathvale. The children's actual mother will also appear to the world to *be* their mother, while Belinda can leave behind a situation no woman should have to endure."

Belinda sent his lordship a considering look. "Why I should allow a liar, thief, and adulteress the privileges of my station? I married Bathvale, I put up with him, I acceded to his cork-brained schemes, and I deserve recompense for wasting years of my life immured in this monument to his ambitions. I tried to make a union of my marriage, an honest, cordial union, but all he could think about was his empty nursery."

Bathvale had the grace to rise and approach his wife. "Belinda, I am sorry. I am not the man you deserve. I am a creature of duty and exactly what I was raised to be. I know you tried, but..." He looked at his boots, then at the woman he'd vowed to cherish. "Become Clara, and you are free—of me, of the Abbey, of the past. Marry Sir Randall, remove to Paris, become the literary hostess that sets London on its ear. Be free."

I could not have stated the case better myself.

"What of me?" Samuel asked. "I'll not leave my boy to the likes of you lot, and if the baby isn't mine, then she's my boy's sister, and that makes her family to me."

St. Sevier gave Samuel a long perusal. "Become his tutor. You say you're educated, and you are devoted to him. I trust his lordship will not object?"

A most excellent suggestion.

"I object," Clara said. "Nobody has asked me what I want, and I don't see where a few misplaced trinkets means that I have to put up with the likes of—"

Without moving, Sebastian took on a looming quality. "Multiple acts of theft, conspiring with another to steal, an entire career of thievery, in fact, mean you deserve the noose, Miss Putnam. Be quiet until Lady Violet bids you to speak."

"But I never—"

"Clara," Samuel said. "You are the mother of my child, and for his sake, I would rather not see you hanged. For the love of God, hush."

Oddly enough, she subsided onto the sofa beside Lord Bathvale.

"I will cheerfully become Owen's governor or his tutor," Samuel said. "Bathvale, do you agree to this?"

"Yes, yes. Are we finished yet?"

The throbbing in my head was taking on peculiar qualities, as if my hair could register sensation, all of it miserable, but I was not yet finished.

"Belinda, will you step into the shoes of your unmarried sister?" I asked. "If so, you will wear her clothes, imitate her penmanship, assume her memories and her abilities."

Sir Randall murmured something into Belinda's ear, and she smiled. "As long as I am free to leave Bathvale, I can accept those terms."

To each her own. "Samuel, you are content to become Owen's tutor, a doting cousin devoted to him for life?"

"With pleasure."

"Lord Bathvale, will you accept the mother of your children as your countess? She will have much to learn if she's to become Lady Bathvale, and you are the only party available to teach her."

"But I—" Clara began.

Sebastian, St. Sevier, and Samuel all spoke as one. "Be quiet."

"Hold your tongue," Bathvale said. "If you are to become my countess, Lady Bathvale to the world, then you will learn discretion, dignity, and decorum. You will learn to manage this household as efficiently as Belinda did, and you will never, by word, deed, silence, or indiscretion, betray the trust I place in you tonight. Do you understand? Even as my wife, you remain a commoner, and subject to the full authority of the law."

She spared a glance at Sebastian, whose smile promised execution in the court of public opinion, if not at Newgate itself.

"I understand."

The room breathed a collective sigh of relief.

"If that's all," Sir Randall said, "then *Miss Putnam* and I will be on our way."

Belinda—the new Miss Putnam, rather—swept the room with a glance, her gaze coming to rest on Bathvale and his recently accepted countess. "Good luck to you both. You will need it."

They left, and I wanted to applaud.

"That's all right, then," Samuel said. "Lord Bathvale, you'll need a new first footman. My advice is to choose a homely fellow who knows what's what. I'll keep to my present post until the house party concludes, but then I'm off to London to buy Owen some decent books."

He left the room after offering me a jaunty bow. For Clara, he had a pitying look, or perhaps the pity was for Lord Bathvale.

"That's it, then," Clara said. "We shake hands, and I'm Belinda, and she's me?"

"No, that's not it," Bathvale said. "My wife will fall prey to a sudden indisposition. You will remain out of sight for the rest of the house party, and I will carry on as host. You can use the next few days to alter Belinda's wardrobe to suit you, take up her correspondence, and familiarize yourself with her duties. Practice her penmanship, for all I care."

"A fine idea," I added, "and you also have a confession to write, *your ladyship.*"

My use of the honorific had an odd effect on Clara. She sat up straighter, and her expression became more reserved, as if she were mentally stepping into the shoes of the departed countess. My scheme, hare-brained and unusual as it was, had a prayer of working.

"Who keeps the confession?" Bathvale asked.

"If I might make a suggestion?" St. Sevier said. "Three copies. One to remain with you, your lordship. Another goes to the marquess, the third will be in the keeping of Lady Violet. An abundance of caution, you understand. And I will make certain that Samuel, in particular, knows to whom each copy has been given. We would not want anything untoward to happen to Owen's devoted tutor."

Clara did not like that suggestion at all, based on her expression, but Bathvale was pleased.

"Three copies it is, and I will be one of the witnesses. I meant what I said about settling a sum on that Upjohn fellow. By way of apology for the misunderstanding."

"Dunkeld," I said, "I will leave that negotiation to you. St. Sevier, if you'd see me to my room?"

Sebastian held the door, and St. Sevier politely offered his arm once we were in the corridor. I took it, not because manners meant a damned thing to me at that point, but because without his support, I would have found myself in a heap upon the floor.

～

To be carried to bed in the arms of a handsome swain was supposed to be romantic, but alas for St. Sevier, by the time I quit the sitting room, my balance was unreliable, my belly was in an uproar, and my headache was a class of agony beyond description. I didn't recall how I arrived to my own apartment, but Lucy was there to tuck me in, and St. Sevier brought by a posset that contained some tincture of oblivion.

Bless the man. He truly did have many wonderful qualities.

I kept to my room for all of the next day and ventured forth on Saturday only to sit in the quiet meadow with a book. I wasn't sorry I'd come to Bathvale Abbey, but I was looking forward to being home.

A shadow fell across the page I'd been staring at for some time. Either St. Sevier's magic elixir had left me with a lingering mental fog, or the events of the week had depleted my energies.

Perhaps both.

Sebastian peered down at me. He was in riding attire, which showed his physique to excellent advantage.

"Your French bulldog said I wasn't to tax you."

"As if dealing with you requires effort?"

"May I sit?"

I patted the worn wood of the bench. "Has Clar—I mean, Lady Bathvale written her confession?"

"That was yesterday's entertainment. I made her rewrite it three times and copy it three times. I do believe she hates me."

"Try not to sound so pleased. I suspect her ladyship hates most men. She and Bathvale will make each other miserable." Though neither party had been particularly happy to begin with, that I could see.

"Not entirely miserable," Sebastian replied. "St. Sevier made a comment that leads me to suspect her ladyship is carrying again."

Well, of course. I'd been denied the pleasure of motherhood, while a woman who saw children only as a means of manipulating men could turn them out like clockwork.

"Let's hope she presents Bathvale with the spare he's so desperate to have, but I am honestly more interested in getting home to my little household in London than I am in any more of Bathvale Abbey's drama."

Sebastian ranged an arm along the back of the bench. "We have the epilogue to endure. Will you save me a waltz at tonight's ball?"

Ye gods, the ball. I had planned to put in an appearance, dance the opening waltz with St. Sevier, and then disappear to my rooms. If traveling on the Sabbath wasn't regarded as half scandalous, I would cheerfully quit the premises on Sunday morning.

"I have only the supper waltz left to give you. If you're still intent on finding a bride, then shouldn't you be saving your waltzes for Mrs. Bonaventure or Miss Waltham?"

Sebastian crossed his legs and leaned his head back to tip his face to the summer sun. What a magnificent profile he had. Strong, lean, nearly harsh in its masculine angularity, but attractive without having anything of prettiness about it.

"St. Sevier says you didn't know I asked permission to court you." Sebastian's eyes were closed as he offered that comment, and his expression suggested he might have been discussing the best places to fish for trout in Bathvale's lake.

"St. Sevier needs to learn some discretion."

"Agreed."

Sebastian would not ask me directly, and if I changed the subject, he'd likely never raise the topic of his youthful ambitions again.

"Papa never said a word. Not a hint, Sebastian. I will have a very pointed discussion with him when next he and I are private."

"Derwent told me that my uncle would get an heir on his new wife or die trying. I had no business offering for an earl's daughter when I was little more than an old Scotsman's insurance policy." Sebastian sat up and scuffed a boot across the grass beneath the bench. "Your father bought my colors. Said he was doing me a favor. He was right."

Papa, how could you? "He was wrong." To send that imaginative, mischievous, thoughtful boy off to war and turn him into this taciturn, serious soldier... Papa had done His Majesty's army a very great favor, but at an enormous cost to Sebastian.

And at some cost to me.

"Perhaps Belmaine had already made his intentions known," Sebastian said.

"Or Freddie's uncle had put plans in train for his nephew. Spare me from interfering old men." Such was the beauty of the day, or such was my relief that the house party was ending, that my anger was muted and sad rather than vitriolic.

Sebastian's arm came around my shoulders. "You'll allow me your supper waltz?" He gave me a squeeze, a friendly hug that lingered for only a moment, then let me go.

"If I must. You shall promise not to sweep me off my feet, though. You are so disobligingly tall, and I haven't danced the waltz since donning my weeds."

"No sweeping, I promise."

We fell to bickering then, about whether rain was on the way, then about whether Sir Randall and the remaining Putnam heiress would get married. I honestly did not care—let the lady do as she pleased for once—but arguing with Sebastian over nothing was a joy I'd never thought to experience again.

As Sebastian escorted me back to the Abbey, I decided that the house party had been a success—for me. I'd broken the spell of ennui I'd been falling under in London, I'd passed some truly enjoyable hours in the fresh country air, and I'd helped unravel a bedeviling situation that could have gone very badly for at least one innocent party.

"But that," I said to Sebastian, "is enough excitement to last me for quite a while."

"Admit it," he said as we approached the back garden, "you enjoyed upending the entire household here and then setting all to rights according to your own scheme."

I had. I very, very much had. "Don't be ridiculous. Peace and quiet are my highest aspirations, and I look forward to attaining them without limit for at least the next twelvemonth."

"I put a fiver on you landing in another imbroglio before the year is out."

He bowed over my hand, for we'd reached the back terrace, and I let him have the last word.

As it happened, Sebastian was absolutely correct—I landed in another imbroglio not three months later, and that fiasco made the house party at Bathvale Abbey look like the merest frolic by comparison...

Though that, as they say, is a tale for another time.

TO MY DEAR READERS

I hope you enjoyed this inaugural who-done-it in my **Lady Violet Mystery** series. I had great fun writing this story and puzzling out the clues, motives, and red herrings. While I read tons of romance, and specifically historical romance, I am also a voracious consumer of historical mysteries. So when Lady Violet Belmaine found herself in the Robertsons' ballroom with a migraine, a grouchy Scottish marquess, and a debonair French physician—also a nakey-nakey fellow who wasn't on the guest list—I decided to see how matters developed.

I waited until I had six books complete to start publishing the series, but I don't think that's going to be enough. We'll see what her ladyship and her friends have to say about that!

Because I have half a dozen titles ready to publish, I'm making books one through six available first on my **web store**, and then (Feb.22, 2022) through the ebook retailers as individual titles. Libraries will also have early access to these titles if all goes according to plan. The print versions are all stand-alone titles, and also available through the usual retail suspects.

If you'd like to stay up to date on my upcoming releases and preorders, following me on **Bookbub** is probably the simplest way to do that. I also have a **Deals** page on my website, which I update around the first of each month to list discounts, web store early releases, and other sales. If you're more the newsletter type, I send mine out about monthly (**sign up here**), and I promise I will never swap, spam, or sell your personal information.

However you like to connect, I wish you, as always,

Happy reading!
Grace Burrowes

Read on for an excerpt from book two in the **Lady Violet Mysteries Series**, *Lady Violet Attends a Wedding!*

LADY VIOLET ATTENDS A WEDDING— EXCERPT

Chapter One

The best way to get to know a man is not to share a bed with him, but rather, to share a coach with him in the middle of a deluge on what is euphemistically referred to as the King's highway.

This experience befell me en route to my brother Felix's wedding. My escort on the journey was Monsieur Hugh St. Sevier, a skilled physician and the most cordial of men under normal circumstances. He sat across from me, his Gallic charm having been jettisoned within an hour of leaving London.

"My lady, in all the vast reaches of the great, untamed wilds of the English language, I could not find profanity sufficiently vile or voluminous to describe my contempt for His Majesty's roads."

St. Sevier, though heir to a French title, had spent many years in England. His accent thickened as his normally gracious manner eroded. At present, that accent was the consistency of the mud miring the wheels of my traveling coach.

"My contempt is reserved for the English weather," I replied, tightening my grip on the leather strap dangling from the ceiling. "I have never seen rain like this."

We'd left London amid a mere downpour, but as the day had advanced, the downpour had intensified, at times creating such a thunderous roar on the coach roof as to render conversation impossible. We had changed teams frequently, for the going was bad enough to tire the stoutest of equines.

"We should find an inn," St. Sevier said. "We must find an inn before one of the horses is lamed by this mud and we are stranded by the side of the road."

He'd assayed that opinion previously, and every other sensible traveler was likely of the same mind. The inns would thus offer nothing but a stinking, clammy trial to the nerves in a crowded common, even for me, an earl's daughter and a widow of means.

I dealt with crowds even less graciously than St. Sevier was dealing with the weather.

"We must press on," I said, trying for a cajoling tone. "We are less than ten miles from Derwent Hall, and my family is expecting us. If I fail to arrive as scheduled, they will fret, and when my family frets, the peace of the realm is at risk."

I was the youngest of five siblings, which was all well and good, but the other four offspring of the Earl of Derwent were male, each one louder and more opinionated than the one before. Felix, the youngest of the brothers, was only the second to marry. My oldest brother, Mitchell, Viscount Ellersby, had been married for more than five years.

Mitchell had yet to sire a son, and Papa was agitating for more grandchildren, of course. Until his sons presented him with grandsons—note the plural—he would not consider the earldom's succession secure.

The coach lurched, and St. Sevier began cursing in a river of low, inventive French.

"Violet, my esteem for you is without limit, but this journey has become a nightmare. We must stop at the next opportunity."

The carriage righted itself, and I breathed a sigh of relief. I loved my traveling coach, from the heavily padded benches to the clever compartments designed to hold food and drink. The lamps were exquisite, the leather sumptuous. The floor held a compartment for heated bricks, and the lap robes were soft merino wool dyed to match the chocolaty leather.

I had good memories of traveling in this coach with my late husband. Good, *married* memories, for the two benches cleverly folded out to create what amounted to a bed. Freddie Belmaine had believed in getting comfortable before we'd passed the first tollgate out of London, though even he would have been hard-pressed to manage connubial joy amid the jouncing I endured with St. Sevier.

"We will be on Derwent land soon," I said. "When the terrain is less hilly, the road will improve."

St. Sevier had tended the wounded on battlefields all over the Continent, and I'd seen him face down Society gossips with only an elegantly raised eyebrow. He was an attractive man, chestnut-haired, brown-eyed, suave, and soft-spoken.

Sitting across from me in the coach, he looked as if he'd been dragged through a hedge backward by drunken demons under a witch's moon.

"You English," he said, in tones that were less than respectful of his host country. "You cannot build a road to save yourself. The Romans, using donkeys and common sense, built roads that yet endure. You are still using the roads they left you nearly fifteen hundred years ago. But depart from the Roman roads, and your country is reduced to traveling cart tracks that no civilized—*Dieu nous préserve!*"

This time, the coach did not immediately right itself, but sat at an awkward angle, the back end of the vehicle slanting downward most alarmingly. Shouting and whinnying sounded above the pounding of the rain. A whip cracked, and the coach heaved back upright.

"Violet, we are being foolish," St. Sevier said. "I did not survive years at war to lose my life in some English ditch."

"St. Sevier, I know you can swim." As could I, thanks to an inade-quately supervised country upbringing, but what good would those skills do us if our coach were to fall into any of the rivers rising so quickly beneath the many venerable bridges we had to traverse?

"We stop at the next inn, Violet," St. Sevier said, his expression grim. "As the escort whom you requested to accompany you on this journey, I am making that decision, and you will not argue with me."

"I have long suspected that steel lies beneath your fine manners and *bons mots*."

"Not steel, my lady, a fervent wish to live to see the dawn."

We said nothing for the next several miles, and I began to hope that we'd reach Derwent Hall in one somewhat bruised and bedraggled piece. My coachman was a tough old Scot who also apparently sought to live to see the dawn, for he took no risks, letting the horses slog along as best they could without foolish displays of speed even when the going was somewhat better.

"We'll be there soon," I said as we clattered out of the village that served my father's estate. The gaggle of buildings arranged around a now-sodden green had fascinated me as a child. I'd watched the smith at his forge and fancied him Vulcan in the underworld. The apothecary and lending library had been full of adult women speaking in half-humorous code about odd ailments and troubled marriages. What would they have said about my union with Freddie Belmaine?

"You truly did grow up in the country, didn't you?" St. Sevier asked, peering at the damp green world beyond the windows.

"I miss it." I'd reached that conclusion some weeks earlier, at a house party I hadn't particularly wanted to attend. I'd found myself stealing away with a book to this or that quiet meadow or pretty garden path. "I've been thinking of leaving London."

St. Sevier left off scowling at the wet countryside. "Leaving London for where?"

I considered him a friend and strongly suspected he was willing to be more than a friend. "Would you miss me?"

"I'd visit you, assuming I was welcome, and assuming all of England does not wash into the ocean in the next twenty-four hours."

I'd visit you. He did not specify in what capacity, and I did not press the matter. As a physician, Hugh had advised me to get out of London for the duration of that house party, and his guidance had been sound. I'd come home a stronger, less-anxious person.

Had I come back happier? "I'm not sure where I'd go," I said, "but I miss fresh air and true quiet. London is never quiet." Nor did London ever smell even faintly alluring much less fresh.

My emotions put me in mind of the stream running beside the road. I'd built my share of dams in that stream. The rains had swollen a placid little burn into a raging torrent surging well past its banks. The current sluicing by the coach was swift and roiling, with branches and debris bobbing wildly in muddy rapids.

That peaceful little country burn was dangerous now, and the restlessness I'd brought back to London with me felt equally untrustworthy.

"Not so long ago," St. Sevier said, cocking his head, "you were reluctant to leave your house or put off your weeds. Now you propose to flee London altogether?"

"I'm not sure what I propose." The coach turned right, toward the Derwent Hall main gates open at the far end of a wide wooden bridge. No gatekeeper came out to welcome us, though I spied a dim light in the window of the gatehouse through the downpour.

"Your brother's wedding will bring back difficult memories," St. Sevier said. "I'm sorry for that."

"Why must you be so perceptive?" I'd been a happy bride, also an ignorant one.

St. Sevier and I shared a smile, one of many that made me feel as if I could tell him anything, and he'd receive my confidences in a spirit of compassion and shared humanity. I liked Hugh so very much, and he was forthright about letting me know that he—

Several things happened in the same instant. A crack of thunder sounded as if God had dropped his fist on the very roof of our coach. Horses whinnied and iron-shod hooves thumped and scrabbled on the wet planks of the bridge. The coach lurched crazily, and a sharp snap accompanied an abrupt slide toward the water roiling beneath the bridge.

St. Sevier dove across the coach to grab for me as the door flew open. Then I was falling, with nothing to hold on to.

Order your copy of **Lady Violet Attends a Wedding**!

Made in the USA
Las Vegas, NV
28 November 2022